WILD PITCH

DAYTONA FURY SERIES
BOOK 1

C.L. ROSE

Copyright © 2024 by C.L. Rose

All rights reserved.

No part of this book may be reproduced in any form or by any electronic or mechanical means, including information storage and retrieval systems, without written permission from the author, except for the use of brief quotations in a book review.

Editing and Proofreading: Breanne at Breezy Book Edits

Cover Design: Breanne at Breezy Book Art

Chapter Break Artwork: Breanne at Breezy Book Art

To anyone who feels like their dreams are too big.

I believe in you…

AUTHOR'S NOTE

This book contains sexual scenes that are rough and primal in nature. They include biting, slapping, spanking, and other acts that may be triggering to some readers. Everything that happens between the characters is agreed upon and consented to, but please use caution when moving forward if you have sensitivities to this type of content.

As always, please research thoroughly before engaging in any type of kink with an experienced partner.

xoxo,

Candice

PLAYLIST

1. mr. sunshine - Arden Jones
2. PUMP THE BREAK - morgxn
3. Bruises & Bitemarks - Good With Grenades
4. She Hates Me - Puddle Of Mudd
5. Needed Me - Rihanna
6. Teeth - 5 Seconds of Summer
7. Bad Liar - Selena Gomez
8. i hope ur miserable until ur dead - Nessa Barrett
9. Please Please Please - Sabrina Carpenter
10. Some Kind Of Drug - G-Eazy, Marc E. Bassy
11. Chills (Dark Version) - Mickey Valen, Joey Myron
12. Small Doses - Bebe Rexha
13. The Devil Wears Lace - Steven Rodriguez
14. Vicious - Bohnes
15. Armor - Landon Austin
16. Wicked Game - Lusaint

17. greedy - Our Last Night

18. High Horse - Kacey Musgraves

19. I Did Something Bad - Taylor Swift

20. skin - Donna Missal

21. Who Do You Want - Ex Habit

22. Animals - Call Me Karizma

23. Bleed - Connor Kauffman

24. All Over Me - KEELIN

25. Shackles - Steven Rodriguez

26. love me - Ex Habit

27. When You Say My Name - Chandler Leighton

28. Starving - Hailee Steinfeld, Grey, Zedd

29. Closer - Nine Inch Nails

30. RUNRUNRUN - Dutch Melrose

31. Bad Things - mgk, Camilla Cabello

32. Fall Into Me - Brantley Gilbert

33. Cravin' - Stileto, Kendyle Paige

34. Animal - The Cab

35. Take It out on Me - Bohnes

36. Don't Freak Out - Huddy, iann dior, Tyson Ritter, Travis Barker

37. Sick To My Stomach - Natalie Jane

38. Horns - Bryce Fox

39. Easy to Love - Bryce Savage

40. I Can See You (Taylor's Version) - Taylor Swift

41. Off My Face - Justin Bieber

PROLOGUE

MONROE - TWO YEARS AGO

"GOD, you have pretty tits. What did you say your name was again?"

"I didn't," I reply on a breath, grabbing him by his collar and jerking him to my mouth. As soon as our lips meet, just like they did in the back of the car on the way to this swanky ass hotel, fireworks explode around us. I moan into his mouth, realizing this is way out of character for the girl I'm trying to be, but I want to melt right into his kiss.

I'm not here to fall in love.

I'm here to get some strange dick.

He pulls back. "You're not going to give me anything?" he questions. "What am I supposed to yell out while I'm fucking you?"

I bark a laugh, surprised by his candor. "Who says I'm going to let you fuck me?" I ask.

"Babe, you're topless in my hotel room and the muscles in your stomach are quivering. We're fucking," he says with a cocky smirk.

This guy is too hot for his own damn good.

I step back, slapping both hands over my abdomen, which is in fact quivering. I can't let my body react like this. I need to stay in control. I gave all of myself to someone once, and it ended with me having to skip town and start all over. I just got here. I'm not doing that again.

"Listen, Val," I say as he steps back in and digs his long, thick fingers into the flesh of my waist. My body goes hot all over again with the way his touch is so firm, biting into me in the most delicious way. As soon as he traces his tongue in a wet line from the base of my throat to my earlobe, I moan loudly, almost losing my train of thought. "I…" I breathe. "I need this to be a one-time thing. No names. No personal details. Just sex."

He trails kisses over the side of my face, working his way back to my mouth. "I already gave you details," he murmurs. "I told you I'm in town for work, that I live in Florida, and that I'm going to blow your fucking mind tonight. The least you can give me is your name."

"How about I just suck your cock instead?" I say, dropping to my knees and bringing my fingers to the button of his dress pants. Hopefully the distraction will make him stop asking so many questions.

"Fuck," he groans, gripping my long, newly chocolate-brown hair. "I'm going to call you Mayhem. Because that's exactly what you look like down there. Chaos. Trouble. Like a riot I know I should run from, but I can't fucking look away."

I keep my gaze on his as I pull his pants and boxer briefs down in one go. My eyes widen and my mouth waters as his cock springs free. It's big and hard, with wide veins wrapping around it and a bead of precum sitting at the tip, waiting for me to drink.

I don't waste a fucking second. I need this so badly after everything I've been through in the past week. Packing everything you own into your small car and leaving the only place you've ever known to start all over by yourself takes a toll on you, and I just want to let go. The old Monroe needs to die so the new one can be born. I have a chance to be anyone I want now, and I'm choosing to be a bad bitch who takes what she wants and doesn't let anyone walk all over her. As far as everyone here knows, that's exactly what I am.

Leaning forward, I lap at the head of his dick before sucking it between my lips. I moan at the way he tastes as I feel myself growing wetter under my panties. Looking for relief, I squeeze my thighs together, but it's nowhere near enough friction to soothe the throbbing ache between them.

"Holy fuck," he rasps, gripping my hair tighter in his fist. "That's it, baby. Suck my cock." The sound of his voice, plus the way he's got his fist clenched tightly to my scalp has me taking him as far back as I can go, fighting against my gag reflex that's telling me to pull back. I've never done anything like this before, and I've never felt more alive.

Looking up, I almost orgasm without even being touched at the sight above me. Val's face is pointed up to the ceiling in pleasure, and I watch his Adam's apple bob as I suck his cock like it's the most delicious thing I've ever tasted. It's not far off. I could live off the flavor of his skin.

"You suck me so good. *Fuck*," he grits out, thrusting his hips into my face. I feel powerful and owned at the same time, and it's making my blood run like lava through my veins.

I feel him get impossibly hard against my tongue and he pulls away with a jerk. A string of saliva connects us as I look up at him through my lashes, both of us gasping for air as we stare into one another.

"Up," he growls loudly. The tone of his voice has me on high alert, and while I should be running for the hills, it makes the throb between my legs intensify almost to the point of pain. I scurry to stand, willing to wait for further instruction, but I don't even get a second to think before I'm lifted off my feet and tossed onto the bed. I push up onto my elbows, watching as he stalks my way with a look in his eyes that I can only describe as predatory. Prowling toward me, I stare, not blinking a single time as he crawls over my body and leans down, pressing his mouth to my throat. I arch up to him, throwing my head back as he licks and sucks, but when he sinks his teeth into the sensitive skin of my neck, I hiss a breath through my teeth as pain radiates down toward my shoulder.

"I want to take you rough," he says. "Are you okay with that?"

I shouldn't be. His voice is dark and chilling…and it's possible that he just broke through my skin when he bit me. But *fuck*. I want more.

"Yes."

I blink my eyes rapidly, waiting for them to adjust to the early morning sun that's peeking through the blinds of the hotel room. Memories from last night slowly come back to me as I lie there, trapped under Val's muscled arm. The biting. The clawing. The way he worked my body until I was a desperate, writhing mess, begging for more pain to go with the pleasure he was giving me.

It was *everything*.

But I can't stay here. I need to sneak out somehow without waking him. He already had a million questions that I wasn't willing to answer last night, so I know if he gets the chance, they'll start right back up. Plus, I don't want to be late for my first day at the boutique, so I need to skedaddle.

Wiggling down the bed, I inch myself out from under his gigantic arm. Whatever this guy does for work has to be some type of manual labor. I bet he can pop someone's head right off their body with the inside of his elbow while chugging a beer with the other hand. I try to hold in my laugh at the mental image as I continue working my way down the mattress.

As soon as I'm out from under him, I rush around the room, picking up my clothes. My shirt and bra are right by the door, where he pulled them off of me as soon as we walked inside, unable to wait another second. I get them on, spinning quickly to look for the rest of my belongings. The pink linen micro skirt I wore to the bar last night is tossed over by the window. I run over, swiping it and sliding it up my legs before tiptoeing to where my panties lie bunched up by the bed. But when I go to put them on, I realize they're completely ruined. Memories of Val literally ripping them from my body flood my brain and I want to swan dive right the fuck back into the bed with him for another round. But I'm just going to have to settle for keeping last night's festivities in my spank bank for future use, because this can't be anything more.

I grab my clutch off the back of the armchair, moving to the door and taking one last look back at Val before reluctantly leaving him without saying goodbye.

Forty-five minutes later, I pull into the parking lot behind Praya, the luxury boutique where I just got hired. The drive from Boston to Hope Harbor wasn't too bad since I made it through the city before rush hour. I had to touch up last night's makeup and steer with one knee while I brushed the wild knots out of my hair, but I managed to make myself presentable.

And keeping an emergency pair of panties in my glove box?

What a power move.

I rush to the door with about ten minutes to spare before the store opens, smoothing my clothes down and walking in like a normal, confident individual who has her life together, even though I definitely don't.

"You must be Monroe!" an adorable blonde girl says as she stands and comes my way. "I'm Grace. I'm the assistant fashion buyer here. It's nice to meet you." I take her extended hand, returning her smile. She can't be more than a couple of years younger than me, if that, and I have a feeling we're going to get along really well.

"Likewise," I say, looking around. "Where is everyone?"

"Oh!" she replies. "The ladies always meet for tea on Monday mornings before they come in, so they'll be a little behind. It's just us for about an hour. Until my brother gets here. He's a professional baseball player and his team is playing in Boston tonight, so he's dropping in to say hello before he has to be at the stadium."

"Oh, that's cool," I offer. "What's his na—"

"Riggs!" she squeals, cutting me off as she runs to the door. She jumps into her brother's waiting arms and I turn around, smiling as I watch them embrace.

"Hey, Bunny," he says, and my blood goes cold when I hear his voice. As soon as she steps back, my eyes lock onto his. Eyes that I was just looking into hours ago as he ripped orgasm after orgasm from my exhausted body.

This lying motherfucker.

ONE
RIGGS

"LET'S FUCKING DO IT, BOYS!" I yell to my team, bouncing on the balls of my feet. It's our home opener, and after losing early in the playoffs last season, I'm ready to head straight through to the World Series. This is the Daytona Fury's year.

We take the field, and as soon as I make my way toward the mound, I notice that something is off. Where the fans would normally be hyped up and cheering, all I hear are loud boos as they fill the stadium.

"What the fuck?" I grumble, looking around.

"Tough crowd," our second baseman, Jackson Blake, says with a chuckle. "Makes sense, though, since we're playing the team from the same city as the dude you knocked out on the field last fall."

Okay. I can explain.

I grew up with Tanner Lake, quarterback for the Boston Blizzard and America's fucking sweetheart. When I found out that he slept with my sister behind my back and broke her heart, I lost my shit. I ditched a very important playoff game, hopped on the first plane from Florida to Massachusetts, and laid his ass out right in the middle of a game.

Sorry, not sorry.

In the end, Tanner and I made up, and he's now my brother-in-law. He and Grace got hitched in Vegas a couple of months ago. I was his best man, and despite the fact that we've done an annoying amount of media appearances to clear the air, apparently the fans of Boston have kept me at the top of their shit lists.

"Football season is over," I say quietly, scrunching my nose in disgust. "They need to move on. Their precious golden boy is fine. They should be focusing on baseball."

Jacks takes his spot on the bag while our catcher, Ace Mathers, squats behind home plate. As I go to throw my first warm-up pitch, the jeers intensify. I get why the Boston fans are pissed at me, but when I look into the crowd, I notice that *everyone* is booing—even the Daytona fans.

The fuck is going on?

I stiffen and roll my shoulders in an attempt to loosen my tense muscles. But the sound only gets louder, making it hard to focus on anything else. My throat goes dry and sweat beads at the base of my neck as I unsuccessfully attempt to drown it out.

"C'mon, Valentine!" Ace yells, punching his hand into his mitt and extending it out in front of his body in invitation. "What are you waiting for?"

I tell myself to calm down, but when I see a bright purple blur in my peripheral vision, I whip my head toward the batter's box, where our mascot, Friggle, is leading the crowd in a chorus of boos. His arms, which are entirely too long for his body, shoot up over his head, giving two furry thumbs down before he points at me and shakes with laughter. I turn my head, trying to ignore him, but he runs back into my line of vision before resuming his taunts. My heart beats a heavy cadence behind my rib cage, and I take another look into the stands, where all the angry faces begin to blur together as their loud sounds of disapproval ring in my ears. And when I see that Friggle has begun to creep even closer to me, waving a hand in front of his bulbous nose to indicate that I stink, that's the last goddamn straw.

I yank my glove from my hand, flinging it into the dirt on the mound before I take off toward the hairy motherfucker at full speed. He stands there frozen as I tackle him to the ground, slamming my fists into his big, googly eyes. Squeaking noises that resemble a dog's toy come out of his nostrils with every strike as I continue raining punches down on whatever the fuck he is. The Fury's mascot is supposed to be a dragon. But Friggle?

Not a fucking clue.

It's not until I feel a set of arms yank me back that I realize what I've done.

"What the fuck, dude?" Jackson says as I stare down at the crumpled-up costume on the ground. I know there's a guy inside it, and I'm afraid I might have knocked him out. I bring my eyes up to the crowd, who are stunned silent as they look onto the field in horror. Backing away slowly, I irrationally hope nobody saw me just attack our mascot, but I only get about two steps before our manager Clyde's voice jolts me back to reality.

"Valentine!" he yells. "Get your ass in the locker room, *now!*"

Eyes wide, still in shock, I walk toward the dugout as angry fans throw their food and drinks at the netting that separates the field from the stands.

"I hate you, Riggs Valentine!" shouts a small voice. I look up to see a little girl with tears streaming down her cheeks, obviously concerned about Friggle's well-being.

Fuck my life.

"Come on in," Taylor, the team's public relations manager says, holding the door to her office open for me. I stand from the chair, wiping my sweaty palms on my pants before heading into the room with my tail between my legs. I was tossed from the game by my own manager and was forced to watch on a TV in the locker room as the Boston Tide embarrassed us on our own dirt.

Apparently, the meeting started before I got here, because the office is already full. I look around, nodding sheepishly in greeting to Clyde, Taylor's assistant, and of course, Friggle. Well, the guy who wears the Friggle costume. He can't be more than nineteen years old, which makes me feel like a total dick. Poor kid just got his ass beat on national television with nothing to defend himself with except his four-foot flappy arms.

"Sorry, man," I grunt as I sit down in the vacant chair

across the room. He just gives me a disgusted look, shaking his head.

"Okay," Taylor says, plopping down at her desk. "Respectfully, Riggs, what the fuck was that?" My eyes widen and I look around the room to see everyone's reaction to her language, but they're all just staring at me as they wait for an answer.

"Ummm," I say, trying to stall. I'm a pro athlete. I'm used to being heckled on the field and should be able to block it out after being in the majors for this long, but I'll admit that my fuse has always been a little on the shorter end. "I lost my temper. I was wrong. It won't happen again."

Friggle scoffs quietly, and I clench my hands tightly over the armrests of my chair so I don't launch myself at him again.

"I have to be honest with you," she begins. "The fans have been calling for your head for months. You leaving the playoff game that ultimately cost us a shot at the pennant so you could attack the most beloved quarterback in all of football wasn't a good look. The owner was ready to make a trade after last year, but I talked him into keeping you. This little stunt may have been the final nail in your coffin here. Unless you have one hell of a reason for what just happened, I can't do much to save you."

Fuck.

If I get traded because of this, the chances of another team wanting me after what I did today aren't great. I'm a hothead, and I literally just attacked an innocent mascot because he pretended to laugh at me. I'm a great pitcher, but those are a dime a dozen in this league. If they shitcan me, there'll be ten guys ready to step in and try to take my place. I need to think of a way to save my own ass or I could be forced to retire at the ripe old age of twenty-seven.

"I…" I say, spitting out the first thing that comes to me. "I'm just really stressed. My girlfriend…I've been trying to get her to move to Daytona and it's been roadblock after roadblock. I guess it finally all just hit me at once."

My fucking *what?* What the fuck am I saying? I don't have a girlfriend. Not unless you count the cleat chaser who sucked me off in the bathroom of Club Wave two nights ago…and then again in the front seat of my car before I went home, which, *I don't.*

I am a proud manwhore. I admittedly sleep around, but I'm honest with the women I bring into my bed. They don't want anything long-term with me any more than I want it with them. Their objective is to say they slept with a professional athlete, and mine is to blow my load all over their tits.

Simple. Fun. Uncomplicated.

"Oh," Taylor says with wide eyes. "I wasn't aware that you were in a serious relationship."

I swallow roughly. "It's…new, but when you know, you know. Right?" I ask.

What. Theeeee. Fuck.

The only thing I know when it comes to women is that if you curl your fingers just right when they're buried inside their pussies, it makes them go off, *like that.* But as far as dating them or knowing when you've met *the one*? Yeah…no thanks. Hard pass.

Sweat gathers on my temples as she relaxes back into her chair, steepling her fingers in front of her pursed lips. Maybe my excuse is working, and she understands the pretend pain I'm going through. With any luck, I'll be back on the field tomorrow for game two of the series.

"As you know, Mr. Durst is a family man," she says, speaking of the team's owner and one of the wealthiest men in the state of Florida. "If we can get your girlfriend here and prove that your priorities are changing, that might just be your saving grace."

Well, fuck me sideways. That backfired.

"I don't—" I say on a nervous laugh, but Clyde cuts me off.

"Oh, shut the fuck up, Valentine. You have a two-point-seven ERA. You have a hundred and one mile-an-hour fastball. If you fuck me out of another World Series this year, you won't have to worry about the fans because I'll cut your fucking brake lines myself."

Yikes. Can we get someone from HR in here, just in case?

As if she didn't just witness a blatant threat to my well-being, Taylor continues. "Let me talk to Mr. Durst. I can buy you some time while you get your girlfriend to Daytona. Bring her around the facility, have her come to some games, and show everybody you're better with her here."

My fingers start to tingle, and I pull at the collar of my jersey because all of a sudden, it feels like it's choking me. What the fuck do I say? I can't agree with this plan, because there *is no girlfriend.* But I can't say no because it could potentially cost me my career. I try one last excuse, hoping I can talk my way out of this.

"She…umm…she's shy," I say, attempting to come up with an excuse for why they can never meet my girlfriend who doesn't exist. "She—"

"Goddamn it, Valentine!" Clyde roars, shooting out of

his seat and slapping his giant hand on the desk. "You better get that girl here before your next start or else! Do you hear me?" The vein in his forehead is threatening to burst as he stares at me with pure rage in his eyes.

I slump in my chair, defeated. "Yes, sir."

"Okay!" Taylor says with a clap. "As long as Brent doesn't have anything to say to you, you're free to go."

"Who's Brent?" I ask, confused.

"Me, you asshole," Friggle pipes up from the corner. "I just want to make it clear that the only reason I'm not pressing charges is because my dad already thinks I'm a disappointment. Pretty sure getting his favorite player arrested would get me kicked out of the house for good this time."

I stay quiet because what do you say to that? Believe it or not, I know when to keep my mouth shut, so I just watch as they get up and prepare to leave. Taylor's assistant escorts the men out of the room, giving the two of us some privacy.

"I'm serious, Riggs," she scolds. "I can't keep pulling you out of these holes you dig for yourself. Get her here and show the Durst family that you're ready to be a posi-tive part of this organization. You're too good of a player to go to waste."

I nod, standing and walking out of the building toward the player parking lot. Hopping into my Jeep, I think about all the things that Taylor said and how right she is. From the moment I picked up a baseball when I was four years old, I knew I was different. Even at that young age, I could feel it. It was going to be my life.

I spent my entire adolescence idolizing professional pitchers. Every time someone asked me what I wanted to be when I grew up, there was never a new answer. I never had a backup plan in case I didn't make it to the MLB. Failure was *not* an option. So, when I entered the draft before my senior year of college, my entire future was riding on whether or not I was chosen. Thankfully, the Fury took me with the third overall pick, and here I am.

I knew coming into this organization that they put a heavy emphasis on being a good person. We're required to attend a certain number of charity events each year and to spend time in the community as part of our contracts. I learned a lot about helping others while growing up in a tight-knit Massachusetts town called Hope Harbor, but I'll admit I haven't done nearly enough of that since I've been in Florida.

When I moved here at twenty-one, I got sucked into the nightlife. Being a professional athlete means getting into the most luxurious clubs and spending nights with the most beautiful women this city has to offer. And even though it's been six years, I'm still having fun with that. I love the freedom that comes with being single. I honestly don't see myself ever settling down for real, which is why I can't believe that was my go-to excuse for losing my shit today.

What the fuck am I supposed to do now? It's not like I can go back to the bathroom at Club Wave and find...*whatever her name was*. I don't know any women in Daytona that I'd feel comfortable trusting with this dilemma, let alone having as a live-in fake girlfriend for however long it takes to convince the team's owner that I'm ready to settle down and take my job seriously.

I'm fucked.

TWO
MONROE

"I HATE YOU," I say to my best friend Grace as I lean on the doorjamb to her almost empty office. "I hope you and your sexy husband have a hundred Lego-loving children who leave them all over your giant mansion, so you step on one every time you walk."

"That was oddly specific and really mean," she says with a grin. "But Tan is definitely sexy."

Grace got married to her brother's best friend, and quarterback for the Boston Blizzard, after their Super Bowl win a couple of months ago. I may give her shit because she's packing up and leaving the boutique to work full-time as a fashion designer, but I couldn't be happier for her. Just last year, she was in a shitty relationship with an absolute douche nugget because she had given up on ever getting a second chance with Tanner. Thankfully, he got his shit together and returned to Hope Harbor to fix what he had broken, showing Grace what she truly deserves. It may seem like they got hitched in a hurry, but after spending five years apart, who could blame them for wanting to start their life together?

It's been amazing watching them rekindle their love, but standing here as she packs up her office? I have to admit I'm a little sad. Not because she's moving. I know she'll be less than an hour away and I can see her as much as I want. It's bittersweet for me because Grace was my very first friend when I moved to Massachusetts from California two years ago. Actually, she's kind of my only friend.

I go out. I hit the clubs in Boston on the weekends. But I wouldn't necessarily consider the group of girls I do that with my *friends*. They're more like acquaintances who have the same goals as I do when we're out.

Drink. Dance. Find a hottie to take home.

Rinse and repeat.

That may sound boring and monotonous to some people, but not me. For twenty-four years, every move I made was with a purpose—and it was *never* for myself. So, when I hit my breaking point and left home, I decided everything I'd do from there on out would be for me, and no one else. For now, that means clubbing on my nights off and banging whoever I want whenever the mood strikes. If there ever comes a day when I get sick of it and decide to settle down, it'll be on *my terms*.

"Hey, girls," Claire says in a somber tone. She owns the boutique, and as long as I've known her, I've never seen her without her signature ear-to-ear smile. I can tell she's holding back tears, so Grace and I give her our full attention.

"What's wrong?" I ask, helping her over to the chair.

She settles in and takes a deep breath before she looks up, wiping the tears that have started to fall down her cheeks.

"I just got back from meeting with my accountant. I may have underplayed some of the numbers to you guys recently. Praya is officially so far in the red, I don't think we can even afford another month of the mortgage here."

Grace stands, rushing over to Claire as she breaks down. I know I should do the same, but I'm frozen in place. This job is the only reason I'm able to take care of myself independently. When I left Rolling Hills, my parents cut me off financially, which I completely expected and had prepared for. After I graduated college, I immediately went to work at a marketing firm in Los Angeles. I stayed under their roof, abiding by their strict rules for as long as I could, pocketing every single dollar I could spare in an account they didn't know about. Even though I hoped to be able to save more, they left me with no choice when they practically sold me away to the richest bachelor they could find.

I know what you're thinking. *An arranged marriage? What is this, the eighteen hundreds?* And *yeah.* That's what I said too. Actually, my exact words were *"Well, blessed be. Thank you for bestowing upon me a man to show me my place in this world."* My dad rolled his eyes, told me I'd never keep a man happy with such a poor attitude, and informed me that I'd be marrying Conrad Astor by the time I was twenty-five if I wanted my share of the Decker family fortune.

I gave it a try. I dated him for as long as I could stand him. But the thing about rich, trust-fund nepo babies like him—they're raised by generations of men who teach them the most closed-minded ways of life. *"Women should be seen and not heard." "A wife's place is in the home." "The man is the head of the family. Women aren't our equals."*

A girl like me can only tolerate the *Stepford Wives* bit for so long before she loses her shit.

So I left. Like a literal thief in the night. I packed up everything I could fit into my small BMW and drove as far away as I could. I had enough money saved to make it to the East Coast, where I had landed a job as the marketing manager here at the boutique.

I still talk to my parents. Well, I still talk to my mom. My dad refuses to speak to me until I come back and marry Conrad. I think he'll come around eventually. I'd like to believe he just wants the best for me, but he doesn't realize the damage that always having to be perfect was doing to me. I'm afraid to think of where I'd be right now if I hadn't decided to leave when I did.

"So, what now?" Grace asks. "I know I'll be in Boston, but if I can help in any way, I will."

Claire shakes her head. "I'm afraid it's time girls," she says, defeat evident in her tone. "It's time to close our doors. I'm eighty-two years old. I should've retired long ago, but I just love this boutique so much. I wanted to do it until I couldn't anymore. I had no idea it would be the economy that took us out rather than me croaking."

Grace lets out a quiet chuckle, wrapping her arm around Claire and squeezing her frail body. It takes me several seconds to snap out of my haze, but I look their way as Grace widens her eyes as if to say *hello, hug her,* prompting me to walk over and join in on their embrace. But internally, I'm freaking the fuck out.

If I don't have a job, I can't pay my bills. If I can't pay my bills, I have to go crawling back to my parents. And that can't happen. Thankfully, I'm good at what I do, so I'm sure I'll find something else, but who knows how long that could take?

I step back, trying my best to remain sympathetic while also attempting to gauge the category of shitstorm I may be in. "How much longer do we have here?" I ask.

"Well," Claire begins. "I spoke with a realtor, and they have someone who's looking to open a day spa. They think this space would work really well for it, and if I let them start making their renovations on the first of the month, I won't have to miss a payment while we go through the process of selling the building to them. So, I agreed."

"That's in ten days," I say, completely shocked. I'm trying to be sympathetic to Claire, considering she's losing her life's work, but I feel like my throat is starting to close up from the anxiety of not knowing what I'm going to do for money. I'll do anything if it means not having to slink back to my parents and Conrad, but a week and a half isn't nearly enough time to line something up.

"I know, honey. I'm so sorry," Claire says as Grace and I back away, giving her some space. "If it puts you in a bad spot with money, I'm sure I can find a way to help you out."

"No," I reply, feeling terrible for worrying her. "I'll be totally fine, Claire. I've been dying to get into freelance marketing so I can travel more. I was scared to make the leap, but I guess this is my sign to give it a shot." It's not a lie. I *have* been wanting to go out on my own, but I had a good thing going here at Praya. I'm far away from home, in a small town where nobody would even think to come find me—not that they've tried—and I've made enough money to take care of myself without needing any help. Not to mention, I love the ladies here. Claire and her sales manager, Etta, may be in their eighties, but I consider them to be some of my closest friends. And Grace is the most important person in my life. Up until she said she was resigning as our head fashion buyer to design clothes full-time in Boston, I had no reason to even consider leaving here.

But now? Maybe I could find a way.

THREE

RIGGS

"OH MY GOD, you are *so funny!*" Jennifer screeches, laughing entirely too hard at my bad joke. She's from Georgia, but visits on occasion to take care of her great aunt that lives in my building. We hooked up last year and the sex wasn't bad, plus she's one of the only hookups I've ever brought to my actual condo, rather than just fucking in my car or a hotel room. So when I ran into her in the elevator earlier, an idea popped into my head. I'd ask her to come up for a drink, and feel her out to see if she'd be a suitable fake girlfriend for this bullshit situation I fucked myself into.

Apparently, I forgot that she's annoying as shit.

Sorry, but she is.

Maybe it was because she was either choking or screaming the last time I saw her, which didn't leave her with a lot of time to speak, but everything out of her mouth since she walked in the door tonight has either been about herself or my job. I stopped listening when she asked if I'd get her and her friends a suite to our next game so they could see all the *"baseball baddies"*. Her words, not mine. Although Ace *does* have an ass you could bounce quarters off of. Normally, I wouldn't care. I'm used to women only wanting me because I play professional baseball, but this is a different story. I need someone who's not only completely all in on the fact that our relationship would be fake, but also someone I can trust. Clearly, Jennifer here isn't the girl for the job.

I won't lie. I'm starting to get a little nervous. I know I need to find someone to do this with me, but it seems as though my fuckboy ways are finally catching up to me. Maybe if I had put a little more energy into finding something more solid with the women I've spent my time with, I wouldn't be out here scraping the bottom of the barrel for someone to pretend to be in a relationship with me until I've shown the Fury organization that they can trust me to lead their team.

"So, you know Hawk Mason?" She asks, and I inwardly roll my eyes.

"Yep. He's my third baseman," I reply on a forced exhale. Can this girl just hurry up and tell me how hot that broody motherfucker is so I can get her out of here and go back to the drawing board?

"Is he really that hot in person?"

There it is.

"Sure is," I say, walking over and gently ushering her to the entryway. "It was honestly so nice to see you, Jennifer. I had a great time catching up, but I have a bunch of stuff to do, so we'll talk later. Send my regards to your sweet Aunt Geraldine." She looks at me confused, sputtering in an attempt to answer as I open the door and lead her into the hallway.

"But I thought we were going t—"

She doesn't even finish the thought before I slam the door, running my hands down my face in frustration. The worst part of it all is that I can't blame anyone for this shit but myself. My big mouth has gotten me in trouble more times than I can count, but this time I've really fucked up. Where am I going to find a fake girlfriend who will not only be okay with going through with whatever this crazy-ass plan brings, but also won't want anything more from me after we're done?

What I need is someone who hates me.

Godfuckingdamnit.

FOUR
MONROE

"FUUUUCKKKKK," I groan as I upload my resume to CareerMonster. The last thing I want to do is look for a new job, but with the boutique closing in just over a week, I don't really have a choice. As much as I'm sure my parents would love to have me back home as the model daughter and future trophy wife to Conrad, that's not happening. So I'll apply for every marketing-related position that pops up. Hopefully I can find something that pays well enough to ensure that I won't have to make any more sacrifices than the ones I've already chosen to make by moving away from home.

I hit *submit* just as my phone rings, and my day immediately goes even further down the shitter when I see the name flashing across the screen. I inwardly curse my best friend for giving her family my number *"in case of an emergency"* when we were on our girls' camping trip last summer

Not today, Satan.

I ice the call, tossing my phone onto the couch beside

me before reaching for the pint of half-melted Chunky Monkey on the coffee table. But I only get a single bite before the phone rings again.

"Jesus fucking Christ, *what?!*" I spit. No idea why I even answered. Nothing good ever comes from an interaction with Riggs Valentine.

"Wow, Mayhem. What did I do to deserve such a warm greeting?" he says flatly. "I see you're still a bitch."

I scoff. "And I see you're still five years old. What do you want, Riggs?"

"I need your help," he says, clearly pained to be asking. I'm kind of enjoying the indignation in his tone, but I also wish he would fall off a cliff and never speak to me again.

"No," I reply.

He chokes on his surprise. "What do you mean, *no*? I haven't even told you what it is yet."

"Doesn't matter," I say, shoving a spoonful of ice cream into my mouth. "You could be on fire, and I wouldn't piss on you to put you out."

"C'mon," he coaxes. "It's the least you can do after you fucking walked out on me without saying goodbye, then somehow ruined my life even more by becoming best friends with my sister."

He did *not* just bring that up. That shit was over two years ago. I told him I only wanted sex and he agreed. So, the fact that he's bent out of shape about me not saying anything before I snuck out that morning is ridiculous. Besides, what good would it have done for us to go another round? He would have asked a bunch of questions, I would have felt obligated to answer in some way, and he would have pushed me and all of my baggage right out the door.

Even if I wanted to spend more time with Riggs back then, I certainly wasn't in a place to do so. I had just left home and was set on living my life the way *I* wanted to, so even a situationship would've derailed all of that for me. I did what I had to do that morning. Not to mention, he wasn't exactly forthcoming with me, either.

"Funny how you get your panties in a wad about me leaving, when you literally *lied about who you were*," I scoff.

He groans in response. "I didn't lie. Val is my nickname. I *do* live in Florida and was in Boston for work that night. So tell me, Monroe, where did I lie?"

Oh my God. This man is the literal devil. I don't understand how he's such a dickbag while his parents and sister are the sweetest people I've ever met. Even his best friend Tanner is caring and thoughtful. How did he end up so far from that?

"The fact that you're even asking me that right now tells me everything I need to know about your character, *Val*," I say, spitting out his stupid nickname like it's the worst tasting thing that's ever rolled across my tongue. *Sadly, I know from personal experience that it's the only part of him that isn't delicious.* "So, no. I won't help you. Bye."

I hang up the phone, tossing it onto the couch and looking into the carton of melted ice cream. It's basically soup at this point, thanks to Riggs and his colossal waste of my time, but I refuse to let him ruin my night.

"Fuck it," I say, lifting the pint to my lips and drinking the cold mush. It's not ideal, but it's still ice cream, so it's not a total loss.

I'll admit that I'm a little curious to know why he called me out of the blue asking for my help. What could *I* possibly have to offer that he couldn't get from the one million other sexual partners he's had? Because that's really all I am to him. Just another hole he stuck his dick in. And I mean that in the best way possible…at least for myself.

Before that night, I had never done anything even close to what I did with Riggs. When he sat next to me at the bar and offered to buy me a drink, I immediately fell into those deep brown eyes. He was absolutely beautiful, with his strong jaw, medium length chestnut hair that curled at the base of his thick neck, and the fullest, poutiest lips I'd ever seen on a man. We kept our conversation fairly surface level, but it all came so easily. When he asked me to go back to his room to keep the evening going, it was a no-brainer. Riggs Valentine was built for a night of sin, and that's exactly what we did. I've never been fucked that way in my life, and I'm certain I never will be again. I've tried to find something even close to it in the time since, but unfortunately, it must be exclusive to lying fuckboy manwhores, because it continues to elude me. And *that,* my friends, is a shitting shame. Because even though I can't stand the sight of him, I've fantasized about the way Riggs took me so many times that I should probably be ashamed of myself.

I'm not…but I *should be.*

"Whatever," I mumble, pushing away all thoughts of Lucifer himself and whatever he was trying to ask me for so I can focus on the rest of the incoming shitstorm that is my life.

FIVE
RIGGS

I PULL my car into the driveway of the modest ranch house, putting it in park and blowing out a breath. After Monroe hung up on me the other night, I almost gave up. I racked my brain for hours trying to come up with another option for someone who can stand in as my fake girlfriend, but she really is the only one. As much as I'd like to say I can do this without her, I can't. Infuriating, but true.

Which is why I'm about to heave myself right into the lion's den.

After talking with Grace yesterday, I found out that the boutique where Monroe works is closing in less than a week. Apparently, it all came out of nowhere, so I'm going out on a limb here when I say she likely doesn't have anything else lined up yet. This is perfect. Hopefully I can convince her to come stay with me in Daytona while she looks for a new job. By the time she finds one, I'll have convinced Mr. Durst that I'm a stand-up guy, and she can fly off into the sunset on her broomstick. It's a foolproof plan. I just need to get her to hear me out.

I arrived in Boston with the team last night for the next game in the series against the Tide. I'm not scheduled to pitch again until next week—if they even let me—but I knew this trip would be the perfect opportunity to pay my future ex-fake girlfriend a visit. It's early because first pitch is at one o'clock this afternoon, so I need to be back to the city in about an hour and a half. This should leave me with plenty of time to sweet talk Monroe into helping me.

I walk up the steps and ring the doorbell, stuffing my hands into the pockets of my Daytona Fury sweatpants while I wait. Shifting from one foot to the other, nerves suddenly wash over me as I hear her approach. The subsequent groan coming from the other side of the door tells me that she's looking through the peephole. I wink, just in case, right before it inches open and she peeks out.

"I'm not interested in any Girl Scout cookies today, but thanks," she says, barely able to open her eyes. Even when she's half asleep, she's still a goddamn smart-ass.

"No cookies, sweetheart," I reply. "But I have a nice, big sausage if you're hungry."

She scoffs. "You're disgusting. Why are you here?"

"First of all, you're lucky I don't remind you exactly how *not disgusting* you thought I was when I was balls deep inside you," I say smugly. "Secondly, I need to talk to you. Can I come in?"

"If I let you in, do you swear to get whatever this is over with and leave me alone?"

"Yes. Girl Scouts' honor," I promise, holding up two fingers as if I'm pledging an oath. "Five minutes of your time. Then I'll never bug you again." That's a boldfaced lie, but whatever. Maybe I'm an asshole, but I get joy out of driving Monroe crazy. It's easy and she's cute when she's mad.

"Fine," she says, sighing in defeat as she opens the door wide enough for me to step inside. As I walk by, I notice that she's wrapped tightly in a thick blanket. It pools on the floor at her feet, and when she walks, prompting me to follow, it drags across the hardwood floor like a queen's cape. One thing I will say about this woman: she may drive me fucking mad, but *goddamn* is she a showstopper. Even when I know she just flung herself out of bed after what looks to be a rough night of sleep, she's still one of the most stunning women I've ever had my hands on.

"Take a seat," she says, gesturing to the couch. "Let me go get some clothes on."

I turn and plop down onto the sofa as she walks through the kitchen, disappearing into what must be her bedroom. She closes the door about halfway, but it's open enough for me to see the blanket that was wrapped around her hit the floor in a pile. My cock thickens in my pants, and I imagine her completely naked on the other side of that wall, looking like a wet dream as she sifts through her dresser. Her tits are definitely fake, but they're so perfect with small, light rose-colored nipples that get so hard they could cut glass. They're also sensitive as fuck. I remember having her on the cusp of an orgasm just from rolling my teeth over them.

Fuck. I'm all the way hard now.

She opens the door and I panic, grabbing a throw pillow and setting it in my lap just as she heads back toward me. I'm going to need to get my shit under control if this woman is going to be living with me. My body still obviously hasn't gotten the memo that she's a miserable shrew who we absolutely can't give any amount of power over us.

"Alright," she says, standing with her arms crossed over her AC/DC t-shirt. A sleeve of tattoos runs from her elbow to her wrist, and just like every other time I've seen her since she started getting them, I try to avert my eyes from the intricate designs so she doesn't think I'm staring. She's got one hip popped out and her spicy attitude is on full display. Not helpful for my...*situation*. If she doesn't knock it off, I'm going to have to replace this throw pillow. "Your five minutes start now."

I take a deep breath, trying to gather my thoughts. I probably should've come in here with a plan, but to be honest, I'm not used to getting so much pushback from women. Monroe is a different kind of beast in that aspect, and I'm not sure what I'm doing.

"So, I got myself into some trouble with the team. I'm sure you already saw the videos since they went viral, but I attacked our mascot and now I need to show the owner that I'm ready to settle down and be an asset to the organization and community." I expect her to have a sarcastic remark, but she stays quiet, raising a brow and imploring me to continue. "I randomly blurted out that I was trying to get my girlfriend to move to Daytona, which had me stressed out, and that's why I went off. That's where you come in."

Her brows furrow in confusion. "How does you beating up that long-armed monstrosity have anything to do with me?"

"It doesn't," I say. "But the girlfriend part does. Will

you come to Daytona and pretend to date me while I try to fix my image?"

She stands there, barely even blinking for what seems like forever. I widen my eyes, hoping I didn't short-circuit her brain as I wait for her to speak. But she doesn't. Nope. Instead, she bursts into a fit of laughter. And I'm not talking the cute type of laugh that some girls do when you tell a joke that's not very funny. I'm talking a full-on, gut-busting, knee-slapping howl. There's even a point in the middle where she's laughing so hard that I think I may need to perform CPR, because the fucking girl looks like she can't breathe.

Maybe I'll just let nature run its course on this one.

I'm completely speechless as she finally reins herself in and stands up straight. Tears are streaming down her face, and she wipes them away before her eyes finally lock onto mine. "Oh my God," she says, her expression going serious. "You're for real?"

I raise my chin, taking a mental inventory to ensure that I still have a set of balls attached to my body before mustering up whatever dignity I have left. "Yeah, I'm for real. Will you help me?"

Her lips press into a thin line, and she immediately starts shaking her head rapidly. "Riggs, no. Can you imagine us attempting to look like we actually like each other? Not to mention, I can't just pack up and move to Florida. I have work."

"Oh, yeah? Where?" I ask. "Because when I talked to my sister, she told me that the boutique was closing, and you're racing to look for a new job."

Her jaw drops in exasperation. "That bitch really gave me up? Does she know about this?"

"Not exactly," I reply. "I told her I was going to see if you would come do some work for me while I try to get back into the organization's good graces. We both thought your background in marketing might help me from a public relations standpoint. You make all those ugly clothes at the boutique look good, so it shouldn't be hard to do the same for me."

I really need her to say yes to this. Even though we have a rocky past and an even rockier present, I trust Monroe not to take advantage of the situation like all the other women I know would. Not to mention, I wouldn't have to worry about her falling in love with me because she hates my guts.

She chuckles. "Marketing and PR are not the same thing. I'm sorry, but you're going to have to find someone else to help you with this."

Fuck.

I stand from the couch, walking toward her. I'm trying to keep my cool here, but her attitude gets me so worked up every time we're near each other, I end up wanting to choke her or fuck her. *Or both at the same time.* Her eyes widen as I stalk her way, but she keeps her chin lifted, fake confidence exuding from her small body. "Come on, Monroe," I say quietly, reaching out and ghosting my palm along her jaw. Her eyes flutter shut, and I swear I see her lean into my hand the tiniest bit, which surprises the fuck out of me. A smirk spreads across my lips. "You and I both know you need me just as much as I need you."

That seems to snap her out of whatever trance she was in. Her deep blue eyes go impossibly dark, and her brows pull tight in anger. She slaps my hand away and pushes at my chest, throwing me off balance and making me stumble backward a step.

"I don't need shit from you or anyone else," she seethes. "I can take care of myself. So why don't you go back to Florida and find some bimbo to be your girlfriend? You'll have a lot better luck controlling someone like that with your money and fame than you will with me. Get the fuck out of my house, asshole."

I'm shocked by her reaction, but scramble to take the words back, not knowing why they triggered her so quickly. "Wait," I rush out. "I'm sorry. I know you don't need anyone. I didn't mean it like that. I just think this situation has the potential to help us both." My apology seems to make her fume a little bit less, but I can tell she's conflicted. Her lips are pressed tightly together and her nostrils flair slightly with every inhale. She fidgets with the hem of her shirt as she shifts from one foot to the other.

"How?" she asks. "What could you possibly offer me besides doing PR for you? I'm not qualified to do that, even if I wanted to."

I let out a breath, thankful that she's not kicking me out. But once again, my lack of a plan has me at a loss for what to say. If I tell her I'll pay her to be my fake girlfriend, she'll lose her shit. She obviously doesn't like the idea of being reliant on anyone besides herself, so I need to tread carefully if I want her to hear me out.

"Have you ever thought about working for yourself?" I ask. I already know she has from my conversation with Grace, but I wasn't given many details, so I'm flying kind of blind here. She narrows her eyes, and her tense arms drop to her sides. Seeing the opening, I take it, continuing to speak before she has a chance to stop me. "What about starting your own business? You could take the time in Daytona to get everything in order, make some fresh new contacts, then you'd have the freedom to go wherever you want with it."

She shakes her head. "Already tried. My credit score isn't high enough to take out a loan. I need more time to save up before I can do anything like that. I just need to find something else and keep putting money away."

Bingo.

"How about this?" I begin. "Come do this for me, and I'll invest in your business as a silent partner."

She chews on the inside of her cheek, contemplating my offer. I internally pat myself on the back for having the wherewithal to come up with something that would reassure her that she'd still be in control of her own life. After what seems like minutes of silence, she finally speaks.

"Okay."

Fuck yes.

"But under one condition," she rushes out.

"What?" I ask, raising a brow in question.

She puts her shoulders back, looking right into my eyes. "Every dime you give me will be paid back, *with interest.* I don't need a handout, and I refuse to take one, no matter how rich and unconcerned you are about your money. It matters to me that I make my own way and don't have anything for people to hold over my head. If you can't agree with that, you can find someone else to help you."

I nod my head rapidly in agreement. "Yeah, of course." I'd love to know why she thinks I'd ever give her money then hold it over her, but that's not important right now. The only thing I'm worried about is getting the fuck out of here before the bitchy side of her personality pops back in and fucks this all up for me.

She shakes her head in defeat. "When did I get this desperate? Pretending to date arguably the biggest dickwad on the planet just to survive."

Okay, drama queen.

"All I heard was *'biggest dick'*," I say with a grin. "So, thank you."

She rolls her eyes, but I don't miss the way she's tamping down a smile. I can't believe I got her to agree to this. That was some Jedi mind shit, right there. I extend my hand out between us for her to shake, but of course she doesn't.

"Rule number one of this arrangement," she says, looking down at my open palm like it's covered in dog shit before bringing her narrowed eyes to mine. "Don't touch me."

I drop it to my side, giving her a tight nod.

"Whatever you say, Mayhem."

SIX
MONROE

I'VE BEEN on the road for almost twelve hours. I'm somewhere in the middle of North Carolina, and even though I left Hope Harbor pretty early this morning, I'm exhausted. It's weird how you can be busy all day and still have energy, but when you sit behind the wheel of a car for hours on end, you feel like you ran a fucking marathon.

A cramp seizes my leg muscle, and I decide that it's time to pull over and get a hotel room. I need to sleep if I'm going to make it another eight hours. Riggs insisted that I fly; then he'd have my car shipped down to Daytona. And while it was a logical idea, I refused. Something about the fact that he was making perfect sense didn't sit right with me.

I was being a bitch. *Whatever.*

The boutique closed two days ago. It was bittersweet, but Claire seemed to be at peace with it. That poor woman has worked her fingers to the bone for decades because she loved that place so much. She deserves to enjoy some rest and relaxation. Grace is living in Boston and making clothes for all the football wives, but she's promised to stop by my house once a week to check on things and grab the mail. I'll be back before I know it. Either I'll help Riggs get out of trouble with his team and return home quickly, or I'll kill the stupid motherfucker and flee the state of Florida without a trace. Both are possible honestly.

Thankfully, I got off at the right exit because it seems to be a main drag, lined with several restaurants and hotels. I pull my car into the first one I see, relieved that the parking lot seems fairly empty. Hopefully it's because it's early on a weekday and the rooms are vacant, and not because it's a shithole with bedbugs.

Within twenty minutes, I'm checked into my room and lugging my two suitcases onto the elevator. The place is clean and doesn't smell like body odor, so I'm happy. Despite being raised in an expensive home with pretentious parents, I don't need to be fed with a silver spoon. As long as I have access to McDonald's french fries and Coca-Cola every now and then, I'm good. To me, *those* are the finer things in life.

My mom would shit a brick if she heard me say that.

I use my key card to enter the room and make a beeline for the bed, tossing my bags on top. I rifle through them for a new pair of underwear, an oversized t-shirt, and my toiletry bag because I feel disgusting from sitting in the car all day. All I want is to take the hottest shower known to man and spend the night watching a trashy Netflix dating show.

I spend a while washing my body and hair, stopping to have an impromptu Bella Simon karaoke sesh before I shave my legs. The fact that my best friend makes game day outfits for the pop star will never stop being cool to me. Grace says she's the most down-to-earth person in the world, which makes her even more amazing in my eyes. Bella was a guest at her wedding with Tanner a few months ago, but I unfortunately couldn't make it because of work. It was a last-minute event after the Boston Blizzard won the Super Bowl, so while I was sad I wasn't there, I understood. I was still her maid of honor via FaceTime.

I turn off the water, wring out my long, dark brown hair, and dry off before throwing on my panties and t-shirt. Just as I plop down in bed and pull up the streaming app on my laptop, my phone vibrates with a text. I look to see the notification from my best friend before swiping up to open the messaging app.

I ended up telling her what was going on after Riggs left my house that day. She already knew he was in trouble with the team and needed to do a quick one-eighty in their eyes, so I don't think she was too surprised when I laid out the plan he came up with. I'm already keeping one big secret from her, and I wasn't about to add to that.

GRACE

Hey sister-in-law! How's the drive treating you?

MONROE:

Oh, fuck off. One thing you can be certain of is that I will NEVER marry your brother. The only reason I'm even helping him is because I ran out of options and need money to survive.

GRACE:

> I still don't understand why you hate each other so much. Trust me, if anyone knows how annoying he is, it's me. But it seems like you guys didn't even give it a chance.

MONROE:

> I know guys like him, Grace. No offense, but he's a douche. I'd rather put my nipples through a cheese grater than be friends with him. This arrangement is strictly business.

GRACE:

> Please don't kill him. I'm not in his will yet.

MONROE:

> No promises.

I KNOW what you're thinking. I should've just been honest with her over the last two years and told her how Riggs and I really met. But every time I started to, I chickened out. Grace is the best friend I've ever had, and I'm afraid that if she knows that I slept with her brother, I'll lose her. Even though it was before she and I met, I don't want that night to screw up the amazing relationship we have. Or worse, what if she loves the idea of us and tries to get us to be together? No thanks to that. Riggs Valentine belongs to the streets. I am not equipped, nor do I have the patience, to turn a ho of that caliber into a husband.

Like I told Grace. Doing this was a last resort. Although I submitted several applications and sent my resume to every marketing firm within driving distance of my house, the responses aren't coming in, so I needed something quick. Could I have picked up a serving job or done some delivery driving? Yeah, probably. But none of those things will get me any closer to starting my own business the way going to Daytona will. As long as Riggs stays in his lane and keeps himself from getting into any more trouble, we'll be fine.

I set my phone down, picking up my laptop and starting the dating game show I've been dying to watch. But I'm so exhausted, I barely make it through the first episode before sleep takes me.

Tomorrow, the shit show begins.

SEVEN
RIGGS

"HOW WAS THE DRIVE?" I ask, standing beside Monroe in the elevator as we ascend to my floor. She's got several bags slung over her shoulder and the handle of a rolling suitcase in each hand as she stares at the door like she's waiting for it to open so she can get away from me. I attempted to carry her luggage in from the car, but she snapped at me and told me to *"back the fuck off"*, then proceeded to load herself up and trudge into the building like a pack mule while I followed with empty hands. The glares I got from all the rich old ladies in the lobby were special.

"Long," she says, blowing out a breath. She looks like she's been through the wringer, and I want to say I told her so about driving instead of flying, but I have a feeling she isn't in the mood to go back and forth with me. So I keep the thought to myself. There will be plenty of time to get under her skin and see how many of her buttons I can push later.

The doors slide open, and I motion for her to exit first,

following and taking a right down the hallway. She pulls her suitcases slowly enough that we're walking side by side, and I catch her off guard when I reach over and take the handle from her grip. She looks up at me with a scowl but doesn't move to grab it back.

We reach the very last door and I press my finger to the digital pad to unlock it. As soon as I hear the faint *click*, I push down on the handle and swing my door open. I let Monroe walk in front of me, expecting a grand reaction to my luxurious condo, but she just heads through the entryway and turns to me without even taking in her surroundings.

"This is nice," she says, but her tone tells me she isn't nearly as impressed as most of the other guests I've had here. Either she's holding back, or she's seen places like this before because even I can admit that the living area alone is awe-inspiring. The floors are bright white marble that gleams even as the sun begins to set. The walls are also white, with recessed lighting along the ceilings to make everything look clean and open. The far wall has a mounted seventy-seven-inch television with a full audio system. Underneath it is a built-in electric fireplace, that's really more for aesthetics than anything else, since the temperature here doesn't drop very often. And the entire back wall is all windows, giving an amazing view of Daytona Beach. The section directly below us is actually reserved as a topless area, which was really a selling point for me. The women here are all knockouts with gorgeous bodies.

Monroe will fit right in.

I clear my throat, not really sure how to handle her nonchalance. "Ummmm," I trail off. "This is obviously the living area. The kitchen is to your left. Help yourself to whatever you want, whenever you want." I tip my head toward the stairs. "Your room is up here," I say. She nods tightly and follows me as I lead her to the room directly next to mine. There are more bedrooms, but this is the only other one that faces the beach, so I thought she'd want it. Unfortunately, we'll share a wall, but I'll take all my *self-care activities* to my ensuite bathroom so she doesn't hear me. This is temporary anyway, and it's a small sacrifice to make when it means getting my job back on track.

"Feel free to unpack into the dresser and closet," I tell her. "The bathroom is right down the hall. I have my own, so don't worry about leaving all your girly shit on the counter. And if you want to decorate a different way, just let me know and I'll have my designer take care of it."

She looks at me, the hint of a smile tipping up one corner of her mouth. It almost makes me wish I could redo the past two years. I don't regret the night I spent with Monroe, but I shouldn't have been so vague with the details of who I was. She obviously had some hang-ups about not wanting to exchange personal information, and I'll admit I deceived her on purpose. I just wanted to be regular guy with her—not a famous athlete.

As much as I love playing the field when it comes to women, sometimes I actually do want to enjoy their company outside of just fucking them. It's rare, but every now and then I feel more than just a physical connection. That night, I did. We talked for a hell of a lot longer than I normally do with anyone at the bar before I invited her back to my hotel. She intrigued me so much with the way our conversation came so easily, and I wasn't ready to let her go. Believe it or not, I had no intentions of fucking her, but when I set my hand on her thigh in the back seat of the Uber, the heat that traveled through my arm and straight to my dick was unlike anything I had ever felt before. I went completely feral at the contact and couldn't stop myself from taking her mouth in the dirtiest first kiss I'd ever experienced. By the time I shoved her through the door to my room, my animal instincts had kicked in, and all I could think about was taking her in the most primal way.

Normally, that's a part of myself that I try hard to suppress. The urges that I get to let go of all logic and give in to my impulses are so hard to control if I let them take up space in my brain that I push them away as fast as they come on. But that night with Monroe?

I gave in.

She let me give her all of me, in my rawest, realest form. And the rush I got when I sunk my teeth into her flesh while I brutally fucked her like an animal is something I haven't forgotten. I don't think I ever will.

I snap out of my thoughts to see her still staring, an almost questioning look burning into me. "Okay," I say awkwardly, shoving my hands into the pockets of my shorts. "I'll leave you to get settled in. The fridge and pantry are full, but just put anything else you want on the list on the iPad in the kitchen and I'll make sure it gets added to the grocery delivery."

She nods her head in understanding. "Got it."

I turn and walk toward the door, stopping to face her again. "Thanks for doing this," I say quietly. "I really appreciate it."

She raises a brow. "Don't make me regret it," she replies, but her eyes dance with playfulness. I haven't seen her like this in so long, it catches me off guard, but I try not to act affected as I give her a tight nod and leave the room with a million thoughts running rampant in my head.

MONROE

Awkward, party of two, your table's ready.

As soon as Riggs closes the door to my bedroom, I let out the breath I was holding, allowing my tense shoulders to sag in relief. What the actual fuck was that? Not only did he thank me and offer to let me redecorate his house, but the way he stared at me for several minutes like he was remembering every dirty detail of the last time we were in a room with a bed together made me tingle all over.

So what if I was thinking about it too? It was hot. *Sue me.*

Anyway, we're going to need to get back to our regularly scheduled insults and indifferent attitudes if this is going to work, because if he starts being sweet and buying me snacks, it's only a matter of time before I fold like a dollar store lawn chair. And that can *never* happen. I need to use my time here to come up with a business plan so I can put it into motion immediately when I'm done fixing Riggs' fuck-up.

I unpack my suitcases into the dresser and hang the dresses I brought in case we end up at any formal events. Claire let me take a few from the boutique that I had been eyeing, so maybe I'll get a chance to wear them. We really didn't discuss all the things he's expecting from me while I'm here, and I'm not sure what to think, but I guess I'll find out soon enough.

It's late by the time I'm done, and all I can think about is how I haven't eaten since I left the hotel this morning. I have enough money saved up to pay my bills for a few months, with a little extra. But I still didn't want to waste funds on expensive food when I knew I could just eat once I got here. I honestly thought I would be done a little sooner so I could hit the grocery store, but it looks like I'm going to have to find something in the kitchen.

I make my way down the stairs, noticing that the house is completely dark and quiet. He must already be in bed. I make a beeline straight for the refrigerator and look inside. It's full of all kinds of fresh fruits and vegetables, but other than that, nothing is looking like it will hit the spot. I'd do some shady shit for a king size Reese's right about now, but the outlook isn't good.

Throwing up a silent prayer, I head toward what I assume is the pantry. I open the door, and the light inside comes on automatically, illuminating the floor-to-ceiling shelving units that are fully stocked. It looks like Riggs might have a bit of a sweet tooth, because although there's no chocolate, there's enough junk food here to feed a small country. This will certainly suffice until I can go out tomorrow.

I settle on a bag of tortilla chips and a jar of salsa, bringing them out to the kitchen and sitting down at the breakfast bar. I pull open the bag of chips, the salty scent filling my nose and making my mouth water. Picking up the jar of salsa, I try my hardest to twist off the lid. But no matter how tight I grip it, it won't budge.

Trying another approach, I walk over to the sink and turn on the hot water, tapping my foot against the marble floor as I wait for it to reach the right temperature. I hold the jar under the stream for a while, tucking it under my t-shirt and attempting to twist again, but it still won't pop open.

"What the fuck?" I whine quietly, getting ready to surrender and just eat the chips by themselves. But before I can even turn away from the sink, a warm breath hits my ear.

"Need some help, Mayhem?" Riggs whispers, making me jump so high that I almost drop the salsa right on my foot.

"Asshole!" I screech, turning around and slapping his chest with one hand while the other clutches onto the jar for dear life. As soon as my hand connects, I notice that he's shirtless. His rock-hard muscles are on full display, being illuminated only by the light coming from inside the pantry. I can't tear my eyes away from him, no matter how badly I want to. Flashbacks of being pinned under his body, his chest pressed tightly to my back as he fucked me flood my memory, making me almost moan out loud.

Goddamn this guy. I don't know if I can live like this.

I'm finally able to pull my gaze away, bringing it back up to his face with a scowl. As if he knows exactly what I was thinking about, he smirks, reaching out and grabbing the jar from my hand before popping it open with ease.

"There you go, sweet thing," he says as he sets the salsa on the counter next to the bag of chips. He's still wearing that same cocky smirk, and I want to punch it right off his stupid face.

"Does that self-assured bullshit really work on women? If so, I'm extremely concerned for the future of the female species," I quip, walking past him and settling back down at the bar.

"You tell me," he says. "Did it work the night I gave you the best fuck of your life? If memory serves, I think it did."

My jaw drops open in surprise, but I recover quickly, pretending to gag and throw up all over my chips. "You're a pig," I say. "I'm not hungry anymore."

Hopping off the stool, I walk away, but stop in my tracks to turn around and grab the chips and salsa from the counter. Because I'm definitely still hungry.

"Good night, Mayhem," he sings on a laugh as I flip him off over my shoulder and return to my room with snacks in tow.

I need to figure out how to fix his problem fast so I can get the fuck out of here.

EIGHT

MONROE

TODAY IS my first game as Riggs' fake girlfriend. He still isn't playing, but he'll be in the dugout with the team, so I'm here doing what we agreed upon this morning. I'm wearing his jersey and I'll be putting on a cute little show for anyone that may be interested in watching us. I plan on throwing a few waves his way, but after the other night in the kitchen, I'm feeling more frustrated than ever that I even agreed to do this.

Although he drives me nuts with his cocky attitude, being near Riggs has made me as horny as ever. Flashbacks of our night together have been playing on a loop in my head, and no matter how much I want them to stop, they just won't. Every time I think I have myself under control, I'll catch a whiff of his lingering cologne and my hormones perk right the fuck back up. I'm convinced the shit is made of one-hundred percent fuckboy pheromones with the way my pussy clenches every time I inhale it.

I'm also convinced that he rolls around in my bed every time I leave the room because while it's faint, I can smell him at night. At this point, it's only a matter of time before I wake up actively humping my pillow. Let's just hope dream Monroe is quieter than awake Monroe. The last thing I need is him hearing me through the wall as I get myself off using a poor, innocent piece of bedding. He'd never let me live that down.

I walk down the cement staircase, double-checking my ticketing app before stopping at the second row of seats. I would've much rather been in a suite because it's hotter than Satan's nutsack out here, but after discussing it, Riggs and I decided that for the first few games, I should be near the field. That way, everyone who's looking will be able to see how we interact, and hopefully it'll give the illusion that he's making changes in his life. Maybe I'll get lucky and it'll only take a couple of these things before we accomplish our goal and I can get the hell out of dodge to begin the next chapter of my life.

Just as I take my seat, Fury players start trickling out of the dugout and onto the field. Some stay off to the side, stretching and jogging along the foul lines. Others run toward the outfield, where they warm up by throwing the ball back and forth to each other. I know pitchers generally stay in the bullpen during pre-game stuff, so I'm surprised to see Riggs walk out in full uniform. My traitorous whore of a body reacts, and I have to clench my thighs together to quell the throbbing between them at the sight.

I've noticed that every player wears their uniform differently. Some have shorter pants with socks pulled up to their knees. Some go all the way down to the ankles and give lots of room to move. But Riggs? Holy fucking fuck-balls. They show off every muscle in his toned body, from his round ass down to his thick quads and calves. I can see every one of them firing off under the tight fabric as he makes his way along the baseline toward the stands. I assume he's coming over to me, but he walks right past, stopping where a young boy, no more than six years old, shyly holds a ball and glove in his little hands about ten feet from where I'm sitting.

"Hey, buddy," Riggs says, getting as close as the wall will allow him. "Do you want to help me warm up?"

A wide smile blooms across the little boy's face, and he nods his head quickly, doing his best to hold the ball while attempting to shove the glove over his palm. When Riggs sees that he's struggling, he takes a few steps back before running up and scaling the wall, pulling himself over the railing and landing next to the kid.

"Where are your parents?" he asks. The boy turns and points behind him to where a young woman is sitting with a baby carrier strapped to her chest. What looks to be an infant wearing a big, floppy sun hat sleeps peacefully against her as she waves down to them with a smile. Riggs lifts his hand in greeting, kneeling down in front of the boy and helping him put the glove on.

"Thank you, Val," he says in the tiniest voice, and I swear I want to melt right on the spot.

"No problem, pal," he returns, ruffling his hair. "How about that game of catch?"

The boy nods enthusiastically as Riggs hops back over the railing and onto the field. I watch as they toss the ball back and forth for several minutes, and I have to admit that I'm extremely surprised to see this side of him. This is the same man who gives me shit every chance he gets, loses his temper on innocent mascots, and always seems to find himself in a heap of trouble. But I can't help but think there's more to him than all of that. Maybe there's a reason he is the way he is.

I'm broken from my thoughts when he walks toward the railing, tossing the ball to the kid one last time and pointing in my direction.

"See that pretty girl over there?" he asks. The little boy looks my way and nods, turning back to Riggs with a smile. "I'm going to go say hi to her, but thank you for helping me warm up. I don't know what I would've done without you."

He turns and walks in my direction, and I have to pull myself together so he doesn't see me reacting to the tender moment. I can't soften for him. That's a recipe for disaster with us living together and having to put on a show for the team. I remind myself that that's all this is as I stand from my seat and make my way to the railing.

"I have to say, you look damn good in my jersey," he says lowly, as more of a growl than anything else. "Any chance I'll ever see you wearing it and nothing else?"

I lean down, putting myself a little closer to him, plastering a saccharine-sweet smile on my face so that everyone who can see us thinks I'm being flirty. "Not a fucking chance in hell," I reply quietly, blowing him a kiss as he grins back at me.

"Keep it up, sweet thing," he says so only I can hear. "I'll pull you down onto the field and fuck you right into this dirt. And we both know you'll love every minute of it."

My eyes go wide, and my mouth falls open in surprise. I want to send back a smart retort, but his filthy threat mixed with the way he looks in that uniform is making words *really hard*.

"And look at you being a good girl for me, opening that slutty little mouth to be filled. I love it when you're agreeable, Mayhem."

Catching me off guard, he hops up and grabs hold of the railing, pressing a quick kiss to my cheek before lowering back onto the field and running toward the dugout. I'm still standing there, gaping like a fish long after he's gone.

RIGGS

"She's pretty," Ace says as we sit on the bench during the bottom of the fifth inning. We're leading the San Antonio Vipers three runs to one, but I've barely been watching the game. I'm too busy focusing on Monroe as she cheers from the second row. As much as I've been begging to play, I'm glad they didn't choose today to add me back into the rotation. Because the distraction of knowing that my last name and number fifty-seven is stretched across her back has made it impossible to focus on anything else.

"Fuck yeah, she is," I say, trying to hold my smile back. "She's funny too. And super smart."

The rookie catcher grins. "She must be if she has the Bad Boy of Baseball all worked up. Damn, Val. You're down bad, huh?"

My instinct is to deny, deny, deny. Come up with some asshole comment about wanting to be balls deep inside her hot body for a night. But then I remember the plan, and I'm thankful I don't have to save face by diminishing her in that way. Here, we aren't enemies. She's my girlfriend and I don't have to act like I'm not a little excited about her being here. I should probably check myself to figure out why I'm feeling anything besides indifference toward her when all we ever do is bicker, but that can be a problem for later.

"I think I am," I say, looking over to see her playing peek-a-boo with the baby brother of my new warm-up buddy. He kicks his feet and reaches out for her, and she waves at him because her seat isn't close enough to touch his chubby hand.

I wonder what she'd look like pregnant.

Whoa. Slow your roll, Valentine.

I shake off the dangerous thought, tearing my eyes off her and returning them to the field just as Hawk Mason steps up to the plate. He grips the bat like he's actually trying to squeeze the life out of it before widening his stance and preparing for the pitch. It's a low fastball, which is the pitcher's first mistake, and before he even connects, I know Hawk is about to add a two-run homer to his tally for the season. The bat makes a loud *crack* and we watch in silence as the ball sails through the air, over the outfield, and drops into the second deck of bleachers past the wall.

He flips the bat, letting it drop to the ground as he jogs around the bases with no trace of a smile to be seen. He just acts like it's not a big deal as the crowd goes wild and fireworks shoot into the air beyond center field. Even though he's a grumpy motherfucker who barely speaks to anyone outside of his best friend, our second baseman, Jackson, we all line up along the dugout to jump on him when he returns. When I turn away to take my spot on the bench again, I can't stop my eyes from returning to the dark-haired bombshell with my name across her back.

NINE
RIGGS

I PACE the floor of the living room, waiting for Monroe to be ready for tonight's team event. We usually don't have a lot going on during the season, but there's a new charity in Daytona that Mr. Durst holds close to his heart, so he's made it mandatory for all players to attend. Generally, this is something I would drag my feet to and complain the entire way, but I feel like it's a good opportunity to show off my new persona as the chill, cool guy of the team.

I nervously run my hands through my hair, checking the clock on my phone to see how much time we have left. She went up there hours ago to start getting ready, and she's still not done. If I didn't know any better, I'd think she hopped right back into bed with her snacks and laptop and is watching some reality dating show on her streaming app.

"C'mon, Mayhem! You're going to make us late!" I yell up the stairs, resuming my pacing as I wait. Seconds later,

I hear her heels clicking along the marble floor at the top of the staircase.

"Keep your pants on, Val," she says flatly, prompting me to turn around with a scowl. The insult that was rolling around on my tongue disappears without a trace as I take her in, her hips swaying from side to side as she descends toward me. It's like she's moving in slow motion as her long, formfitting black dress drags behind her.

Her dark hair falls in large curls over one shoulder, accenting the delicious column of her neck. A high slit runs up her toned thigh, and I swear I stop breathing as I watch it peek out with every step. Her full tits are pushed up, making me want to sink my teeth into the creamy flesh of her cleavage. She's absolutely breathtaking, and even though our relationship is fake, it's crystal clear that I've outkicked my coverage by a fucking mile. I feel like I've swallowed an entire bag of cotton balls as she finally hits the bottom stair and stops in front of me.

Clearing my throat, I try my best to play it cool, as if I'm not thinking a million degenerate thoughts about what it would be like to tear the luxurious fabric from her body. I may be able to convince myself that I hate this woman, but *fuck*. My dick damn sure isn't falling for it.

I need to get this shit under control.

"You ready?" I grunt, refusing to make eye contact with her. I know if I lock onto those blue pools, there's a possibility that I'll throw her over my shoulder and we won't make it to this event. She may fight me all the way, but the joke would be on her because I'm into that shit. Especially knowing that she'd definitely want everything I'd be giving her. I don't miss the way Monroe looks at me when she thinks I'm not paying attention. She can tell herself she can't stand me all she wants. But I can smell it.

"Yeah," she replies, and I can't help but notice that she looks a little deflated. Is she disappointed that I didn't compliment the way she looks? Trust me, I want to. But I also need to make sure I keep enough distance between us that we don't end up blurring the lines of this arrangement. If I'm reading her all wrong, that would be even worse, because being nice to her would make things more awkward than they already have been since she moved in. I need to stay within the lines of our agreement because I can't lose my job. Hopefully, after tonight, some of the heat will be taken off me, and I'll have a little room to breathe.

I reluctantly put space between us, turning on my heel and walking toward the door as Monroe follows, her stilettos clicking against the floor as she does. I pull the door open, letting her walk out, and she keeps her eyes glued to her feet as she passes me.

Fuck. I've definitely upset her.

I pull the door shut behind me, waiting for the faint *click* of the lock engaging before we walk side by side to the elevator. I motion for her to step in first, following her and settling toward the back of the metal box right before we're enclosed inside, all alone. I try my best not to focus on the scent of her perfume as we lower down to the parking garage. I can't put my finger on what she smells like, but it's definitely a mixture of something and *her*. It's the same scent I remember from the night I spent with her. The one that turned me into a feral beast that could barely control himself.

I wish I could stop those memories from flooding my

mind every time I'm near her, but it's getting harder and harder to do the more we're in close proximity to each other. Part of me wishes I could erase it from my mind forever, but it was easily the best sex I've ever had, so the other part of me never wants to forget.

The ride to the event is quiet, and I notice that Monroe has made herself small in the passenger seat of my car. Her knees are angled toward the door, and her head is facing away from me as she looks out the window, watching as the city passes by. Her hands are fisted in her lap, and I have the urge to reach over and pull them apart.

When I can't take knowing I've hurt her feelings any longer, I twist the knob on the radio, turning the music down.

"You look really pretty tonight," I say softly, hoping that she can hear the sincerity in my words.

She slowly turns her head in my direction, lifting her eyes to me while she fidgets with the fabric of her dress. "Thank you," she says as a visible blush spreads across her cheeks. The tension in her shoulders dissipates and she lets out a quiet sigh as she sinks back into the seat.

I return my eyes to the road, but my mind is swirling with thoughts about why Monroe, who is generally so hard and confident, reacted that way to my dismissal of the way she looks. It makes me want to rewind everything and tell her the truth—that I have to tear my eyes away from her sometimes so I don't give in to the urges I've had since she moved here. I know I'm supposed to hate her. It's easier that way, especially since I know she hates me right back. But that doesn't mean I can't see how stunning she is. I have perfect vision, and she seems to get more beautiful every time I blink.

I pull into the valet area of the event center and step out, handing my keys to the attendant before rounding the hood to open Monroe's door. But before I even make my way to the passenger side, she's out on her own. She rises from the seat, smoothing her floor-length dress over her thighs before walking toward the staircase that leads to the entrance of the building. I quickly swing the car door shut and run behind her until we're side by side.

"Remember, you're supposed to be my girlfriend," I say quietly. "You have to at least *act* like you can stand to be around me."

She continues walking, forcing a smile. "Don't worry, *Val*," she says. "I'm great at wearing a mask at these things." I cock an eyebrow in question because I have no idea what she means by that, but she just pushes her shoulders back and walks straight down the middle of the room. I settle a hand on her lower back as we make our way down the aisle, noticing that every guy stops what he's doing and stares as she passes by. I don't fucking blame them because she's a goddamn knockout. But if they keep it up while she's very clearly here with me, I'm going to add another fight to the long list of reasons I'm in deep shit with the team.

As we approach our table, Taylor turns away from the bar, catching my eye. I'm reminded of everything that was said in our meeting after I assaulted Friggle, and my mind starts going in a million different directions at once. As the panic starts to settle in, I grab Monroe by the arm and run to the nearest corner, spinning us so that her back is toward the room while I look beyond her shoulder nervously.

"What the hell are you doing?" she says, pulling away from me.

"I can't!" I whisper-yell, shaking my head rapidly. "They're going to know!"

Her brows pull together in confusion. "Know *what?*"

I force an annoyed exhale, although I'm not sure why. It's not like she can read my mind, especially when I was as cool as a cucumber ten seconds ago. I swallow, doing my best to stop the dry heaves that are threatening to make an appearance before I explain. "My dumb lie got us into this mess! What if they ask questions about our relationship and the word-vomit just starts coming out? I can't be trusted, Monroe! I'm a *liability!*"

I'm about to go into a full-blown panic attack when she grabs hold of my shoulders, giving me a stern shake. "Look at me, Riggs." As soon as she says it, I bring my eyes up to hers, and even though she looks annoyed with me, it's calming. My heart rate slows, and I take a deep breath in through my nose, exhaling through my mouth as her gaze stays on mine.

"It'll be fine, I promise. Just follow my lead, okay?" I nod my head as she takes my hand, weaving our fingers together and walking back toward the table full of Fury employees. Heat travels up my arm with every step, and I almost walk into several people because I can't stop staring at where we're connected. Even though I touched this woman on almost every inch of her body that night, for some reason, holding her hand feels more intimate than any of that.

"Valentine," our shortstop, Dante Cole says with a nod. I lift my chin in greeting as Monroe slides over so her side is pressed against mine before extending her hand.

"Hi," she says with a bright smile. I turn my head, taken aback because I've never actually seen this expression. I've seen her laugh like she does with my sister. Or the way she giggled at the baby she was playing with at my game the other day. I've obviously seen her pissed. I've even seen her cry via Facetime during Grace and Tanner's wedding. But this—whatever kind of smile this is—is new. "I'm Monroe Decker, Riggs' girlfriend." They exchange a handshake, and she moves on to each person sitting at the table, introducing herself and striking up an easy conversation. I watch in awe as she captivates everyone, outwardly showing how interested she is in what they have to say.

While I love the way she's leaning into her role, it's unsettling how comfortable she is in what would otherwise be a very *uncomfortable* situation. We came in here fifteen minutes ago and she didn't know anybody. Like it was something she'd been doing all her life, a mask of positivity slipped over her face as she initiated introductions with my colleagues and teammates before I even had a chance to tell them who she was. How did she get so good at faking the woman I'm watching right now? Because in the time I've known her and all the situations I've seen her in, this isn't Monroe.

Just as she's wrapping up her conversation with my centerfielder, José Maiello, Taylor makes her way over to the table. "This must be the girlfriend," she says, a kind smile blooming across her face. "I've been dying to meet the woman that managed to tame this wildcard." She motions to me, and I smile nervously. I'm just hoping I can get through this conversation without blurting out that none of this is real and that I'm not tamed. That Monroe is only here because I bribed her by offering to help her start her business.

Thankfully, my new girlfriend once again takes the reins and does her own introduction. "Well, I don't know if I've tamed him, but I'm certainly working on it," she replies with a grin, wrapping her small hands around my arm and leaning into me. My muscle flexes under her touch, and I wish I could will away the sparks that are firing off under the taut sleeve of my dress shirt. "Monroe Decker," she says, putting her hand out for Taylor to shake. She does, and then looks up at me with an expression of approval.

"It's very nice to meet you," Taylor replies. "I'm sure I'll see you around at the stadium. Have a great night, you guys," she says to the table, and they all wave as she turns and moves on to the next group of people awaiting her. I breathe a sigh of relief, internally patting myself on the back for keeping all my nervous words inside my body.

Now that one of the people I need to convince is out of the way, I relax a little, pulling out a chair for Monroe to sit in. Playing the part, she gives me a sweet smile before moving to lower herself into it. But before she gets there, Taylor calls for her.

"Monroe!" She says, waving her hand. "Come over here and meet some of the ladies!" The overly happy expression that had fallen from her face goes right back on as she stands to her full height, kisses me on the cheek, and walks toward the group of women. I recognize some of them as the wives of my teammates, but I think some of the others are probably just here because it's a charity event and they have a lot of money. I let her go, sitting in the seat that was waiting for her.

"She seems like a good one, Val," José says, jutting his chin out to where Monroe is now waving her hands animatedly in conversation. "I guess your luck never runs out, huh?"

"She is," I reply, unable to take my eyes off her. "I think I'll keep her."

TEN
MONROE

"WHERE ARE YOU FROM ORIGINALLY?" Dana asks as she holds her champagne glass gingerly between her manicured fingers. I learned that she runs one of the children's charities the baseball team works with, so she's here to thank everyone whose donations make a difference in the lives of the kids she works with. She seems nice, but something about her has been rubbing me the wrong way since I came over here.

"Well, I'm originally from California. But I met Riggs in Boston, where I've been living for the last two years," I reply.

"We were all so surprised to hear that he actually has a girlfriend," she says. "To be honest with you, for a while there, we thought maybe you weren't real."

"It was a whirlwind at first, but he ended up winning me over. Now I can't imagine my life without him," I say, glancing over my shoulder at the table where he's talking to his teammates. It's not a complete lie. Our night together was definitely a whirlwind. So what if the events that have happened since aren't exactly the stuff of fairy-tales? Fake it till you make it, right? I'm just here to make him look good so the team stops putting so much pressure on him to straighten up.

The woman next to me—Sasha, I think her name is—scoffs quietly. I slide my eyes over in her direction, narrowing them slightly because *what the fuck is this bitch's problem*? Ever since Taylor called me over here, I've felt a negative energy coming from her. I'm really good at reading vibes, and hers suck.

"What?" I ask, every nerve in my body on high alert as she slowly takes a sip from her glass and lowers it.

"Oh, nothing," she says with a fake-as-fuck smile. "It's just that everybody knows that Riggs Valentine doesn't generally keep the company of a woman longer than a few hours. I know from experience that that man isn't capable of giving more than a couple of orgasms before he makes his way to the next unsuspecting victim."

I look up at the other women, expecting them to be shocked at her words, but aside from Taylor who now has her eyes averted to another part of the room, they're looking back at me as if this is old news. As if they're all in agreement that there's nothing more to Riggs than what he does in the bedroom. But they're wrong.

He and I may have our differences, and maybe we'll never mesh, but I've watched him with his family and friends. I know that when his sister was younger, he and his best friend included her in everything they did, no matter how annoying she was. I know that when his dad had back surgery, he used almost his entire offseason to help him run their construction business, refusing to take any money in return. I also know that since I've moved here, I haven't added a single thing to his grocery list, yet all my favorites continue to show up in the delivery order.

There's so much more to Riggs that these people have never seen. They don't know who he really is.

I straighten to my full height, mustering up all the confidence I can find. "That man over there," I say, lifting my chin back to the table where he sits, "is amazing. He's selfless, loving, and would give the shirt off his back to anyone in need. It's a shame you're too bitter and spiteful to see it." I turn to the others. "It was nice meeting you all. I should get back to my date now."

I turn on my heel, making a beeline straight for Riggs. He catches me out of the corner of his eye and turns to face me as I approach. Without even giving it a second thought, I put one hand on the back of his chair, lean down and press my lips against his. I'm sure they're all still watching, so I put on a show, using my tongue to trace his plump lower lip until he opens for me. His hand ghosts over my waist as we kiss, and just that simple touch is a reminder of the way he made me feel two years ago.

I haven't forgotten what it felt like to be with him. Quite the contrary, in fact. I'm not shy about my sexual explorations. I was raised to be prim and proper, never giving my body or pleasure away to whoever I wanted. I lost my virginity to Conrad, but he never gave me what I needed. It was only about him. I was just a tool he used to get himself off. So, being with Riggs the first night I was in Massachusetts? That was the first time I really felt like what I was doing was for me. And I haven't been able to replicate that since.

I've been open to new partners. I've told them what I liked, and they've tried to give it to me, but they've never matched up. I think that's part of the reason why I'm so angry with Riggs, and why his mere presence in my life makes me want to rip my own hair out. It's not even his fault. He tried to get me to open up to him. He tried to get me to share more of myself than just my body. I didn't want that. I still don't. But the fact that he still has such a hold on me this long after we were together isn't an easy pill to swallow.

Those women weren't wrong. He does sleep around. It's something he's quite proud of, and that's fine. He never leads anyone on, and they know the score before they make the decision to have sex with him. But the way that they spoke about him, like that's all he has to offer, was fucked up. I have no problem showing them they're wrong.

He growls into my mouth and his hand on my waist tightens almost to the point of pain. I whimper quietly and that breaks the spell that he's under. He quickly rips his head back but never loses eye contact as he stares at me with a look that's equal parts confusion and heat.

"Fuck, Mayhem," he says on an exhale. He's still in shock, and I barely register the fact that everyone at the table is staring at us until someone clears their throat.

I slip back into character, the corners of my mouth lifting in a sweet smile. "I was gone too long," I say, just loud enough for everyone around us to hear. "I missed you." He swallows thickly, nodding before grabbing my wrist and pulling me down into his lap. I can feel his thick cock pressing up against the back of my thigh. I try not to act surprised, but can't help the wetness that begins to gather in my panties, knowing that one kiss turned him on so much. He must've wanted me to feel it, otherwise he would have just let me sit down in a different chair.

My instinct is to say something smart—to try to piss him off. But for some reason, I settle into his chest and wrap my arms around his neck loosely. The table slips back into their quiet conversations, and we move on as if this is all so normal for us. Like we won't be at each other's throats the second we're alone, just like we always are. It's just…*us*.

But I'll be damned if I don't make it clear to all these people that they're lucky to have a guy like Riggs Valentine on their team.

ELEVEN

RIGGS

IT'S EARLY MORNING, and I'm sitting at the kitchen table getting ready for the day. The team has to be at the stadium several hours before game time for media, so I'm trying to multitask—drinking my coffee, answering emails, and clipping my toenails. Gross, but I'm not a heathen. It has to be done.

I'd love to say I'm flying through all my morning tasks, but I keep getting distracted by everything that went down at the charity event last night. The more I try to wrap my head around all of it, the more confused I am.

The first thing that has me messed up is how quickly Monroe slipped into the role of my girlfriend, commanding an entire room full of people and making them fall in love with her. That's not something you do if you don't have years worth of experience. So where did she learn that?

The other thing that has my mind going a million miles an hour is that kiss. One minute, she was talking to that group of women, and the next, her mouth was pressed to mine, sucking every breath from my body. Once I got over the initial shock, I practically had to hold myself back with the need to take her in front of everybody at the table. And the small whimper when I tightened my grip on her luscious hip? I was instantly hard for her. I had to pull her down into my lap to hide the steel rod under my dress pants. It was like I was fourteen again, unable to control my body as her tongue slid against mine.

She hates me. I'm supposed to hate her right back. But last night made it impossible for me not to think about how explosive things would be if we didn't have such animosity between us. We both know how fucking good we are together physically.

"Please tell me you're not doing what I think you're doing at the table where we eat," a groggy Monroe says from behind me. I immediately shove the nail clippers under my thigh, hoping I can convince her that I'm not.

"Checking my email and enjoying a cup of coffee before I have to leave for the day? Because if that's what you think I'm doing, you'd be right." I swallow nervously as she approaches before stopping right next to me and reaching out for my leg. I squeeze my thigh against the hard wood of the chair, the metal of the clippers biting into my skin through my thin sleep pants.

Her eyes go wide as she grabs my arm and attempts to pull me up, but I resist. "You're clipping your toenails in the kitchen!" she shrieks. "That's disgusting, Riggs!"

My jaw drops in faux indignation, hoping I can convince her that I would never do such a thing. "I am not!" I turn my body, doing my best to drag the clippers under my leg, but she doesn't let up. She just continues wiggling her hand between me and the chair, squeezing her fingertips in only inches from where the evidence of my crime is hidden.

"Lift your leg, then!" she grits through her teeth as she continues her assault. Every muscle in my body is rigid, because there's no way in hell I'm letting her under me.

"You're acting crazy!" I say as her nails dig into my skin. I hold my ground, refusing to let her move any part of me until she's finally so gassed out that she gives up. As if she didn't just use every bit of her energy, she stands to her full height, blowing a rogue strand of hair out of her face before pulling her phone from the pocket of her shorts. She's got a hip jutted out, her sassiness on full display as she begins typing on the device with one eyebrow lifted in defiance.

"What are you doing?" I ask, not loving the smug expression on her face.

"I'm texting your mother," she replies. "Imagine how disappointed sweet Libby Valentine will be to know that her pride and joy is out here acting like he was raised in a barn. You're going to break her heart, you know that, right?"

I narrow my eyes at her. "You wouldn't dare."

I hear the *whoosh* of the message being sent and I bare my teeth at her in frustration. And to think I was almost softening for her a little bit. She's the same snarky bitch she's been since I've known her. Clearly, that'll never change.

I only get a few seconds to begin plotting my revenge when my phone rings on the table beside me. Monroe chuckles quietly as we both look over to see my mom's name and photo flashing on the screen. I stare at it for a few rings, hoping she'll hang up, but I already know she won't. She's on the other end of that line in Hope Harbor, waiting to scold me for my actions.

"Are you going to answer it? It's your mom," she says with a saccharine smile across her face.

"I know who it is," I grumble, swiping the phone up and pressing the green button to answer. "Hello?"

"Riggs Sebastian Valentine, please tell me you aren't clipping your nails at the table in the presence of a lady!" my mom yells, practically blowing out my eardrum. The woman is a saint, but if she knows we're doing something we shouldn't be, she's the first to call us out.

"I'm not," I deadpan. "I'm doing it in the presence of Monroe."

The wretched creature beside me chokes on a gasp and I look up to see her jaw practically hitting the floor. Even though I'm getting yelled at by my mother, who can still manage to make me feel like a child from a thousand miles away, the shock on my fake girlfriend's face at my response is worth all of it.

She growls quietly, spinning on her heel and walking toward the coffee maker as my mom continues laying into me. She gives me a proper scolding on my actions and reminds me to be a perfect gentleman now that there's another person living in my house. I verbally affirm all of her points, knowing damn well that I'll continue doing whatever I can to piss Monroe off because it brings me joy.

When we're in public, I'll make goo-goo eyes at her and tell everyone how smitten I am. But inside these walls? Not a chance.

TWELVE
MONROE

I WAKE UP FAMISHED, feeling like I haven't eaten in weeks. I had some yogurt and a banana before bed, but the loud growl coming from under the comforter tells me my stomach didn't think that was nearly enough. I know that even if I attempt to go back to sleep, it wouldn't work. Maybe working on my business plan for a while this morning will make me tired enough for a nap this afternoon. Riggs has to leave for some away games later today, so the house will be quiet, and I can relax in peace.

I turn, swiping my phone from the nightstand and checking the time. It isn't horribly early, but I could've definitely caught an extra two hours of sleep if I wasn't so hungry. Sitting up, I raise my arms above my head in a stretch before standing and walking toward the dresser. I've been sleeping in just a tank top and panties while I've been here, so I open the bottom drawer and pull out a pair of shorts to put on before I go downstairs. Even though Riggs has seen me naked and in a bathing suit a few times during barbecues at his parents' house, I would feel weird walking around here without being fully clothed. I can't wait to get back home so I can wear nothing but my birthday suit when I get up to eat breakfast.

Hands down, it's the best thing about living alone.

I step into the cotton bike shorts, pulling them up my smooth legs. I decide to throw a gray crewneck sweatshirt over my tank since it's tight and my nipples can probably be seen through the thin fabric. The last thing I need is for them to react to Riggs' gravelly morning voice and reveal all my secrets—that, even though he annoys the fuck out of me, that sound elicits fantasies of what he could do to me if we didn't hate each other. He'd never let me live it down.

I toss my hair up into a messy bun, using one of the thick, black scrunchies I have lying out on the nightstand. Once I'm presentable enough, I open the door and walk down the hall, heading toward the stairs. I can hear the sounds of his shower through the wall, so I know he's awake and probably getting ready for work. I do my best to ignore the mental image of him naked, with suds lazily sliding down the ridges of his defined abs, but I fail miserably, internally smacking myself and vowing to get my shit together as I enter the kitchen.

I want to say living with Riggs has made it easier to be turned off by him. I've heard horror stories of couples moving in together after getting engaged and never making it to the altar because they couldn't handle each other's gross habits. Even after catching him clipping his toenails at the table the other day, I still have unwelcome dreams at night about him sneaking into my room and putting his mouth all over me. Don't get me wrong, it *was* disgusting, and I'll be eating my meals at the breakfast bar for the duration of my stay, but it didn't have the effect it probably should have.

I open the refrigerator, pulling out a carton of fresh strawberries that were delivered yesterday. As soon as I took them out of the bag to put them away, I knew they'd be delicious on top of some oatmeal. They're huge and perfectly ripe, which means they're probably so sweet and juicy.

There's a little extra pep in my step as I make my way to the sink, laying out a paper towel so I can dry the fruit after I wash it. As soon as I reach for the faucet handle, something black wrapped around the sprayer catches my eye.

Apparently, my text to Libby the other day struck a nerve, and I unknowingly started a prank war. Well, I would have if Riggs wasn't such an idiot. The rubber band on the sink sprayer trick is the oldest one in the book, and I've fallen victim to it more than once at the hands of his sister. It must be a family thing, because neither of them knows to use an elastic color that blends in with the hardware, which is why I'm not soaked from the chest up right now.

He wants to prank me? I'll prank him right back.

Uno reverse, motherfucker.

I wait, listening quietly as the shower turns off. I'm starting to memorize his morning routine, so I know I have about seven minutes before he moseys down the hallway, making his way to the kitchen for coffee and a bagel. I go over the details of my plan in my head until I hear his bedroom door open. Scrambling back to the sink, I angle the sprayer down so it doesn't hit my face before pulling the lever and letting the water soak my shirt. I turn it off, spinning around and slapping the counter loudly with an open hand. Crying out in fake pain, I dramatically fall to the floor, throwing both hands over my right eye.

"Monroe!" Riggs says, rushing toward me and kneeling down at my side. I tuck my head down because, as much as I wish it were, fake crying is not a skill I was ever able to master. "What happened?" he asks, panic gripping his words as he reaches out and pulls me to him. I immediately notice his still-damp skin pressing against me, and I have to focus on my plan to avoid being distracted by it.

"I—I," I stutter, sniffling to really drive things home. "The sink…it sprayed me and I slipped. I hit my face on the counter."

"Oh my God," he whispers, and I can feel his whole body shaking as he holds me tighter. "I was pranking you. *Fuck. I'm so sorry.*" He's in full panic mode, and now I feel kind of bad, but he brought this on himself, so I stay committed to the fake injury.

He pulls away, placing his trembling hands on the sides on my head, carefully turning it toward him. "Can I see it, sweetheart?" he asks, trying to remain calm but failing miserably. "I need to know if I should call an ambulance. Are you dizzy at all? Please be okay. I'm so sorry." His voice cracks with his apology, and I pull my hands down, exposing my perfectly untouched face to him. His expression, that was twisted in fear just moments ago, morphs into one of relief as he checks me like he's not sure if he's seeing things right. I laugh as he exhales a quiet breath, hanging his head for a moment before looking back up at me. As soon as I see his face, I grow serious.

"Riggs, I'm fine," I say, trying to reassure him as he brings his hands over his face. "It was a joke."

"A fucking *joke*, Monroe?" he says loudly, dropping his hands to the floor and pushing himself to stand. "Yeah, it's real funny to fake a head injury! I was scared out of my fucking mind that you were hurt!"

"Whoa," I reply, standing to join him. "You started this! I *could've* gotten hurt for real with this dumb shit if you actually knew how to pull it off without being caught!" I stab my finger into his chest. "Don't get pissed at me for turning it back around on you!"

He takes a few breaths before his angered expression softens. "I'm sorry," he says, pulling me into a hug. I stiffen at first because I definitely wasn't expecting this, but eventually, I melt into the embrace. He leans down, pressing his lips to the top of my head quickly before pulling back.

"It's okay," I reply quietly. "I'm sorry I scared you."

He huffs a forced laugh, shaking his head from side to side as if he can't believe the results of his little stunt. "Let's call a truce, alright? At least on the pranks. Before I have a heart attack."

"Hmmm," I say, tapping my lower lip as I pretend to mull it over. "I'll tell you what. You make my oatmeal, and I'll consider abandoning my plan for revenge."

He smiles, walking toward the sink. "You've got yourself a deal, you little shithead."

THIRTEEN
MONROE

I SIT ON THE COUCH, opening my laptop and pulling up the back end of what will soon be my marketing company's website. Even though Riggs has agreed to be a silent partner and invest the funds I need to get started, I'm still trying to cut every corner I can. I took a web design course in college, so while it may take me a bit to get it done without a professional, I know I can do it.

I don't think it's really hit me yet that I'm doing this. But honestly, this is a dream come true. Knowing that I'll be in charge of everything when it comes to my work is something I've always wanted. I want to shake up the marketing industry, showing smaller business owners that they can go toe to toe with bigger corporations if they think outside the box.

Working at the boutique was an amazing learning experience for me. Since it was just a small shop located in a rural beach town, it was almost like I had a blank slate when it came to how I would get people to walk through our doors. Instead of sticking to the same old advertising plans that have been in use for decades, I decided to begin relying heavily on targeting a younger crowd with social media. I planned to make influencers want to work with us by using all sorts of trendy photos and videos to spark their interests. Claire may have been in her eighties, but she was open to all my new-age ideas and believed me when I told her I could succeed. Unfortunately, these things can't be built overnight, and I couldn't save Praya in time.

I refuse to let another small business go under on my watch. That's why I'm so excited to get this thing off the ground.

I hear the door open and close, checking the clock in front of me and seeing that it's five in the evening. I've been here for a few weeks now, and I'm starting to feel like maybe I should offer to cook dinner or do chores around the house, but everything is still a little awkward between me and Riggs. He just got back from almost a week on the road, so I haven't really been forced to work through my feelings about the kiss from the charity event. Which is fine with me because it's definitely easier to act like he's the bane of my existence than it is to admit that kissing him was the hottest thing I've experienced in a long time. So hot, that I had to fuck my fingers in the shower later that night just to make the ache between my legs go away. I followed up by giving myself a stern scolding about why we don't let our hormones control our impulses, just for good measure.

Then, there was his reaction to me getting hurt in the kitchen the day that he left. I understand where he was coming from with the fact that it isn't a joke to fake an injury like that, but the way he held me and kissed my head wasn't something I expected. Now I don't know what I'm feeling. I'd like to say that nothing has changed in the way I see him, but that could definitely be a lie.

"Just wanted to let you know I'm home," Riggs says, stepping into the living room where I'm camped out against the arm of his wraparound sofa. "Did you eat dinner?"

I look up at him, and it takes my brain a couple of seconds to realize that he asked me a question. He's wearing a tight black Daytona Fury t-shirt that rides up slightly at the hem, gray sweatpants that hang so low, I can see the delicious V of his abs peeking out from under the waistband, and a fitted white baseball cap, turned backwards.

Damn it. This guy is as slutty as they come.

I rip my eyes away from his body, doing my best to form something that sounds at least a little bit like a coherent sentence. "No. I didn't even realize the time. If you want me to make something—"

"Oh, no that's okay," he says, cutting me off. "I was about to place an order for delivery, but I don't know what you like."

I give him an awkward smile. "Ummm, I'm not very picky. A chicken Caesar salad would be great." It's nice of him to offer. To think of me when he doesn't have to. He's just doing it so he doesn't look like a dick eating in front of me, but it's still a nice gesture. I've been noticing how thoughtful he is since I've been here. Just another reason he pisses me off. I want to hate him, but it's not as easy when he keeps showing me sides of him that I find admirable.

"Yeah, I think I'll go with that too," he says, pulling up

the delivery app on his phone and making the order. I think he's going to leave, but instead, he rounds the sofa and takes a seat next to me. "What's this?" he says, jutting his chin out to where I have my website pulled up on the screen.

At first, I want to close my computer so he doesn't see that there isn't much done. But he's investing his money in this business, so he has a right to know how it's coming along. "I'm trying to build my website," I tell him. "It's going to take a while because I don't have a lot of experience doing this, but I know my way around the back end and think I can get it done. I'm at least going to try before I hand it over to a web designer."

He reaches over me, dragging his fingers along the trackpad and scrolling down the page. "Not bad, Mayhem," he says with a smile. "So, tell me a little bit about what you're trying to do with this thing."

"That's probably something you should've asked before you offered to partner with me, huh?" I joke. He chuckles quietly, still looking at the computer. I turn my head toward him. "I want to make a difference for small businesses. Big box stores and huge corporations have all the marketing resources at their disposal. Somebody needs to help the little guys." I shake my head. "When the boutique closed, part of me felt like I had failed. Even though I was doing my best to change their entire marketing plan, I couldn't scramble to get it done before it was too late. Claire worked her whole life for that place. It's just sad that she had to close her doors because I couldn't get people through them fast enough." I avert my eyes, looking back to the screen in front of me in shame.

"Hey," he says, using one finger under my chin to turn

my gaze back to his. My brain is telling me to pull away in defiance, but I can't deny that his touch is comforting. "That wasn't your fault. Hope Harbor businesses have struggled to stay afloat since before I can remember. Once it became more of a tourist attraction than a home for so many people, it was impossible to build and keep relationships with customers. Praya stuck around longer than any of them, but there was nothing you could do. If anything, you helped them stay open longer than they should've."

My heart flutters in my chest. I'm not sure he's ever used such softness with me. We went from a night of wild sex to hating each other in the snap of a finger, it seems, so we never really got a chance to talk like we are now. And since he knows Claire and the history of the boutique, his words are a healing balm to my heart. I've been struggling with the guilt of feeling that if I had just done more, the shop would still be open today. I know that's ridiculous, since I was an employee for a lot less time than everyone else there, but I couldn't help feeling like a large part of the failure was on my shoulders.

"Thank you," I say, smiling up at him softly. No matter how hard I try to unlock my eyes from his, I can't. Butterflies take flight in my stomach, hoping that he'll just lean in and kiss me. Hating him has become increasingly harder in the short time I've stayed here because I'm seeing parts of him that I didn't know existed. I mean, I did, but they've never been used toward me like they are right now.

His eyes flash with heat, and I think he's finally going to end this streak of hatred between us. But as if a spell has been broken, he shakes his head, blinking quickly. The harsh reality that the moment has passed hits me like a bag of bricks, and I turn my head to face the computer screen in front of me.

He clears his throat loudly, shooting up from the couch and dragging his palms down the front of his sweatpants. "I'll leave you alone to work. I'll let you know when the food gets here."

"Yeah, okay. Thanks," I reply, trying as hard as I can to mask the disappointment that shakes my voice.

Without looking my way, he hightails it out of the room. As soon as I hear the door to his bedroom close, my body sags, and I allow myself to feel the loss of what could've been something amazing.

It was easy to dislike Riggs when I thought the same thing as everyone else—that he's just a manwhore who does what he wants and usually gets away with it. But now that I'm here, living in his house and spending my days around him, I know that's not right. I'm seeing a side of him that's so much more than I ever expected, and now I have to figure out how to avoid screwing up all my plans by falling for him.

FOURTEEN
RIGGS

I ENTER the lobby of my building, exhausted from a long day of practice. I'm finally back in the rotation, so I spent the day preparing to take the mound for the first time this season. We got home yesterday from the first three games of our series in New Orleans, and we play here in Daytona tomorrow night.

I spoke with Taylor, and she told me that although we didn't get to interact with the Durst family on the night of the charity event, everybody noticed a change in my demeanor. She's been lobbying hard for me, and her words of praise combined with the way Monroe commanded the entire room have certainly paid off. I don't know if trading me is still something they're considering, but the fact that I'll be pitching tomorrow night is a positive thing.

"Yes, I have a delivery for suite seven forty-two," I overhear a young woman say as I pass the concierge desk. I turn in her direction immediately.

"I'll take that," I tell her. "That's mine. My girlfriend must have made an order." I'm a little shocked at how quickly the term rolls off my tongue, considering I've really only had a couple of chances to use it in public, but I guess it's better than slipping around others and forgetting who Monroe is supposed to be to me.

The girl looks back to the concierge, who gives a tight nod in agreement. She extends her arm, the plastic drugstore bag dangling from her fingers for me to take as I reach forward.

"Thank you," I say before turning and walking toward the elevator, pressing the button to go up and waiting for the doors to slide open. My curiosity gets the better of me and I peek into the bag, finding a box of tampons and some ibuprofen.

"Great," I mutter to myself. Although she's been pretty sweet lately, I imagine that a menstruating Monroe is some kind of a beast. My sister Grace used to have very heavy and painful periods when she was younger, and she always made sure the whole house knew she was feeling less than her best. It got to the point where Tanner and I scoured the internet for home remedies so she'd stop being so mean to us. That was why I did it, at least. But I have a feeling that he just struggled with the fact that she was suffering. He's always been so protective over her, and now that they're married, all of his actions throughout our younger years make a hell of a lot more sense.

The doors slide open, and I enter the elevator, nodding to the attendant who presses the number for my floor. The ride is short since we don't make any other stops. It's a little later than I normally get back from practice, so most of the people who live here have probably been home from work for a while.

I prepare myself for whatever attitude is about to be slung my way as I finally reach the door to my condo and push my way in. The first thing I notice is how eerily quiet it is. For the past few weeks that Monroe has been here, she's usually perched against the arm of the sofa at this time, working on her website or business plan. But when I peek into the living room, she's nowhere to be found.

"Mayhem? Are you here?" I ask, already knowing that she is. We have assigned parking spaces in this building, and hers is right next to mine. Her BMW was exactly where it was when I left this morning, so I know she's home.

My heart starts racing in my chest as I walk toward the staircase, hoping she's just in her room or something. But when I get about halfway up, I hear a pained moan coming from the hallway. I'm immediately on high alert, picking up my speed and racing to the top. As soon as I turn I see a sight that terrifies me to my fucking core.

Curled up in a ball on the floor right outside the bathroom is Monroe, wearing only an oversized t-shirt and a pair of panties. I can tell immediately that this isn't like the day in the kitchen when she was faking an injury. This is serious. She's completely still, but rapid, shallow inhales are moving her back up and down, so I know she's at least alive and breathing. I drop the bag from my hand, run to her side, and kneel down.

"Hey," I say, carefully placing my hand on her shoulder. A low groan comes from her body as she slowly turns toward me and opens her eyes. "What happened? Are you okay?"

"I'm fine. I just don't feel good," she replies weakly, attempting to turn herself and push up onto her hands and knees. She moves to crawl toward her room, but I stop her with a hand on her arm.

I know she probably doesn't want to let me in on the fact that she's having her period, but since I already know, I reach down and scoop her up into my arms. She half-heartedly tries to fight me but ends up sinking into my body and laying her head on my shoulder as she whimpers quietly.

I crouch down, briefly letting go with the hand supporting her back to pick up the drugstore bag from the floor and head down the hall. I bypass her room completely, turning into my own and gently laying her on the bed. She goes to protest, but I interrupt before she can. "This room has an attached bathroom, so it'll be easier for you. You won't have to walk as far."

She shakes her head. "I can't lie in your bed, Riggs. I might—"

"I'll grab a towel for you to lie on if that makes you feel better," I say, letting her know I understand why she's not feeling well. "But I promise you, a little blood doesn't scare me."

Her eyes go wide with worry for just a moment, but I can tell she's too weak to argue with me. I don't need an answer from her anyway. She's not going anywhere.

I take the bag into the bathroom, pulling out the ibuprofen and filling one of the small glasses next to my sink with water. Opening the closet, I find a dark towel because I have a feeling that if she does happen to stain it, it'll make her freak out more. Tossing it into the warmer for a minute, I bring her the meds.

"Can you take these for me?" I ask, helping her sit up so she can swallow them before making my way back to the bathroom and setting everything on the counter. I wash my hands quickly and grab the warm towel on my way out the door. I don't have a heating pad upstairs, but hopefully this'll ease some of her pain.

Returning to the bed, I gently pat her tattooed thigh. I fight to stop myself from focusing on the large piece because there's so much detail that I'm sure I could study it for hours. Maybe someday she'll let me.

"Lift for me," I order softly, and she obeys, pushing her hips up off the mattress. She goes to grab the towel, but I don't let her as I slide it under her body. She drops back down, swallowing thickly as she looks at me through tired eyes. I can see the gratitude in them, even if she doesn't want to admit it out loud.

"Anything else I can do to make you feel better?" I ask, hoping she'll be honest with me. I've seen my sister fight through this so many times, and if there's something I can do to ease Monroe's discomfort, I want to help.

She shakes her head. "I just have to wait it out. The first couple of days are always the worst, but this one is on another level. I promise I'll be fine in time for your game tomorrow."

I choke on a laugh, surprised that that's what's on her mind right now. "If you're still feeling like this tomorrow, there's no way in hell you're getting up to go out. I won't have you leaving to parade yourself around in front of people who don't matter when you're in pain." She's out of her goddamn mind if she thinks I'll allow her to show up at the stadium when she can't even walk right now.

She gives me a small smile, but it's cut short as she

pitches forward, both hands around her abdomen. She groans in pain, and my primal instinct to protect her kicks in before I can stop it. I rip my shirt over my head and slide my sweatpants down so I'm standing in only my boxer briefs before lying next to her in the bed. Her body goes stiff, and she tries to push away from me, but I don't let her.

"Please," I beg, my voice trembling with the adrenaline coursing through me. "Let me help you." She wants to defy me by putting space between us, but she's too physically weak. I want to kick my own ass for making her feel like she can't trust me to care for her. I shouldn't have fought her anger about my omissions with more anger that day at the boutique. I should've just explained to her that I wanted to get to know her without my job being the elephant in the room. I had never experienced the desire for more with anyone before that night, and I definitely didn't handle the rejection well.

I see the moment she finally accepts my offer as the tension in her shoulders loosens. She takes a deep breath and nods, snuggling into my warm skin. I know I shouldn't, but I press my nose into her hair, inhaling the scent that's haunted my dreams since that night in Boston. My cock wakes up, beginning to harden under my briefs, but I will my erection away. The last thing she needs is to know what having her here in such a vulnerable state is doing to me.

"Can you roll over with your back to me?" I ask, knowing it'll be easier to keep my body's natural reaction a secret, but I also feel like I can ease her pain better if I have access to her back.

She nods her head and rolls over onto her side. I gently

ghost my hands under the back of her shirt that's already ridden up to her waist and start by applying a small amount of pressure at the bottom of her spine. She sighs in relief, so I take my time massaging her tight muscles.

Just as she starts to relax into the mattress, her body jolts, and she pulls her knees up toward her stomach. I know her cramps must be terrible, so I take a chance and slide my hand to the front of her abdomen. At this point, she doesn't even have the energy to protest as I smooth my hand over her velvet skin, rubbing light circles right above her panty line.

"Go to sleep, Mayhem," I whisper, pressing my lips to the back of her head and letting them linger. I feel her breathing slowly begin to even out as she drifts off, and there's not a single thing that could stop me from following with her in my arms.

MONROE

I wake slowly, attempting to fight it because I haven't been this comfortable in a long time. The bed is like a cloud, making me feel warm and secure under the thin down comforter. I crack one eye open to find rays of sunlight bleeding through the curtains. I can't believe I slept that long.

Moving to roll onto my back, I realize I'm being held in place by a strong, muscular arm. Memories from last night race back into my brain, and I recall Riggs finding me on the floor in the hallway. I inwardly groan because I must have looked like such an idiot, unable to handle a few measly cramps. In my defense, these are the worst ones I've ever had.

When I was sixteen, I was diagnosed with polycystic ovarian syndrome. My periods were all over the place, and sometimes the symptoms were so debilitating that I couldn't even go to school. I went through several brands of birth control to keep it at bay, and while the one I'm on now does the best job of them all, sometimes it's still a struggle. I had a feeling last week when I knew it would be coming that it was going to be a bad one, and I was right. I went through so many tampons yesterday, that I had to order a box for delivery because I was in too much agony to drive to the drugstore. All I wanted to do was sleep until it went away, but the fact that my uterus was in revolt kept me from doing so. It wasn't until Riggs started rubbing my back and belly that I finally felt good enough to doze off.

Being trapped under him brings me back to the night we spent together. The following morning, I had to slip out from this same grip to leave before he woke up. Thankfully, now I know how heavy of a sleeper he is, because I'm going to have to pull that maneuver again to go to the bathroom.

This time, I'm less graceful as I pick his arm up and roll away. It drops back onto the bed, and he mumbles something unintelligible before his body relaxes into the mattress. I slide my legs off the side, looking back to make sure I didn't leak while we slept. Thankfully, my flow has obviously slowed, because the sheets and towel are clean. Unfortunately, the cramps still seem to be in full force, making it hard to stand up straight when my feet hit the floor.

I make my way into the bathroom while keeping steady pressure on my abdomen with my hand to quell the nagging ache. Closing and locking the door behind me, I spot the new box of tampons on the counter. I quickly do my business, wash my hands, and head back out.

For a moment, I consider going to my own room. But I know if I do, I'll just end up feeling as bad as I did yesterday. Having the weight of him behind me definitely helped, so even though I know I probably shouldn't, I crawl back into bed and slide under his arm, letting him spoon me. He tightens his hold on my waist, and I sink back into his chest with a contented sigh.

He inhales deeply, and his thumb immediately begins moving back and forth across my lower stomach. "Did you sleep okay?" he asks, and even though I feel like it could fall out of my body any minute, my pussy clenches at the deep rasp of his tone. Good fucking God, I need to get myself in check. I happen to know from experience that this man's penis is almost as big as my forearm, and the last thing I need right now is to have it shoved inside my already pissed off body.

I clear my throat. "Yeah, still crampy, but not as bad as yesterday."

"Mmmm," he hums, burying his face into the back of my hair like he did when he first got in bed with me. "I have an idea, but you have to promise to hear me out before you shoot it down."

I immediately want to say no, because if he has to preface it like that, I already know it's bad news. But he took such good care of me last night when he didn't have to, so I'll give him a chance to explain himself before I disagree with whatever his plan is. "What?"

"Let me give you an orgasm," he says calmly.

I choke on a gasp. "No! Are you crazy?" I ask, attempting to move away from him. But of course, he just tightens his hold. "We're definitely not doing that!"

"C'mon, Monroe," he argues. "It's a scientific fact that uterine contractions are a great remedy for period cramps."

I want to dispute this claim, but I'm pretty sure he's not wrong. "How do you know that?" I ask.

I feel his arm move as his shoulder shrugs behind me. "Grace used to get really bad cramps, so Tanner and I would research ways to make her feel better. He always joked with me that he could try giving her an orgasm to help her. Looking back now, though? He was probably being serious."

I can't help but giggle, because now that the two of them are married and we know they've been in love practically their whole lives, I imagine that teenage Grace would've been totally down with that plan.

"It doesn't have to mean anything, Monroe," he says quietly. "Just let me make you feel good."

I want to resist. My brain is telling me to shoot this idea down, go to my room, and give it a try on my own. But when his pinky finger dips under the waistband of my underwear, my clit throbs with need. Even just the small movement has me so turned on, that a quiet whimper leaves my body as he pushes a little lower.

"Riggs, I'm bleeding. It's gross," I say on a harsh exhale. I'm trying my best, but failing to make him stop. Probably because, subconsciously, I don't want him to.

"I thought I told you I'm not scared of a little blood," he says into my ear, making me shiver. "It's quite the opposite, actually." I'm not sure what he means by that, but words are getting harder to comprehend by the minute as he rubs his fingertips back and forth over my shaved mound. "Can I?" he asks again.

My breath is coming out in shallow pants as I finally give in, nodding my head in consent. He lets out a low hum against my ear as his middle finger finally makes contact with my already swollen center. My legs spread on their own accord, allowing him to sneak a knee between them, wrapping his ankle around mine and pulling me wider.

"Look at you, being such a brave girl," he says softly as he continues working my clit, exploring my piercing but not saying anything about it. "You're going to feel so much better after this."

I whimper at his praise, getting more worked up by the second. When we were together last time, he wasn't like this. He was full of need, going from zero to feral almost in an instant. But now? He's gentle and encouraging.

"Does this feel good, sweet thing? Will you be able to get there?" he asks, prompting me to nod my head. I know I'll be able to come like this. I'm already on my way.

I try not to think of how awkward things will be after this is over, and just let myself enjoy the break from the pain I've been going through for the last couple of days. My hips tip forward, trying to create even more friction, which he gives by pressing harder against my warm, sensitive skin. He doesn't slow down or change tactics as I near the summit, heat coiling tightly in the pit of my stomach. I feel like a rubber band that's being pulled to its absolute limit, ready to snap with every passing second of his touch on my body. I moan loudly as my orgasm barrels through me, making sparks explode behind my closed eyes as I shake uncontrollably. Riding the wave of pleasure, I succumb to the floaty feeling and try to hold onto it for as long as I can. He keeps going as the spasms inside me begin to subside, and he was right. I can feel the cramps melt away, leaving my body buzzing with satisfaction.

I expect him to stop, but he just keeps going, rubbing me with a gentle pressure right to my overstimulated bundle of nerves. My thighs instinctually try to close, but he tightens his ankle around my leg, keeping me spread open. I try to fight him off because it's way too much, but he only doubles down, tugging on the barbell that decorates my clitoral hood before massaging it with fervor. "Come for me again. Give me another one," he growls.

"I—I can't," I whimper. I've never orgasmed back-to-back without a break in my life, and I doubt I'll be starting now.

"You can," he argues. "Fight through the pain. I promise you'll come harder than you ever have."

As he continues, I feel the discomfort as it blooms into an intense pleasure. At first, I'm in disbelief that I'm so close to falling over again already, but when he licks a hot line from my neck to my ear, sinking his teeth into my lobe, I go off like a fucking firework. My legs tremble and open impossibly wide as I come, giving him access to wring every last ounce of the climax from my body. I'm pretty sure I black out for a minute, because the next thing I know, he's pulling his hand from my panties and resuming his gentle circles on my abdomen.

But I don't even need it. My cramps are completely gone.

"You did so good," he praises quietly as I turn to mush, sinking back into his chest. "Feel better?"

"Mhmm," I sigh contentedly, closing my eyes and drifting back off, too satisfied to worry about the aftermath.

FIFTEEN

RIGGS

I DON'T FALL BACK ASLEEP after making Monroe come. Instead, I lie there holding her, enjoying the feel of her in my arms while my mind goes a million miles a second, replaying every detail of what just happened.

I honestly didn't expect her to say yes to my offer. She was so hell-bent on me not touching her unless we were in front of the team that I figured she'd tell me to fuck off and hightail it out of my room. So, when she nodded her head, giving me consent to rub her sweet little pussy, I took it.

I wish I could say my intentions were completely pure, but that would be a lie. Ever since that kiss at the charity event, I haven't been able to get her out of my head. The urge to do it again has been almost unbearable, and it's taken all my self-control not to try every time we're alone. It was a lot easier to forget how explosive the sex was when I didn't have to see her every day, but now that she's here, I can feel the feral beast inside me gnawing at the bars of his enclosure.

I can usually keep that part of myself at bay, but with

her? It's just *different*. Especially this morning, when she was weak and helpless, melting into me while I took care of her. I'm walking a fine line doing shit like this, but I can't stop. She fucking owns me right now, even if I don't want her to. I just want to continue with the original plan and get back to the single life I love so much.

But do I really love it, or is it just a great defense against women who don't like me for who I am, rather than what I do?

I shake the thought from my head, focusing on the slow, shallow breaths that tell me she's fast asleep in my arms again. I catch sight of the clock on the bedside table and know that I'm down to a few minutes before I have to get up for work, so I gently press my lips to the back of her head, inhaling her scent like a did several times throughout the night. This time, though, instead of just lingering for a moment before backing away, I allow myself to kiss her hair. An incoherent sigh falls from her lips when I do, and it makes my whole body hum.

Fuck.

I've never dealt with feelings like these before. Normally, I find a random woman who's in agreement with our adventures being completely physical, so we can get each other off and I can move on with my life. Not exchanging personal details is generally a dream situation for me. Monroe is the only person I've ever attempted to get to know, but she was an anomaly, refusing to give me more than just a quick fuck before she took off, thinking she'd never have to see me again.

That shit hurt more than I cared to admit. So, when I saw her later that morning and heard the anger in her words, I pushed back.

"You're a little early!" my sister said, pulling out of my

embrace. But my eyes were already locked onto the same blue ones that I had been looking into the night before. I couldn't believe she was in front of me.

I woke up that morning in my hotel bed, rolling to the side in an attempt to get back inside the goddess that had consumed my dreams. I could feel my morning wood rubbing against the cool sheet, and before I even had a chance to form any type of lucid thoughts, my body was already aching for her.

But when I reached out to where she had been lying as we both passed out from exhaustion hours earlier, she was gone.

My eyes shot open and I sat up, inhaling deeply. Her scent still permeated the air, so I knew she couldn't have been gone long. I quickly got out of bed, raced to my suitcase, got dressed and grabbed my rental car keys before heading out the door. I ran to the elevator, pushing the button rapidly like a madman, but it took forever to arrive at my floor while precious minutes ticked by, separating me from her. By the time I got down to the lobby, it was bustling with people who were going about their day as though the woman of my goddamn dreams hadn't just slipped out the door while they watched.

I knew I couldn't go back to my room when I could still smell her there, so I left. I got into my car and drove to see my sister in Hope Harbor, giving the housekeeping staff time to wash away all the reminders of what was easily the best night of my life.

But there I was at Praya, staring at the very last person I expected to see.

"I, uhhh..." I trailed off, trying to get my shit together. "I woke up before my alarm. Just wanted to get a jump on the day."

Grace smiled, completely unaware of the shitstorm that was brewing in the air as we stood there. "Well,"—she turned her body, inviting the other woman into our interaction—"this is Monroe. It's her first day at the boutique!"

I stepped forward, noticing the way her fists were clenched at her sides as I approached. "Nice to meet you, Monroe," I said, letting her name roll off my tongue while extending my hand out for her to shake. "Riggs Valentine."

She looked down at my offering, hesitating for a moment before finally reaching out and sliding her warm palm into mine. Neither of us blinked as electricity shot straight through my body at the contact, and I wondered if she felt it too.

"Oh!" my sister said, causing us both to look her way as she pulled her phone from her back pocket and checked the screen. She smiled and a blush crept over her sun-kissed cheeks. "It's Cash," she told us, speaking of her douchebag boyfriend, who I only tolerated because he made her so happy. "I have to take this." And with that, she walked into the back room, leaving me alone with Monroe.

"You left," I said quietly, hoping for an explanation as to why she didn't wake me or say goodbye.

"You lied," she shot back.

My eyes went wide. "I—" I cut myself off, because I didn't lie, but I also didn't tell the truth.

She scoffed, pushing her hands through her hair, the scent of my cologne probably still lingering from the way I had wrapped it around my fist. The motion exposed her neck, where a clear bite mark was still very visible against her creamy skin. My dick hardened slightly at the reminder of how she let me fuck her in a way that I've only ever dreamed of doing.

"It doesn't matter," she spit. "All I wanted was a night of fun, anyway. So, thanks for that, but how about we forget it ever happened?"

I flinched at her request but recovered by barking a sarcastic laugh. "Great idea, Mayhem. I really appreciate you letting me off the hook. I thought for sure you'd be one of those needy girls the morning after, but I took my chances because you suck cock like a fucking porn star."

As soon as the words were out, I wanted to take them back. I knew I shouldn't have degraded her like that, but being rejected was not something I had much experience with, and I reacted before my brain could sort through the emotions.

"Sorry about that! Where were we?" Grace said cheerfully as she bounced back into the room, cutting off the heated interaction before I could do any more damage than I already had.

Every time I've seen Monroe since, her hatred toward me seemed to get more and more intense, so I matched her energy. She didn't want me anyway, so what was the point of trying to fix things? But now that we're here, living together, and I can feel her soft body pressed to mine, I realize how fucking stupid I was. Even if she didn't want anything else from me, we wasted two whole years fighting when we could've at least been friends. Just knowing how she's helping me by pretending to be my girlfriend, I can tell that she's loyal to a goddamn fault, and when she says she'll do something, she puts her entire heart and soul into it.

"Riggs," she moans, backing her ass into my body. I watch as her thighs rub together, soft whimpers coming from her lips as she shifts onto her back, then turns toward me.

"Yeah, sweet thing?" I say quietly, but she doesn't answer. "Monroe?" She breathes slowly and steadily as I wait for a response, still completely asleep.

Is she dreaming? About me?

Holy fucking shit.

"Mmmm…" she hums, and I clench my jaw tightly as she slings a leg over mine so that my thigh is pressed against her warm center. I'm trying to figure out a way to get out of this without waking her, but when she begins grinding her hips, I abandon that plan—because like hell I'm leaving. She's obviously needy, and the orgasms helped her earlier, so letting her get herself off on me is the nice thing to do. Right?

Fuck. I know I shouldn't. This is wrong.

"Riggs," she mumbles again, and my morality flies out the fucking window as I surrender, staying as still as I can while she rides my thigh. My arm is draped over her waist, where it has been all night, but I pull back slightly so that she can move more freely.

"There you go, Mayhem," I say so quietly, that even if she were awake, she could barely hear me. "Grind that hot pussy on me. Make that little clit nice and tingly." I'm playing with fire here, but I can't fucking stop myself from talking her through it. If she hears me and wakes up, I know she'll cut my balls off. Yet, I continue.

"Fuck, baby," I whisper as her breathing becomes more labored, her orgasm clearly building as she rides. "If you were awake, I'd pull that tampon out and push my thick fingers so deep in your tight cunt, you'd come all over my hand."

The thought has me lightheaded, and I have to count backwards from ten just to regain control of myself. I need this to be over. I shift my thigh just barely, applying more pressure to her clit as she stills, her body trembling as she finally falls over the edge of her orgasm. A guttural moan leaves her lips as it crests, and I watch in wonder while she comes against my leg.

She's fucking beautiful.

Eventually, the pleasure ebbs away and she relaxes

back into the pillow with a sigh. She's still fast asleep, so I wait another couple of minutes before I slip out from under her, pulling the thin blanket over her body. I immediately turn with my back facing her in case she wakes up. I can't really explain away the steel rod that's straining against my briefs right now.

I tiptoe into the bathroom and take a cold-as-fuck shower because, while I just lost my grasp on right versus wrong out there, I'm not that much of a piece of shit that I'd rub one out two minutes after Monroe unconsciously fucked my thigh.

I move as fast as I can, washing my body while the freezing water makes my dick deflate. After drying off and wrapping the towel around my waist, I quietly make my way to the closet, where I get dressed in a pair of basketball shorts and a black Fury t-shirt. Then I quickly slip on my slides, grab my duffle bag and sling it over my shoulder.

Thankfully, she's still out cold as I pass back through the room. I look down at her one last time before reluctantly heading out the door with a secret that I'm positive I'll be thinking about for the rest of my fucking life.

SIXTEEN
MONROE

"THE WAGS' suite is this way," Taylor says as I follow her down the long, carpeted hallway. If you had told me yesterday that I would be feeling well enough to come to the game today, I'd have told you to lay off the sauce. But Riggs was right. The two orgasms he gave me did the trick, and I woke up feeling like myself again.

I have to admit that sleeping next to him was different than I had expected. Sure, I've done it once already, but that wasn't the same. That was sex. But this? I don't know what it was, but between you and me...I really fucking liked it. I inwardly groan at the thought.

I opened my eyes, expecting to feel lingering cramps, but they were completely gone. I sat up carefully, just in case, and looked around to find myself all alone in the room. I knew he had to be at the stadium early, so I took my time getting out of bed and made my way to the kitchen for some much-needed food and caffeine. Sitting on the counter was a bag of Mini Reese's Peanut Butter

Cups, the bottle of ibuprofen I ordered yesterday, and a glass of water sitting on top of a note.

> *Mayhem,*
>
> *If you aren't feeling better this morning, stay in bed. I don't want you leaving unless you're back to your snarky, sarcastic, radiant self.*
>
> *Take the ibuprofen, eat the chocolate, and I'll rub your tummy...and any other parts of you that you ask me to...later tonight.*
>
> *xo,*
> *Val*

I wanted him to be the asshole that I made him out to be in my own head so badly. But he just *isn't*. I've seen him with family and friends, so I knew he had a caring side, but when I was the one needing help, I expected the bare minimum. When he picked me up from where I collapsed in the hallway and didn't leave my side all night, I was shocked. Then, finding my favorite candy and a note that was equal parts snide and sweet, made my heart thump harder in my chest.

We approach a dark wooden door, and Taylor swipes a card over the digital pad beside it. She waits while the lock disengages before pushing it open and walking in with me following closely behind. There are several women and children moving around the room, some of whom I recognize from the charity event. I slip the same mask of confidence I used that night over my face and smile at them as she leads me to my seat.

"Help yourself to any food or drinks. Everything is

catered and it's an open bar," she says with a smile. "Friggle will be up here to visit with the kids soon, so try not to fight any of your boyfriend's battles with the poor guy." I chuckle, recalling the videos of Riggs teeing off on the mascot's creepy-looking face.

It's not funny, but it kind of is.

She lowers her voice so only I can hear. "He's an amazing guy. A little misunderstood, but I'll fight to keep him on this team until my last breath. Having you here has already helped so much, and you haven't even gotten to meet Mr. Durst. Word is getting around though, so you can probably expect him to pop in and say hello."

I nod my head in understanding. I did my research on the team's owner, and on paper, he seems like your run-of-the-mill billionaire. He was born into wealth, just like me, and has been running his family's successful finance and investments firm for almost fifty years. That may seem intimidating to most people, but I've been rubbing elbows with people like him since I was a kid. I may have left that life behind, but I learned a few tricks along the way. I should be able to handle him with no problem.

"If you're all set, I have to head down to the field. Riggs knows you're up here, and he asked me to make sure you had everything you needed before I left," she says, and there goes my heart again.

"I'm good," I tell her. "Go wrangle those giant children before another innocent mascot gets knocked out."

She laughs. "Enjoy the game, Monroe."

Taylor exits, and I stand from my seat to look out the window. Players are funneling out from the locker rooms, and butterflies take flight in my stomach as Riggs runs onto the field like he owns it. I'm not sure what to expect because it's his first game back since the whole debacle, but I breathe a sigh of relief when the crowd doesn't boo him. They don't cheer for him either, but it's a step in the right direction. In an effort to be closer to him, I grab some food and head out the glass door at the front of the suite, where a row of luxury seats awaits behind a short wall that separates them from the fans. I'm surprised when I look over to see that I'm completely alone out here. None of these women want to see the game from outside their cushy *all expenses paid* glass box?

Whatever. More room for my snacks.

By the time I'm settled in with my popcorn, the first batter is stepping up to the plate. Riggs leans forward, watching his catcher for the signal, and nods in agreement when he sees it. He winds up, lifting his front knee and firing the ball straight down the middle of the strike zone. The batter doesn't swing, but he also doesn't look affected as he takes his stance, getting ready for the next pitch. Just like last time, Riggs waits for Ace to give him the call, then sends it low and outside. This time, the guy swings and misses. The crowd, who had been fairly silent before, begins clapping and cheering as pitch number three goes right into the catcher's mitt before the umpire calls the batter out.

The second person up gets a piece of the first pitch, but it pops up, flying behind home plate. Ace shoots to his feet, throws his mask down, and waits as the ball descends, falling into his mitt with ease.

That's two.

The next batter looks to be about seven feet tall with thighs bigger than my entire body. His biceps are straining against the fabric of his jersey, and the look on his face is a thing of nightmares. But Riggs just stands there staring at him, completely unbothered. Just like the other two, he gets ready and makes the pitch. It's really high, but the guy swings anyway, sending the ball down the third base-line. I hold my breath, watching as it flies over the back wall, just out of play. The words *Foul Ball!* light up on the Jumbotron, and the batter returns to the box. The next pitch is a strike, followed by another. Riggs does a fist pump before running to the dugout with his team.

"Way to go, Val!" I yell loudly before I can stop the words from coming out. I look around, but then I realize that I'm supposed to be doing stuff like that anyway. I *am* his girlfriend, after all.

The next few innings go by in a flash, and the Fury are up three runs to none. Riggs is pitching great, and the fans are back to cheering for him. He's smiling and having a great time out there, which warms my heart because he really does deserve it.

Just as I go to open my second bag of Twizzlers, someone takes a seat next to me. I look over to find Randolph Durst in a three-piece suit, holding tightly to a giant bag of Cracker Jacks.

"Out here all alone, huh?" he says, popping one into his mouth as a Fury batter steps up to the plate.

I look around. "Seems so," I answer. "I don't know why everybody wants to stay cooped up in there. Being outside at a baseball game is where it's at."

He chuckles. "I couldn't agree more. Randy," he says in introduction, extending his hand between us.

"Monroe," I reply, placing my palm in his and shaking it firmly.

He pulls back, popping another piece of the caramel

corn into his mouth and chewing. "I've heard so many good things about you. I'm glad you could join us here in Daytona."

"Me too," I tell him with a smile, surprised I'm not acting when I say it. As much as I fought the move, it really isn't so bad. The weather here is amazing, and it almost reminds me of the better parts of California. The parts that I actually miss.

"So, tell me about yourself, Monroe. You must be a pretty special girl to have caught the eye of our star down there."

I'm skeptical at first, because I don't know if he's being sarcastic or not. At this point, the next person who disrespects Riggs in front of me is catching these hands—billionaire or not. But when I look over at him, his eyes are sincere.

"There really isn't much to tell," I reply. "I grew up in California. When I graduated from college with my marketing degree, I decided to try something new. I moved across the country to a little beach town outside of Boston and worked at a small boutique until it closed a little over a month ago. As far as your star," I say, looking down to the field where Riggs is leaning out of the dugout, hyping up his teammates as they go up to bat, "he's my best friend's brother." Obviously, I'm not going to tell him how we really met, so this seems like a way to explain how we ended up together without having to lie.

"Ooh, I love that trope," he says, catching me off guard. I raise an eyebrow in question. "My wife listens to smutty audiobooks while she drives. One accidentally started playing through her Bluetooth one day when I was in the car with her, and I've been hooked ever since." I choke on a laugh and he smiles in response. "Best friend's brother with a little forced proximity?" he says before kissing the tips of his fingers like a chef.

I can't help but laugh harder at the gesture, and he joins in just as we hear a loud *crack*, turning in time to watch the ball sail over the outfield and land in the bleachers behind the far wall. We both stand with our arms in the air and turn to high five one another in celebration. Every plan I had for wooing this guy flies out the window, because he's not like *them*. He's like *me*. He may have all the money in the world, but that's not what's important to him. You don't see that very often anymore, and I feel like we're kindred spirits up here in our empty row of seats.

We watch together for the next couple of innings before a young woman sticks her head out where we're sitting. "Mr. Durst, the men from the homeless shelter are settled in the luxury box down the hall. They've already met some of the alumni players, and they're just waiting on you now."

"Thank you, Alicia," he says, standing and brushing the crumbs off his expensive suit as he turns to me. "It was so nice meeting you, Monroe. We'll have to do it again soon."

"I'm looking forward to it," I reply with a smile before he ducks back into the suite, leaving me alone again. I watch as Riggs gets another three and out, cheering loudly in hopes that he can hear me. I'm pretty far away, so I doubt he can, but I try my best anyway.

The rest of the game flies by, and Taylor walks in just as I'm headed to find a trash can for all of my snack wrappers. "Hey!" she says excitedly. "Your boyfriend just pitched one of the best games of his career, and I'm here to bring you down to see him."

I swallow thickly as the butterflies return, flapping around like lovesick morons at the thought of him. I toss my garbage and follow her out to the elevator.

Minutes later, I'm perched outside a steel black door by myself, waiting for someone to tell me where to go next. Taylor got a call that pulled her away, but she told me to stay put while she took care of business.

Several people exit, and I nod, smiling at each of them as they walk past me. It feels like hours have gone by, even though I know it's probably only been about twenty minutes, before Riggs walks out. As soon as he sees me, his face splits into an ear-to-ear grin, and he runs toward me. His excitement is contagious, causing me to giggle loudly as he wraps his arms around me and lifts me off my feet.

"I think you're my good luck charm, Mayhem," he laughs. "I haven't come that close to a no-hitter since my rookie year!" He sets me back down but doesn't let go as we stare into each other's eyes.

"I want to kiss you right now," he says quietly, and my heart speeds up behind my rib cage.

"Is it against the rules to kiss your girlfriend in this hallway?" I whisper softly.

The corner of his mouth turns up in a knowing smile. "I don't think so."

"Okay," I breathe, and his lips are on mine before I can even form another thought. It starts soft, and I wonder for a moment if he's really just putting on a show for anyone who might walk out, but when he backs me into the brick wall, pressing his body tightly to mine, I know that this is just for us.

I moan quietly as he lowers down, licking and sucking at the sensitive skin of my neck while he grinds his hardening cock into my stomach. My clit throbs at the contact, and I'm glad we're in public because I wouldn't be able to stop myself from begging him to fuck me if I knew we wouldn't get caught. His hand slides up my body, cupping the underside of my breast, and a deep growl leaves his throat as he squeezes firmly. The contact has me leaking into my panties, lifting my leg around him in an attempt to get some friction.

"Oh my God, I'm so sorry," a voice says from down the hall, causing Riggs to jolt away from me. We turn to see Taylor shielding her eyes as she turns her body away from us. "I didn't mean to interrupt your celebration, guys," she laughs. "I just wanted to make sure you found each other. I'll be going now," she rushes out, shuffling quickly in the other direction. As soon as she's out of sight, we both sag in relief, then burst out laughing.

"Mayhem is the perfect nickname for you," he quips, wrapping an arm around my shoulders and leading me down the hall. "You've got me acting crazy out here."

SEVENTEEN

RIGGS

"I'M HOME!" I yell from the entryway, setting my duffel bag down on the floor. We played our last home game against New Orleans the day after I pitched, then it was off for another three nights on the road. We won two and lost one, but now we get a full day off before heading out for two more games. I'm looking forward to spending some time with Monroe since we didn't get to do that after our kiss in the hallway at the stadium. That night, we both fell asleep on the couch watching a movie, and I carried her to my bed right before I had to leave again. She was out like a light when I got home after my game that night, and I had to catch an early flight to San Francisco the following morning. We've texted a few times, but we haven't talked about us at all.

If there even is an *us*.

I don't know where her head is at, but for me, that kiss in the hallway at the stadium was real. I wanted to celebrate, and I wanted to do it with her. I certainly wasn't expecting it to become as heated as it did, but that seems to be the norm for us.

I'm glad things haven't been super awkward, but that could just be because we haven't been around each other. Traveling for days at a time like I do means putting important issues on the back burner. That's why it's been so easy to live the single life for as long as I have. Most of the women I've been with only liked me because of my job, and I honestly don't blame them. It's not like I gave them a reason to think I had more to offer. It was never something I wanted.

But now?

Maybe.

I'm not saying I've changed overnight and want to get married with two-point-five kids and a picket fence, but being around Monroe has shown me that my initial impulse to learn more about her wasn't wrong. She's beautiful, sexy, funny, strong, and independent. If I were looking for something beyond just a situationship, I already know she'd fit into my life perfectly. Whether or not I'd fit into hers remains to be seen, because her past before she moved to Hope Harbor is still a mystery.

I head up the stairs, walking down the hall to see that her bedroom door is wide open and she's nowhere to be found. I start to get nervous but remember how she told me yesterday that she was going to check out the gym in my building, which is likely where she is since her car is here. It's the middle of the day and it's gorgeous outside, so there's also a possibility that she went for a walk or something.

I take off my jeans and t-shirt, pulling on a pair of mesh

basketball shorts before going back downstairs, dropping onto the couch, and putting some game highlights on the TV. It feels like forever since I had a minute to relax, and *fuck me*, this feels good.

My phone buzzes with a text notification. I lean forward to grab it from the table, hoping it's Monroe, but it's Tanner instead.

TANNER

Hey, bro! Great series this week. Your arm looked great.

RIGGS

Thanks. It's good to be back.

TANNER

Soooooo…

RIGGS

Here we go.

TANNER

How are things with the old ball and chain?

RIGGS

Jesus Christ. Your nosy ass wife tell you to ask me that?

TANNER

Nope. Just wondering if your near-perfect game was inspired by a certain spicy brunette.

RIGGS

It's strictly business, Lake. There's nothing going on between us.

TANNER:

Been there, told that lie.

RIGGS

Yeah. To me, you fuck.

TANNER

It worked out, because you ended up with the world's best brother-in-law. You should be thanking me for fucking your sister.

RIGGS

Hold your breath on that one, Tan. With any luck, you'll drop dead.

BYE.

I toss the phone onto the couch beside me, getting up and walking over to the window. He riles me the fuck up every time he mentions what he and Grace do in their free time. No matter how much I say I don't want to know, the goofy fucker just keeps doing it.

It's gross.

I watch as the electric blue waves meet the shore, swallowing the sand briefly before pulling back. The topless beach below is pretty dead for it being such a nice day out. There are a few people who are fully clothed walking along the shore, and one topless woman lying face-up on a beach towel. I shouldn't look, because I'm supposed to have a girlfriend, but I'm a weak man, and this particular set of tits is fucking spectacular—nice and full with hard, rose-colored nipples. I'm not so far up that I can't see the little barbells that decorate the tight buds as they glint in the sunlight.

Fuck, she's hot.

She's perfection.

Wait, I know those tits.

"Monroe?" I growl as my brain finally registers what I'm seeing. I blink rapidly, rubbing my eyes and refocusing to make sure I'm not imagining things.

But I'm fucking *not*. It's her. Out there almost naked, where anyone could see.

In a flash, I'm out the door and running toward the stairwell, knowing that the elevator will take way too long. I practically fly down each flight, shoving the door to the lobby open and racing toward the exit that leads to the beach. I'm seeing red as I bump into random bodies, not even bothering to apologize as I bulldoze through the obstacles that are slowing down my pursuit.

By the time my feet hit the warm sand, I'm fucking *feral*. My only concern is getting her away from this beach and back inside before anyone else looks at her tits the way I just was. I run as fast as I can, only stopping when I'm hovering over her.

"What the fuck do you think you're doing?" I say through clenched teeth. My body feels wound tight, like it's ready to spring into action at any moment as I angle myself between her and the building in hopes of hiding her from potential onlookers. Unaffected by my presence, she cracks one eye open and smiles up at me sweetly.

"I wasn't expecting you until later. How was your flight?" she asks as if I'm not about to rip her to shreds right here.

"What. The. Fuck. Do. You. Think. You're. Doing?" I ask again, enunciating every word as my fingers curl into fists at my sides. My chest is heaving with my heavy breaths, and my heart feels like it might explode at any second.

"Ummmm, sunbathing?" she replies as if the answer is obvious. Which, it is, but I'm too blinded by anger to see that.

"Get up," I command.

Her eyes narrow. "I will when I'm done," she says.

"Get up, or I'll throw you over my shoulder and carry you off this beach." My body feels like it's on fire as angry heat radiates from my skin. This is it. This is where I snap. And once I do, there's no going back. I give her another few seconds to reconsider going against my orders, but she just looks up at me, never breaking eye contact as she lifts to her elbows and drags her pink tongue across her top teeth. She's doubling down.

Big. Fucking. Mistake.

In one fluid motion, I lean down, grab her by the torso, and toss her over my shoulder as I stand to my full height. Breath whooshes from her lungs, and I can feel the metal of her piercings as they rub against me.

"You're fucking crazy, Riggs!" she shouts, kicking her feet. But her attempts are futile because my grip on her is so tight that she may actually have marks on her tomorrow. "Put me down!"

"Shut the fuck up," I grit out, looking around because I know we won't make it back to my condo before my control breaks. Spotting a row of empty outdoor shower stalls, I head straight for them, my rapid heartbeat mixing with her protests in my ears.

I step inside, close the door behind us, and turn the lock. There's a small space at the bottom where our feet would be visible to passersby, and the top is tall enough so they'd only be able to see part of my head. But they'd be able to hear *everything*.

I slide her down my body, and she brushes along my erection, her eyes widening in surprise as it grazes her thigh. "What the fuck, Riggs?" she yells. "You can't just pick me up and carry me off the beach like a goddamn caveman! You don't *own me*." Her nostrils flair with every breath and her jaw is clenched tightly as she rebels.

I step into her, so that her tits are pressed against my bare skin. She looks up at me, pupils blown completely wide, and I watch her throat roll as she swallows thickly.

I've got her right where I want her.

"You see, Monroe. While you're here pretending to be my girlfriend, these," I say, reaching up and squeezing her tits in my large palms, "are mine." She gasps, but it quickly turns into a moan when I pinch the barbells, giving them a firm tug. Her knees buckle, and she tucks her lips tightly over her teeth in an effort to stop the involuntary sounds from escaping, but it's no use. I catch her, wrapping an arm around her waist for support as my free hand lowers down, releasing the tie on her bathing suit bottoms and letting them fall to the ground at our feet.

"And this," I say with my lips pressed to her ear as I ghost a fingertip over her pierced clit, "is mine."

"I hate you," she says on a shaky breath, but I can tell they're empty words.

I answer by stuffing two fingers inside her. She whimpers in response, and her inner muscles immediately suck me in further. "Your pussy is a drooling mess for me, Mayhem. It doesn't matter if you like me. *She does.*"

Her body melts into me for a moment when I start

pumping in and out, and it only takes a couple of thrusts before her arousal begins to drip down my palm. She lets herself enjoy it for a few more seconds before her fight returns, and she tries to pull away from me. She slips out of my grasp, so I reach out, spinning her roughly until her back is facing me. Pushing between her shoulder blades, I press her against the wall of the shower stall before sealing myself to her back.

"Mine," I growl, yanking my shorts down enough for my hard cock to spring free. I grab the base, dragging it up the cleft of her ass, and she widens her stance, giving herself to me.

I chuckle darkly. "What a needy little slut you are, Mayhem. You say you hate me, but you open right up when I pin you down. You wanted this, didn't you? You wanted me to lose control."

"What I want is for you to fuck off," she replies, not even trying to get away anymore.

"Nahhh," I chide, completely aware of the fact that she's full of shit. "I know your secret, Monroe," I whisper against her ear. "I know you haven't been properly fucked since that night. Guess what? *Neither have I.*"

She gasps as I thrust inside her without warning. Her body struggles to adjust, and I'm doing everything I can to hold onto the very last thread of my self-control so I don't hurt her. "Tell me to stop at any time," I say quietly.

"Okay."

Jesus Christ. She needs this just as badly as I do.

I give her two long strokes before she goes rigid in front of me. "Condom," she rushes out, and *holy fuck, I can't believe I forgot.* "I'm on birth control, but are you—" she stops before finishing her question.

"My wallet is inside," I say through clenched teeth, trying to stay still inside her. "I'm clean. I've never fucked raw, and I haven't been with anyone since you agreed to come here. It's your call."

"I'm clean, but pull out just in case," she replies. That's all it takes for me to finally let go.

I grab a fistful of her silky hair, making her back arch as I fuck into her from behind. Her hands are against the wooden wall in front of us, her nails digging into it so hard that I'm worried they might break off. But my concern is fleeting as her pussy clenches down on me.

"You're not going to come already, are you?" I ask. She doesn't answer, so I land a tight slap to her clit, which makes her jolt forward. But she doesn't go far with the way I'm holding her head in place. "Answer me, Mayhem," I order. "Tell me you've missed this cock so much that you're about to slut yourself out and come all over it when we've barely even started."

"I'm not," she grits out, clearly fighting to prove me wrong as I continue thrusting. Anyone who walked by right now would be able to hear the way my pelvis is slapping against her full ass as I fuck her. I hope they do. I want the world to know she's mine.

I pull harder on her hair, arching her back even more as I brush my lips against her earlobe. "Liar," I say quietly, my hot breath ricocheting off her sweat-soaked skin. "I can make you go off right now and you know it."

She shakes her head rapidly in defiance. She thinks she can hold off. And maybe she can with other guys, but I know what she needs.

I growl before leaning in and sinking my teeth into the side of her neck. I bite down hard, feeling an intense euphoria shoot through me, starting at the base of my spine and spreading throughout my body.

This is how it's supposed to be.

Raw. Primal. Carnal.

It only takes another second before Monroe squeezes around me, her entire body shaking as she orgasms so loudly, that I'm sure it'll carry far beyond this beach. I fuck her through it, letting go of her hair and pulling out of her body as soon as I'm sure she's spent. Wrapping my hand around my steel cock, I stroke furiously as my vision goes white, shooting rope after rope of cum all over her ass. It goes on for what seems like forever, and I jerk myself until I have to stop from the overstimulation.

Her head hangs forward, pressed against the wall, her back heaving as she struggles to regulate her breathing. I gently wrap my hand around her throat and carefully tilt it enough so that the bite marks I left behind come into view. Leaning into her, I drag my tongue along them like an animal cleaning a wound, soothing the angry skin as she whimpers quietly.

"Are you okay?" I whisper, taking my time to inspect her neck and back for any signs of injury before turning her to me.

"Mhmmm," she hums, barely able to keep her eyes open. I lean forward, brushing my lips gently against hers and she sighs, melting into me as she returns the kiss.

"Let's clean you off," I say, doing my best to support her with one arm while turning the shower on with the other. The cool water hits our skin, feeling amazing as it starts to slowly warm. Using a travel bottle of shampoo that the beach keeps stocked in these things, I carefully wash her, watching as the evidence of our pleasure slides down her body and disappears into the drain. The sight makes me want to cover her with cum again. To make her smell like me so everyone knows who she belongs to.

Because whether she likes it or not, she's mine just as much as I'm hers.

EIGHTEEN

RIGGS

"GOOD GAME, BABY!" Jackson says, slapping me on the back.

I laugh, looking up from where I'm grabbing my bag from the locker. "I didn't play, but thanks." I pitch tomorrow, so I spent tonight in the dugout, hyping the guys up as they beat the Philadelphia Kings four to three. His one-run homer in the ninth inning sealed the deal for us, so the happy fucker is even more chipper than normal.

"There's no *I* in *team*, Val," he says with a boyish grin. "We're all going down to the hotel bar when we get back. I know I don't even have to ask, but I assume we can count you in?"

He's right. Normally, I'd be leading the pack. I'm usually the one pushing the guys out the door in an attempt to get first pick of all the women in the place. My routine is to stay until the bartenders tell us it's time to go, then take whoever I have on my arm up to my room for some one-on-one time. I've gone out a couple of times since Monroe moved in to help me, and I've engaged in some surface level conversations with women while sitting and nursing my one or two drinks, but I haven't invited any of them back to my room.

At first, I told myself I was just doing it to keep up appearances. I couldn't very well be telling the team that I'm a whole new man, then turn around and pull the same old stunts. They think I'm in a relationship, so I'm just playing the part.

But after the other day on the beach, I'm starting to wonder if that outlook is evolving into something different. Because tonight, I don't even have the desire to go.

I stand, raising my arms above my head in a stretch. "I don't know, man. I'm kind of tired. I think I might pass tonight. Gonna hit the sack early."

He laughs, rolling his eyes. "Yeah, right," he says sarcastically. "You haven't missed a post-game celebration since I've known you. Just one drink, then you can get back to texting your girl like the whipped little puppy dog you are."

I take a deep breath in, exhaling slowly. "One drink. Then I'm out."

"Nice," he says with a toothy grin, giving me a fist bump before he takes off toward the shower.

I'm not even going to entertain his comment about Monroe. So what if they all think I'm whipped? I know I'm not. I probably won't even text her when I get back tonight.

I'm a fucking liar. I'm definitely texting her. I want to hear about her day.

I didn't get nearly enough time with her after we had sex in the outdoor shower. We went back inside like it was just a regular day, chilled on the sofa, and I brought her to my bed when she fell asleep in the middle of the movie she chose. Next thing I knew, I was out the door again. This job makes it impossible to nurture any type of a new relationship, which is just another reason I don't bother with them. How can I learn enough about a person to know whether they like me for me, when I can't even spend more than a day at a time with them? It's hard to know who's genuine and trustworthy, and who's just playing you because they want money or notoriety. So, I've leaned into that. Embracing that reality has been the easiest way to avoid getting hurt or hurting anyone else.

But with her? Things are different. I can't deny that anymore.

I don't know what Monroe is thinking about what happened between us, but I can't stop wondering if she'd be open to seeing where this thing could go. I'm not saying I'm ready to wife her up, but I also know that my feelings toward her have shifted since she's been here, and I feel like hers have done the same.

An hour later, the boys and I walk through the doors that lead to the hotel bar. As usual, we're swarmed by women that are dressed to the nines for a night out. I'm thankful that we aren't in Daytona, because at least here, we aren't as much of a hot commodity. But nonetheless, it only takes about three minutes before an attractive blonde sits on the empty barstool next to me.

"You looked kind of lonely over here," she says, prompting me to smile politely. I immediately notice all the ways she *isn't* Monroe. Her golden hair is cut into a long bob with blunt edges. Her hazel eyes have flecks of green, but I couldn't see myself falling into them like the deep blue pools that have captivated me on more than one occasion. Her lips are pink and full, but the thought of kissing them makes me sick to my stomach. Not because she isn't gorgeous—because she is.

But she's not Monroe.

Ace was right. I'm down bad.

"Is that right?" I answer. "I figured I'd stop in a for a few minutes before I hit my room."

She turns in her seat, crossing one leg over the other before tilting her head. "Well, I'm glad you did. I spotted you when you walked in and just had to come introduce myself. I'm Chloe." She extends a manicured hand my way, and I quickly shake it before busying myself by pulling the label from my bottle of beer.

"Riggs," I offer. She already knows who I am. I can tell. This happens all the time. Girls pretend like our meeting is just some random run-in, then act surprised when I tell them what I do for work. I've gotten pretty good at knowing when I'm being bamboozled. It doesn't exactly feel great, but I've continued to benefit from it by fucking around with them, so I can't blame the women for doing it.

"What brings you to Philly, Riggs?" she asks, brushing my calf with the toe of her stiletto. The gesture would normally be the green light I need to know that we're on for a night of fun, but instead, I jolt out of my seat in an attempt to get away from it.

"I uhhhh," I fumble, trying to think of an excuse, because I need to get out of here without hurting her feelings. In an act of quick thinking, I stuff my hand into my pocket, fishing out my phone and waving it in the air. "I have to take this call!" I yell triumphantly.

"It's not even ringing," she says, raising a dubious brow.

Fuck.

"It's on vibrate," I say, shrugging my shoulders. I pretend to press a button before bringing it to my ear. "Hello?" I say to absolutely nobody before turning back to Chloe. "It was nice meeting you. Have a great night." I don't even give her a chance to reply before I'm hauling ass out to the lobby of the hotel.

As soon as I'm inside the elevator, I breathe a sigh of relief, letting my tense shoulders sag as I ride up to my floor. I try not to think about the physical reaction I had to being touched by a woman who isn't Monroe, because I don't want to sort through the reality that maybe I'm further gone for her than I thought. I'd like to say it's just the way our kinks line up, resulting in mind-blowing sex, but since that kiss at the charity event, the thought of any other woman has affected me the same way. I don't want them anymore.

I want her. In any way that she'll have me.

If she'll have me.

I understand that there's a lot about Monroe Decker that I don't know. And to be honest, I get that, because my behavior hasn't earned me the privilege of being trusted with her backstory. But I want it. I want to know why she hasn't dated anyone since I've known her. Why she ran from me after refusing to give me any personal information in Boston. Why she got upset with me the night of the charity event when I didn't compliment her...and why, minutes later, she morphed into the picture of positivity in front of my colleagues.

I've never been more frustrated by another person in

my life. And I've definitely never been more intrigued by one, either.

I want to know her. Like, really *know her*.

I wave my key card over the lock, pushing my way into my room. The only thing I want to do right now is take a shower and text Monroe. I hope it's not too late. I bet she's snuggled up on the sofa, surrounded by snacks, with her website pulled up on her laptop and a movie playing in the background. I love how she's made herself so comfortable in my space. Sometimes I forget that our relationship is fake, and she isn't really a permanent fixture. Although, I don't think either of us can deny that it's feeling more real by the second, whether we expected it to or not.

I shower quickly, dry off, and throw on a pair of black boxer briefs before sliding into bed with my phone in hand.

RIGGS:

How was your day, Mayhem?

I send the message, toss my phone onto the mattress next to me, and stare at it for a few seconds before picking it right back up. I don't know how this girl managed to turn me into a giddy teenager, but she did. When she doesn't reply right away, my mind starts wandering until I can feel the panic and doubt slowly creeping in. While things didn't seem awkward between us before I left, maybe she's not responding because she's had more time to think about it and doesn't like what we did.

Fuck. What if she regrets it and it sends us right back to square one, where we can't even be in the same room together without arguing?

Maybe I took it too far on the beach. Monroe is a

strong, independent woman and I threw her over my shoulder and fucked her like a caveman because I couldn't stop my possessive side from taking over. But when I saw her lying there topless where anyone could see, I lost control. I just wanted to mark her so that everyone knew she was mine…even though I'm not sure she wants to be.

My stomach clenches and flips with anxiety as my mind goes through every bad outcome. And while I know I won't be able to sleep feeling this way, I turn off the lights and pull the covers over my waist in an attempt to get some rest. But the only thing I see are those deep blue eyes that pull me in every time I look at them.

Just as I'm about to obliterate every ounce of self-respect I have left by double-texting her, my phone vibrates, lighting up the space beside me. I unlock it quickly and find a text from Monroe.

Thank fuck.

MONROE:

Not bad. Just got back from a walk on the beach.

RIGGS:

It's a little late, isn't it?

MONROE:

Yeah. Needed to clear my head.

I sit up, turn the light back on, and settle with my back to the headboard before pulling up her contact info and pressing the button to FaceTime her. If she's struggling with something, I want to help.

She answers after two rings, her makeup-free face filling the screen. She's so fucking beautiful like this, and it's a challenge not to say it out loud. Her long, brown hair is gathered into a bun on top of her head, with little wisps hanging down, framing her heart-shaped face. Her plump lips shine, probably with that berry flavored lip mask she keeps on the bathroom counter, and I wonder what it would taste like if I kissed her right now.

"Hi," she says softly, and I immediately notice how red and tired her eyes look. When I saw her last, she was well-rested and content, but whatever happened has her looking like she's been through the wringer in the short time since I've been gone.

"Hey there, sweet thing," I reply. "Wanna talk about it?"

She sighs, and I watch as she makes her way through the house, following her with my eyes as she pulls back the covers on her bed. Part of me is disappointed that she didn't go into my room, but why would she? Technically, we're nothing more than a fake boyfriend and girlfriend who've fucked a couple of times. I can't expect her to sleep in my bed while I'm away, no matter how much I'd love it if she did.

"I'm just struggling with my business plan," she says. "The bones of the website are done, but it looks exactly like every other marketing firm out there. No matter how much I try to come up with ways to set myself apart, I'm still going to end up lost in a sea of competition. I need to stand out as someone who truly wants to help small businesses succeed, but how can I do that when there are thousands of other companies trying to suck their budgets dry? Short of literally giving them free marketing plans to prove what I do has the potential to work for them, how can I get their attention?"

She looks defeated and I wish I could take it all away. I hate that she's doubting herself like this when I know how amazing she really is. I think carefully before replying. "What if you *did* give them free marketing plans?" I ask.

Her brows pull in. "Then we'd never make any profit. You may as well just flush money down the toilet at that point. I'll make sure to tell you what bridge I'll be living under when I lose everything I own, so you can come visit me."

I bark out a laugh. "Glad to see your bratty fucking attitude is still alive and well," I quip. "I'm serious, though. When I was a kid, my mom used to bring us to the grocery store every week. Grace, Tanner, and I would practically be vibrating with excitement by the time we got to the aisle where the workers were handing out free samples. It didn't matter what they were—we wanted them. And nine times out of ten, we talked her into buying whatever we tried. Couldn't you give out small samples of what you could do for them, so they could see it before they decide between you and someone else?"

She pauses for a second, considering my story. "It could work, but that would take up a lot of time. Every business is at a different level of marketing. Some of them have a good grasp on it, but others have been barely surviving on word of mouth. In a perfect world, they'd all be set up with social media and have a basic idea of what to do before they hire a—" She pauses, and her eyes go wide. "Oh my God, that's it," she says, a smile blooming across her face.

"What?" I ask, smiling back because she's so fucking pretty, I can't help it.

She straightens, adjusting herself so she's sitting on the

bed with her legs crossed. As she moves, the phone briefly points down, and I have to stifle a groan when I see what she's wearing. A tight white camisole stretches across her braless tits, her piercings visible through the fabric. A thin strip of her creamy skin peeks from the bottom, leading to the waistband of her pink lace panties.

Fuck. Me.

Her face comes back into the frame, and I do my best to ignore the fact that my cock is reacting to that split-second glimpse of the body that I'm already missing so much. God, I wish I was holding her right now.

"So, the worst thing about starting with a new client is not knowing if they have a social media presence or if you'll have to spend time doing that before you can get into the good stuff. The main problem small business owners have with setting up those accounts is that they either don't know how to do it, or once they figure it out, they don't know how to get followers and keep them engaged. This seems simple to the younger generation that was raised with social media, but to some of the older clients, it's overwhelming. If I could cut that part of the process out and have it already in place when I step in, I wouldn't have to waste valuable time doing it when I could be focusing on bigger things."

"Okay, so how can you do that?" I ask.

Her smile gets bigger, her eyes sparkling even more with excitement. "How-to videos on my website," she says as if it's the most obvious thing in the world. "I can do a weekly series on how to set up accounts on each platform, get followers, and drum up engagement. I can show them how to connect with influencers and post about their products or services, so that if they decide to work with me, the groundwork is done. It's like a free sample of my work that also makes my job easier in the end."

"Sounds like you just solved your own problem, Mayhem," I say, smirking at her. "I might be able to retire early once this thing takes off and you're making the big bucks."

She scoffs. "Don't even think about it, Val. If I'm being forced to pretend like I can tolerate your cocky ass, you're staying on that team until you physically can't pitch anymore."

"I don't know, sweet thing," I chide. "I think you kinda like me."

She rolls her eyes playfully but doesn't reply. My pulse speeds up and a blanket of calmness covers me as I scoot down in the bed and turn onto my side, propping my phone up on the pillow next to me. She dims the lamp before doing the same, and because we sleep on opposite sides, it's like we're together, lying face-to-face.

"Do you feel better?" I ask softly, hoping this conversation has eased some of the weight off her shoulders.

"Yeah, I do," she says with a sleepy smile, her eyes growing heavy as we just watch one another in silence. I should say goodbye so she can get some rest, but when her eyes close, I slide my hand over on the mattress, pretending I can feel the softness of her skin as I ghost my thumb over the sheet.

"Goodnight, Riggs," she says, making no move to hang up.

"Goodnight, Monroe," I reply, watching as her breathing slows and evens out. I fight to stay awake, not wanting to miss a single second of seeing her this peaceful, but finally fall under to the sounds of her soft snores.

NINETEEN
MONROE

MY PHONE RINGS on the counter, and I wipe my flour-covered hands on the dish towel before using my pinky finger to answer it. "Hello?"

"Hi, honey," my mom says, her high-pitched voice sing-songing as if she's completely unaware of the miserable life she lives.

"Hi, Mom," I reply, putting it on speaker before returning to the other counter where I have a ball of dough ready to be rolled out. Riggs won't be home from his Philly trip for another thirty minutes, and I promised him my homemade, from-scratch pizza for dinner. He's been so insistent that I focus on my business plan, but I'm starting to go crazy not helping out around here, so I didn't take no for an answer when I told him I'd be cooking tonight.

"You didn't tell me you're in Florida now," she scolds, making me freeze where I stand. "And you have a new boyfriend? Why am I finding this out from the ladies at the country club instead of from my own daughter? Do you know how embarrassing that is?"

I don't bother wiping my hands again as my fingers begin to fly across the screen of the iPad Riggs keeps in the kitchen. I type *Riggs Valentine girlfriend* into the search bar, and several results appear, all containing the same set of photos from the last home series. It was after our kiss in the hallway, when we walked out to the player parking lot holding hands. One of the pictures is a grainy close-up of me looking like a fool in love while he held the car door open for me. Another is a blurry shot of him leaning over the center console, where he stole one last quick kiss before driving us home. The lot has heavy security, but the photos look like they were taken from far away with a high-speed zoom lens. There's also one of us that I've already seen from the first game, where he climbed the wall to kiss my cheek. At the time, the article called me a *lucky female fan*, but now that there's more evidence of us being together, the media is putting two and two together.

Fuck.

"Monroe Elizabeth, did you hear me?" she says, reminding me that she's still on the line. I don't owe her an explanation, but I also wasn't prepared for her to ask because other than team events that only select reporters are allowed to attend, we haven't been out in public as a couple. But it's out now, so I may as well address it.

"I heard you. Yes, I'm in Daytona right now, staying with my boyfriend for a while." I don't go into detail about how I ended up here because I don't want her running back to my dad. If he found out that I'm starting my own business, he'd get it shut down before I even had the chance to make my first dollar. I also can't tell them that this thing between me and Riggs isn't real. They'd use that against us in a heartbeat if they knew. Especially if it meant getting me to go back to California, which I will *never* do.

"Everyone's talking, you know. Saying he's trash. You know those professional athletes have women in every city, right? I'd hate to see you get cheated on, honey," she says, as though my dad hasn't been caught in compromising positions with more than one administrative assistant over the years. It's a way of life in their circle, even though none of them talk about it. The women at the country club don't marry for love anyway. They do it for money or social status.

Which is why I couldn't bear to go through with marrying Conrad. He'd have cheated, and I'd have been expected to hide it, pretending everything was fine. What kind of life is that? I'd rather be single forever. In fact, that's why I chose to keep all of my interactions with guys in Massachusetts completely casual. I wasn't raised in a household that showed me a good example of a loving marriage, and Conrad treated me more like a business partner than a future wife. I'm sure I'll be ready to take that step when I find the right guy. But for now, there's no shame in having fun.

"Mom," I say on an exaggerated sigh. "I don't care what those asshole friends of yours think about me. I thought I made that pretty obvious when I skipped town and left the Decker family fortune in my rearview."

She gasps, and I'd bet every cent I have that she has her hand on her heart in fake shock. "Monroe, that language isn't very ladylike. I raised you better than that."

"Actually," I reply smugly, "you didn't. They're bitches. Every last one of them can eat my ass."

She chokes on another gasp, sputtering as though I've

offended her instead of telling the honest truth about the women she pretends are her besties. She knows damn well that they'd tell her to lose their numbers if she woke up tomorrow with a few less figures in her bank account. "When did you get so disrespectful? I think you should come home. You've obviously lost your way."

"Thanks, Mom. But I'm already *home*," I snap. "Now if you'll excuse me, I need to finish making dinner for my very faithful boyfriend. Bye." I end the call, resting my elbows on the counter and dropping my head into my hands.

I haven't had a conversation with my mother in two years where she didn't attempt to get me to move back to Rolling Hills. It's never *Hey honey! How's everything on the east coast?* or *We'd love to come see the house that you bought on your own, with no help.* It's always her scolding me about what I've done wrong and telling me the answer is to drop the life I've built and go back to the one I risked everything to leave behind. It sucks that my parents can't just be proud of me for doing such a big thing.

"Hey there, sweet thing," Riggs coos, stepping into view. I was so lost in my annoyance with that phone call that I didn't even hear him come in.

"Oh my God, the pizza!" I cry, standing up straight and rushing to the counter where the ball of dough sits and pressing it flat. "I'll be fast, I promise! I'm sorry it's not ready yet!" I move quickly, kneading my fingers into it, flattening the crust with panicked, jerky movements. Just as I go to reach for the bowl of tomato sauce, gentle hands snake around my waist from behind.

"Hey," he says quietly, pressing his cheek to mine. "Slow down, Mayhem. It's not a race." He ghosts his lips down my face, nuzzling into my neck and biting down gently. I sigh as his teeth graze my skin, and when he tightens his arms, I sink back into his warm chest. A sense of calm washes over me as I relish in his protective hold, and all the weight I was carrying from the conversation with my mom just minutes ago falls away.

"Everything okay?" he asks, and I turn my head, giving him a reassuring smile.

"It is now," I say. "But I really do have to get this pizza in the oven, or you may wither away."

He chuckles. "We wouldn't want that." He backs away, and I miss his touch immediately as he turns to the sink and washes his hands. He slides in next to me, ready to work. "You do the sauce and cheese. I'll do the toppings."

I raise a dubious brow. "Can I trust you to place the pepperoni evenly?"

He scoffs. "What do you take me for? Some kind of degenerate?"

I shrug, and he reaches out, swiping some leftover flour from my forehead. The gesture is sweet, and my heart picks up speed at the way he's looking at me as if none of this is fake. It doesn't even *feel* fake anymore, to be honest.

After we left the beach the other day, we didn't really talk about what happened. We came inside, changed our clothes, and snuggled up on the couch to watch a movie. That seems to be our go-to activity on the nights he doesn't have games, and even though we had rough, semi-public sex just minutes prior, none of it felt awkward. I woke up the next morning in his bed, where he had carried me after I fell asleep on his shoulder, feeling him kiss me goodbye before he left for the airport for another two nights away.

We fell asleep on the phone last night, and I woke up to a dead battery, feeling all kinds of things about how he helped me figure out a solution to my problem, even though he was probably exhausted himself. Today is his first day back, and although I feel like we'll eventually have to talk about us, I've had enough heavy conversation for the night.

We work as a team, preparing the pizza as though we've done it a million times before. When it's done baking, Riggs makes me stay put as he takes it out, cutting it into slices before serving it to me where I'm curled up in the cozy corner of the sofa.

We eat and laugh, making the stress from earlier a distant memory as we lounge without a care in the world. The reality of this arrangement is so much different than I expected in the best way, and I'm actually feeling grateful that I agreed to do it.

I can't believe I'm saying this, but I'm having an amazing time with Riggs Valentine.

TWENTY
RIGGS

I TURN OFF THE SHOWER, stepping out and taking a towel from the warmer before drying myself off. We don't have a game today, but it's Friends & Family Appreciation Day, so the whole team will be bringing their loved ones to the stadium for a bunch of organized activities. Then, the gates open to the fans so we can all interact with them. In the past, I've usually begged my parents and Grace to come so I wouldn't be alone, but this year, I decided that it's another good opportunity for the team to see how much I've changed now that Monroe is in my life.

I woke up the morning after our phone conversation feeling like a huge weight had been lifted from my shoulders. Although it was only business related, it felt good to know that she trusted me enough to tell me what was on her mind so I could help her through it. Not that I did much, but it was nice to be a part of it.

When I got home, she seemed happy to see me. She didn't run and jump into my arms or anything, but she returned the hug I gave her, and I didn't miss the way she melted into me when I wrapped my arms around her waist from behind. When bedtime rolled around and I asked her if she wanted to sleep in my bed, she said yes, surprising the shit out of me since she was in her own the night before. Nothing happened, but I got to hold her until morning, which felt better than I expected after being away for a couple of days.

Everything just feels so…*domestic*. And as much as I thought I'd never want anything like this, I'll admit I don't hate it.

I make my way to the closet, opening a drawer and taking out a pair of black boxer briefs. I pull them on before reaching for my black track pants with the Fury logo. I finish off the outfit with a teal t-shirt—because *team spirit*—and turn to head downstairs, where Monroe was busy making breakfast when I came up here to shower. I don't even hit the bottom stair before she hurries through the room like a woman on a mission. She runs straight into me, staring down at her phone with a look of panic on her face.

"Whoa, Mayhem," I say, grabbing her shoulders to steady her. "What's wrong?" I immediately think it's the worst-case scenario, that something bad has happened to one of her family members or something, but it doesn't take long for her to clear things up.

"You didn't tell me about the charity basket!" she screeches in a voice that only dogs can hear. "There's less than an hour before we have to be out of here, and I don't have anything prepared!"

"The what?" I ask, genuinely confused because I have absolutely no idea what charity basket she's talking about.

"The basket of stuff all the WAGs bring to Friends &

Family Appreciation Day to auction off!" She's completely distraught, hands shaking at her sides as she looks around the room as if it has all the answers she's looking for, before training her eyes back on mine. "Taylor just called and said they do it every year. It's this big competition between all the wives and girlfriends of the players. Whoever's basket goes for the most money gets bragging rights for the whole year. I'm not letting those bitches beat me, Riggs! I have to win!"

I raise a brow. "That's what has you down here foaming at the mouth like a fucking bulldog? A charity basket?" I ask and immediately regret it, because by the look on her face, that was the wrong question. I can hear her back teeth grinding as one eye twitches, and I'm not sure I've ever been more scared of this woman since the day I met her. I put both hands up in surrender, hoping like hell that she doesn't rip my nutsack off in a fit of rage. "It's no big deal. We can stop on the way and pick some stuff up."

Apparently, that wasn't the right thing to say either. Because she scoffs as she shoves past me, running up the stairs like her ass is on fire. I exhale, rolling my eyes and letting her do her thing while I get something to eat. No matter what I say, I have a feeling it'll be wrong in this situation, so I'm staying out of it.

Thankfully, there's some food left over for me when I get to the kitchen. I take my time plating some eggs and bacon, adding a little extra salt and pepper because no matter how much Monroe has been telling me I need to chill on the sodium, she'll have to pry these shakers from my cold, dead fingers.

Just as I sit down at the table, a white jersey and

permanent marker are shoved into my face. "Sign this," she demands, popping one hip out in a spectacular show of attitude. I want to say something smart to rile her up more, but I think better of it, uncapping the marker and scribbling my autograph across the front of the garment.

"Thank you," she says, leaving the room again while I get back to my food. I make quick work of eating because I'm still not ready to go, setting my plate and fork in the sink and heading back upstairs. I can hear her rustling around in my room before I even get there, and to be honest, I'm a little nervous about what I'm going to find. Sure enough, the place has been ransacked, and in the middle of it is my Mayhem, digging through the drawers of my dresser.

I step into the closet doorway, leaning against the frame and crossing my arms over my chest. I watch her for a few seconds, unable to stop a silly smile from pulling at the corners of my lips. I'd never say it out loud, mainly because it would probably piss her off, but she's adorable like this. She's standing there in one of my shirts that barely reaches her thighs, and a pair of panties. Her messy bun still hangs lopsided on her head because she hasn't showered yet. Monroe is a knockout, seven days a week. But first thing in the morning, when she's all mussed from sleeping? That's when she's the most beautiful. I love the way she does her makeup for a night out, but there's something about her bare face and wild hair that drives me crazy.

Mine.

"What?" She says, looking up at me from where she's leaned over into one of the drawers. I didn't realize I had been staring for so long, but apparently she did because she's looking at me like she's waiting for an answer. One that I absolutely can't give her right now.

I love the way you look in my clothes.

I love the way you look in my house.

You make me want more.

"Nothing," I say, pushing the heavy thoughts from my mind. Just a couple of months ago, I was sleeping my way around Daytona, thinking I was living the high life. But now I know that I was just trying to fill an empty space while attempting to protect myself from people with bad intentions. There was never a doubt in my mind that I could trust Monroe. Even though we started this thing as enemies, I don't think either one of us is feeling that anymore. And now that it's been stripped away, we're left with the exact thing I wanted the very first night I met her. I felt it then, and it's even stronger now.

She's the piece I've been missing my whole life.

I swallow thickly, clearing my throat. I don't know if she'll ever want to hear the things that are going on in my head, but now is definitely not a good time to discuss them. "Is there a reason you're rifling through my shit?" I ask, attempting to lighten the mood. For myself, because my mind is going in a million different directions that I never expected it to, and for her, because she looks like she's about to come unglued over an auction prize.

"Don't you worry about me, Val," she says confidently. "I'm about to make the best basket any of those bitches have ever seen. They'll be sorry they ever stepped into the ring with Monroe Decker."

I bark a laugh, proud of her competitive spirit. "Atta girl, baby," I reply. "I'll leave you to it so I can finish getting ready. Let me know if you need anything else from me."

"I will," she sing-songs, digging her hand into the bottom of the drawer and pulling out a random t-shirt.

I turn away, heading toward the bathroom to shave and brush my teeth. I know I need to deal with all the feelings I'm having for her right now, but I really want to have a good time today, so I do my best to compartmentalize them. It doesn't have to be that serious. We're having fun, and that might be all this is. Monroe has made it very obvious that she loves being on her own, and there's a good chance that she isn't having the same thoughts as me. It wouldn't be the first time, but I'm hoping that the shift I've felt between us has at least made her think twice about how good we could be together.

I quickly shave, rinse the razor, and set it back on the counter before loading my toothbrush with toothpaste. I hear more rustling around as I continue getting ready, spitting into the sink and rinsing my mouth with water. Just as I put the brush back into the holder, another piece of clothing and the marker are thrust into my hand.

"Sign, please," she says, and I start to obey but stop when I realize what I'm holding.

"This is my shirt," I say, slightly confused. "My *used* shirt."

"Uhhh, yeah. Your *used* Bella Simon concert tee. These things were going for like, eight-hundred dollars on the internet at one point. Why do you even have this?" she asks, tilting her head in question.

"First of all," I say, "I don't love your judgmental tone. Bella Simon is the voice of our generation. And don't even get me started on her songwriting. Plus, she's my sister's friend. I wanted to be supportive."

She quirks a brow. "Then you won't mind if I auction it off. For charity, of course."

Little brat. I know she isn't doing this because of the charity. Monroe loves helping people, but I can tell when my girl wants a competitive edge. I fucking love this shirt. But I love seeing her happy even more.

I roll my eyes playfully, scribbling my signature onto the fabric before handing it back to her. An ear-to-ear grin splits her face, and she stretches up onto her tippy toes, pressing her lips to mine in a chaste kiss. "Thank you!"

"Mhmmm," I reply, pretending to be annoyed as I pick up my bottle of mouthwash and unscrew the top. I've barely taken a swig before her hand reaches back out and snags it from my grip.

"Okay, byeeeee!" she sings, leaving the room with half my shit as I stare in shock. This girl is a literal storm, and I couldn't be happier to be standing in the middle of it.

Two hours later, we walk through the player entrance at the stadium, Monroe vibrating with giddiness as she clutches onto her offering for the charity auction. I stopped paying attention after she tried making me autograph a little league participation trophy from when I was in third grade, so God only knows what else she put in there.

Poor girl. There's no way she's winning this competition.

"Hey, you two!" Taylor says, walking our way. The mask Monroe normally wears at these things is nowhere to be seen, but that's because she seems genuinely happy today. I've seen her in all her forms—pissed off, annoyed, indifferent, sad, defiant. But *this?* This is my favorite. I still can't believe I get to experience her like this, and it's not something I'll ever forget.

"Hi, Tay! Where should I put this?" Monroe asks, holding up her basket. I didn't realize these two were at the stage of their relationship where nicknames were involved, but then again, she slid right in and won the entire organization over just like I knew she would. I'm beyond grateful to her for setting aside her hatred for me to do this. I know it was beneficial to her since I offered to help her start her business, but she could've easily told me to eat a dick and gotten a job somewhere else. She and I both know she would've achieved her goals with or without me. All I did was put her on a faster track.

"Over here on the table," Taylor says, leading us across the room. She moves an oversized crate containing a pair of brand-new cleats, several gift cards, and a signed Fury throwback jersey. I drag my eyes down the table seeing several more, each one fuller than the last. There's some pretty stiff competition, but anything's possible. Maybe people will want my random used shit.

Honestly, I'd spend a fortune buying it all back if it made her smile, so that's always an option.

Monroe sets her basket down and rearranges the

contents so everything can be seen better. She carefully fans out every item, and I can't take my eyes off her as she stares at it triumphantly.

She turns toward me, her expression filled with pride, and I don't stop myself from stepping into her and wrapping my arms around her waist. She slings hers around my neck, and I lift her off her feet, pressing my mouth to hers. "Good job, Mayhem," I murmur against her lips, causing her to smile against mine.

Fuck. There's no way she doesn't feel this. The chemistry between us is explosive, even in the most ordinary moments.

"Monroe!" a familiar voice says from beside us, breaking us from our moment. "How's my favorite girl doing?"

"Randy! It's so nice to see you again!" she says excitedly, breaking out of my arms and moving into his for a hug. I'm shocked at first because she's on a first-name basis with the owner of the team, but again, what's not to love about this girl? Anyone who's blessed with a chance to spend five minutes with the real Monroe Decker doesn't stand a chance at getting away without feeling *something*. Least of all, me. She's everything I never expected her to be when I asked her to be my fake girlfriend.

"Riggs," he says with a smile, extending a hand in greeting. I take it, shaking firmly as he brings his other arm over Monroe's shoulder and squeezes. She eats it up as if she's starved of this type of attention, which makes me wonder even more if her parents or other family members ever made her feel as special as I know she is. "You taking care of this one or do I have to trade you to Detroit?" he says playfully, but it makes my balls shrivel a little bit. I know I'm still not completely in the clear after all my fuck-ups, but I hope I've at least cleaned up my image in his eyes a little bit.

I swallow thickly, pasting on a smile. "Yes, sir," I reply. "I'm doing my best." She must be able to sense my unease, because she slides back over to me, wrapping her small hands around my bicep and leaning her head onto my shoulder.

"I can confirm that he's been a model boyfriend," she says, looking up at me. "I'm a very happy girl." Her eyes sparkle and she gently presses her nails into my skin, sending warmth flowing through my entire body. I lean down, inhaling her scent, a sense of calm washing over me almost immediately.

When we started all of this, I told them that I wanted Monroe here to chill me out. When I said it, I was just trying to excuse my wild behavior, but the truth is that that's exactly what she does. She makes me want to be someone that this organization can be proud of. That *she* can be proud of. This relationship may not be real, but there are pictures of us out in the world as a couple now, and I don't want her to look back at them someday and be embarrassed. Before, I would've never cared what others thought. But my instinct to protect and care for her extends far further than just being a physical thing. I refuse to let her look like a fool for being my girlfriend.

"That's what I like to hear," he says with a grin. "Glad to see you on the straight and narrow, Valentine." My chest pulls tight with emotion as I nod, unable to find the words to express how relieved I am without sounding like an idiot. "I have to make my rounds. Enjoy your day, lovebirds."

I watch as he walks away, letting out a huge breath and bowing my head for a second before peeking over at Monroe, who's looking up at me with a satisfied smirk. "What?" I ask, raising a brow in question.

"I'm basically a miracle worker if that sweet old man thinks you're on the straight and narrow. I know a certain outdoor shower that would say otherwise."

I can't stop the cocky grin that blooms across my face as I turn and drop my mouth to her ear, speaking quietly enough so only she can hear. "I'm only a bad boy for you now, baby," I reply, nipping at her lobe as she lets out an almost inaudible gasp. It makes me want to drop to my knees right here and worship her until she explodes, marking every inch of my face with her cum. I look around, making sure nobody's looking before I press into her, showing her how my body reacts to her hot little sounds. Her eyes widen in surprise, and she slaps my shoulder, making me bark out a laugh.

"Ow!" I say, rubbing my hand over it, pretending she hurt me. "Why are you hitting me? It's your fault for being so sexy!"

"Oh my God, Riggs," she replies, rolling her eyes. "Can you at least control yourself until we get home?" That straightens me right up. I'll be the best boy she's ever seen if it means getting inside her again.

She may be the boss here, but tonight, I'm in charge.

TWENTY-ONE
MONROE

"DID you see the looks on their faces?" I say on a laugh as we walk down the hall toward Riggs' condo. "Not only did my basket make the most money, but it wasn't even *close.*"

"Trust me, Monroe. Nobody was more shocked than me that someone bought my half-empty bottle of mouthwash and a to-do list that's been sitting in the kitchen drawer since my rookie year," he replies. His tone says he's annoyed, but the proud smile on his face as they announced that my basket raised twelve thousand dollars for charity told me everything I needed to know.

He thinks I'm a fucking genius. Which, obviously, I am. I'm good at what I do, and that goes beyond analytics and content creation. Thinking outside the box is a huge part of having a successful marketing strategy, and those tactics can be applied in other parts of life.

In other words, horny rich women will drop stacks to put their mouth anywhere Riggs Valentine has put his.

He unlocks the door, pushing it open for me to walk

through. I barely even have my shoes off before his arms snake around me and I feel his lips coast across the already heated skin of my neck. I melt into him, tilting my head to give him better access and waiting for him to bite, but he just continues teasing, darting his tongue out and dragging it toward my ear. Goosebumps trail behind it and I moan as his hands slide up my body, cupping my breasts. Arching into his touch, I can't stop myself from grinding my ass back into his hardening erection.

"Do you know how much it turned me on seeing you win tonight?" he murmurs, squeezing my nipples gently. "You're so fucking hot when you're competitive. But I think you owe me for helping."

"Oh yeah?" I reply innocently. "How can I possibly repay you?"

He chuckles. "It's probably going to take all night, but why don't you start by going to the bedroom, stripping off all those clothes, and getting on your knees?"

I look over my shoulder, locking eyes with him for a few seconds before slowly moving away. I don't look back, but I can feel the heat of his stare burning into me as I take my time making my way up the staircase before disappearing down the hall to his room.

I quickly get undressed, thankful that I shaved from head to toe last night. I take a brief look in the mirror, fluffing my chocolate-brown hair before dropping to my knees and resting my hands in my lap. My clit throbs between my thighs at the thought of him being rough with me again.

As volatile as our relationship has been since that night in Boston, and as many people as I've been with since then, nobody has ever given me what I've needed the way

Riggs has. I tried so hard to tell myself that it was a fluke, or that it just felt that way because I hadn't been with anyone other than Conrad up until that point, but I knew I was lying to myself. I chased that euphoria weekend after weekend, hoping I'd find it with someone eventually, but I had already been ruined for everyone else. My body knew what it wanted. It still does.

I'm practically vibrating with anticipation by the time he stalks into the room, and my stomach does flips as soon as our eyes connect. I don't have to wonder what he's thinking, because I can feel it radiating from him.

He's *there*. The switch that makes him turn into an animal has been flipped, and the sweet guy that was kissing my neck just moments ago is long gone. I almost moan out loud as he prowls toward me, reaching out to grip my chin between two fingers as soon as he's close enough to touch me. I feel a drop of arousal slide down my pussy lips and toward my ass as he stares into me with dark eyes.

"You say stop, we stop. *I* say stop, we stop. Understood?" he says, and I can tell he's on the verge of snapping completely. I'm thankful he's making that clear, but in this moment, he'd have to rip me limb from limb before I'd put an end to any of this. I need it just as much as he does.

"Yes," I say in response, and as soon as the word leaves my lips, he's violently ripping his clothes off, practically shredding them before he throws them aside. I swallow thickly, my pulse speeding up as he looms over me, deep breaths making his thick chest rise and fall quickly.

His cock is already rock hard, and he takes it by the base, rubbing it along my lips. I open my mouth, needy for the bead of precum that's leaking from the tip, but I barely get a taste before he lands a tight slap to my cheek.

"Uh-uh, baby," he scolds. "You don't get to suck my cock yet. Not until I'm sure you smell like me. Close that slutty mouth and wait until I give you permission to open it again." I do as I'm told, pressing my lips together tightly as I await his next move. I look up at him as he steps in, dragging the swollen head across my cheek before moving to the other side and repeating the motion. I can feel the wetness smearing over my skin, growing more and more annoyed with the thought of him letting it go to waste instead of allowing me to taste it. I whine in frustration, squeezing my thighs together as he rubs his scent all over my face and neck before finally pressing himself through my slack lips.

I relax my jaw, letting him use me, knowing I need to wait until he tells me I can take over. He makes me sweat it out for a while, lazily thrusting in and out. He's so big that my eyes water almost immediately, and I have to focus on not gagging. But when he takes a particularly long stroke, there's nothing I can do to hold it back. My throat constricts around him at the intrusion, attempting to force him out, but he does the exact opposite, fisting the hair at the crown of my head and holding me still. I fight it, knowing that if I really want to stop, all I have to do is slap his thigh. But the panic that's setting in from being unable to breathe is making me so aroused, that I'd rather pass out than do that.

Just as I think I'm going to succumb to the lack of oxygen, he pulls out. I gasp for air, coughing and sputtering while my lungs attempt to fill back up. A string of saliva hangs from my bottom lip, connecting to the tip of his cock, and I do absolutely nothing to break it. I just continue looking up at him, telling him without words that I'm ready for more. He quirks a brow, and even though I should be scared by the way he instinctively reads my mind every time, I'm not. I've never felt safer and more protected than I do in this moment, with this man who could break me in half if he really wanted to.

"You ready to suck me, sweet thing?" he asks, and I have to stop myself from begging and panting like a fucking dog. I nod my head rapidly, and he takes mercy on me, pushing back into my mouth. This time, I close my lips around him, hollowing my cheeks and slowly bobbing my head back and forth. He lets me set my own pace, but I can tell he needs more by the way his ab muscles flex and release every time I pull away. Wanting to make him feel good, I speed up, increasing my suction until I hear him begin to growl above me.

He returns his hand to my hair, gripping onto a thick chunk as he meets me thrust for thrust, snapping his hips roughly. I'm drooling and gagging as we work him toward his release, and I notice that I'm on the cusp of my own. There's no contact to my clit whatsoever, but his sounds and the way he's brutally fucking my face is enough to have me ready to come right here.

His noises become deeper and louder as he yanks my head back, making me pop off of him. I sit there, desperate for more while he jerks himself furiously, just out of my reach. "You ready to swallow me, Monroe? I want to own every one of your holes." I nod frantically, right before he lets go of my hair and squeezes my cheeks, forcing my jaw open. "Don't fucking move," he grits out, leaning down and spitting into my mouth. My clit throbs harder at the lewd act, and I barely get a chance to register it all before he steps back in, grunting loudly as his orgasm tears through him. He paints my lips and tongue before he angles his cock down, emptying even more of the warm liquid onto my chest.

I expect him to let go of my jaw, but instead he drops to his knees, pushing his tongue into my mouth that's still full of his spit and cum. He kisses me wildly, wrapping his arms around my waist and taking me to the floor before lying between my parted legs. His still semi-hard cock rubs along my swollen clit, and I climb toward my own climax, pushing my hips up toward him. I whine into the kiss, and as if he knows what I need, he pulls away, lowering down my body. He stops to lick my tits, gathering the remnants of his release while looking up at me with his pupils blown completely wide.

He ghosts his lips past my belly button and down my slit before entering me with his tongue. Just the thought of him pushing his cum into me this way has me wound ripcord tight, ready to explode all over his face. "We taste fucking incredible, baby," he rasps. "Come for me and I'll show you."

I moan loudly, focusing on the pleasure as he tugs on my piercing with his teeth before latching onto my aching clit. I reach down, fisting his hair and bucking off the floor as he feasts like a starving animal. Between the sights, sounds, and feeling of him devouring me, I'm on sensory overload, not sure whether I want to pull him closer or push him away. But I don't get time to decide, as my vision goes white and my orgasm erupts, making every muscle in my body spasm violently. I feel like I'm floating away, but Riggs has a hand pressed to my abdomen, holding me in place as I slowly return to earth.

"What a beautiful mess you made, Mayhem," he says. "I've never seen anything prettier than you when you come." He gently pushes his tongue back inside my overstimulated pussy, and although I involuntarily whimper at the sensation, it still feels so good. I look down, watching his eyes roll back, triggering an aftershock that I know he can feel.

He pulls back, crawling up my body and dropping his mouth to mine. He was right. We taste amazing. Everything about this moment is perfect, and I know he feels the same shift happening between us as our lips move against one another in the most passionate kiss we've ever shared. It makes the things I've felt for him in the past pale in comparison to the rioting emotions that are raging inside me right now.

Being here with him like this makes me wish I could go back to Boston and redo everything. I still don't think I was in the right place for a new relationship, but the way I went about leaving wasn't right, and I robbed us both of a chance to see where this thing could go. If I had just been honest with him, I'm sure he would've been patient with me. But instead, I lied and omitted.

I still am.

I know I should tell Riggs why I am the way I am. That I was controlled and dismissed all my life, and that I moved to Hope Harbor to escape that. That way, he'd understand why I've pushed him away and fought everything so hard. Even though I said it out of spite for those bitchy women at the first charity event, I wasn't lying.

He's the kindest, most selfless man I've ever met, and he deserves the world.

He moves back down to my neck, kissing and licking at my sensitive skin while he mumbles praises against it. "You're fucking perfection, Monroe. Thank you for letting me be who I am with you. I've never let go like this with anyone else," he says quietly, making my heart crack in my chest at the confession. The fact that I have this part of him that nobody else has seen makes me feel grateful in a way I refuse to unpack right now. Because I know if I did, I'd have to face the reality that my feelings and apprehensions about why I've been so against relationships are making less sense with every minute I spend here.

I inhale deeply, breathing out an exhausted sigh as he backs away and stands, scooping me up into his arms and carrying me to the bed. My head is telling me I should be smart and stop this before I get more attached, but my heart is winning the war tonight.

I know I'll have to deal with the conflicting emotions I've been feeling sooner or later, but for now, I just want to pretend this is our real life.

TWENTY-TWO
RIGGS

I DRIFT AWAKE, refusing to open my eyes because I want to stay in this exact place forever. The warmth of Monroe's small body is like a weighted blanket draped over my chest, and I can feel her soft breaths as they puff against my skin. I smile like an idiot because I've never woken up feeling so complete in my whole life.

After what was easily the hottest oral sex I've ever gotten—or given—I took my time kissing and praising her before I carried her to the bed and did it some more, only stopping once I knew she had succumbed to exhaustion and fallen asleep. I followed shortly after, resting peacefully with my arms protectively wrapped around her.

I've never fully given in to these instincts before, and now that I have, I don't think I can ever go back to hiding myself. I was a goner for Monroe the moment I met her. I've finally admitted that to myself. But now that I have a full understanding of how perfect she is for me, I need to figure out a way to break down her walls. To find out what I can do to convince her to give us a real shot. I'm done pretending I'm not really falling for her.

She stirs, groaning quietly as if she's fighting the fact that her body is waking up. I laugh to myself at how cute she is before rolling her to her back and pressing my lips to her warm cheek. She groans again, but it's less convincing this time as I slide my body on top of hers and kiss her gently.

"Good morning, sweet thing," I say against her mouth, settling myself between her spread legs. My dick hardens as the warm metal of her piercing teases it, and I grind down, letting it stimulate us both. She moans in response. "Fuck, I love that little barbell," I breathe, continuing to move lazily against it. "It's like a gift for us both."

"Mhmm," she whimpers, clearly enjoying the sensation.

"What made you decide to get it?" I ask. It's not exactly a common piercing, and I was intrigued from the moment I first felt it slide along my fingertips the day she let me ease her cramps. I've been wondering why she's made so many modifications to her body in the last two years. Don't get me wrong; I love them all, but I'm dying for the stories behind them.

She opens her eyes and gives me a sleepy smile. "I thought it would make sex feel better." She pauses, thinking for a few seconds before exhaling a flustered sigh. "I shouldn't even tell you the rest."

That gets my attention.

I stop moving my hips, raising a curious brow in hopes that she'll continue. She huffs, annoyed, before rolling her eyes playfully. "I only slept with one person before you. It wasn't great, and he never cared if it was good for me. I barely ever got to orgasm, and even when I did, it was so weak that it fizzled out before I really even got a chance to enjoy it."

I grit my teeth, unsure of whether it's because I hate the thought of her with anyone but me, or because he didn't fuck her properly. Had I known this in Boston, I wouldn't have given in to my instincts the way I did. I'd have been more careful.

She continues. "After you, I tried being with other guys, and it was better than before, but something was still missing. I thought I was broken, so I did some research on ways to boost sensation, and this was one of them. I had already done my nipples, so I figured why not?"

I shoot her a cocky smirk, and her brows pull in. "What?" she asks.

"What I'm hearing is that I'm the best you've ever had," I reply. She smiles a little, but it falls quickly as she breaks eye contact. I can tell something is still bothering her, and I feel like a dick for my dumb response.

"Hey," I say, using two fingers to turn her chin back so she's looking at me again. "What's wrong?"

"I still feel broken," she whispers. "I don't enjoy vanilla sex the way I should. Am I really never going to be able to come hard without being bitten and clawed at?" She looks crushed, and it gives me a desperate need to prove her wrong.

"Listen to me," I say firmly. She trains her sad eyes on mine, and I resume thrusting my hips against her, earning a small sigh. "You're not broken. Even if that were the case, and you *did* require those things during sex, that's okay. It's the guy's responsibility to do whatever it takes to make sure you're getting what you need. If he can't, he doesn't deserve you. Right?"

She nods her head weakly, but I know she's still not convinced. My words aren't enough. I need to show her. I want her to see the amazing things her body is capable of when it's properly cared for.

"Baby, let me show you how perfect you are," I say, hoping she sees the sincerity in my eyes. I need her to say yes to this.

She swallows thickly, considering my offer before she finally consents with a small nod. "Okay."

I grin triumphantly, leaning down to kiss her as I grind against her faster. I can feel her growing wetter with every thrust, making it easier to slide my cock along her slit. I swallow the soft moans that escape her, refusing to break our connection as I angle my hips down, pushing my crown inside her pussy slowly. She whines as I bottom out, stilling so she can adjust to the stretch. I'm seeing stars already, and I haven't even moved.

God, please don't let me come before she does...*several times.*

"You're so fucking warm and tight," I say, carefully pulling out and sinking back in. "I've never felt anything like the inside of your cunt. It's heaven."

I pick up my pace, but keep an even tempo, letting her orgasm build gradually while her breathing becomes more labored. Leaning down, I suck a pierced nipple into my mouth, toying with the barbell as she arches into me.

"Fuck, Riggs," she moans. "It feels so good."

"That's because I know this hot little body like the back of my hand," I reply. "I've fucked my fist more times than I can count thinking about that night."

Her eyes go wide with surprise right before she brings her hand around the back of my neck, forcing our lips together. I devour her mouth, pouring every single emotion into the kiss because I sure as fuck can't say them out loud. I can't tell her I'd get on my knees and beg for a shot if I thought she'd say yes. That I've stolen glances every chance I could get when we've crossed paths in Hope Harbor, and she's taken my breath away on several occasions. That the only reason I even touched anyone else after her was to erase the memory of how she felt, knowing I'd never have her again.

I move my lips to her neck, sucking gently on the sensitive skin below her ear. My instincts to take her roughly are still there, hanging in the back of my mind, but the overwhelming urge to protect and comfort her takes center stage, and I refuse to give her anything other than what she needs right now.

"I can feel you getting tighter, sweet thing. You're getting close, aren't you? You're going to come all over my cock just like this. Then I'll flip you over and start again. I'm going to make this beautiful body fall apart for me so many times, you'll forget anyone else has ever been inside it."

She clenches against me, and I double down, moving in and out of her like a man on a mission. Wrapping my hand around her thigh, I pull it over my hip, spreading her even wider as I grind my pelvis against her clit. That's all it takes for her to detonate, her first orgasm of the morning flowing through her so intensely, that I can feel it vibrating my entire body.

When I know she's finished, I slow for a moment, allowing her to recover. "You're doing so fucking good,

Monroe," I say softly, sweeping a sweat-soaked strand of hair from her cheek. I lean down, kissing her lips that are still parted as she gasps for breath. She looks wiped out already, but I'm not letting her leave this bed until there's no doubt in her mind that she's flawless in every way.

"Get on your tummy," I instruct, pulling myself out of her and helping her turn over. She groans as if she doesn't have the energy to even move, making me chuckle. "Keep your legs together for me," I say, swinging one of mine over her ass, so I'm straddling her. When I push myself back inside her warm, wet pussy, I have to clench my butt cheeks to stop from coming.

"Holy shit, baby," I grunt. "You're gripping me so tight, I can barely see straight."

I begin thrusting again, using my hands on either side of her head to support my weight. I look down, watching myself disappear between her thighs before pulling back to see my cock covered in her cum. This woman fucking owns me, and wearing her pleasure is a privilege I'll never take for granted again.

She moans and whimpers under me, and I can tell it feels good, but it isn't giving her what she needs. So, I pull out, yanking her hips up before shoving her knees apart and entering her again. *Fuck.* No matter what position we're in, she feels so good.

It only takes another thirty seconds before I start to feel her walls flutter around me. "There she is," I say. "There's my perfect girl. You ready to come for me again?"

"Mhmm," she whimpers into the pillow, sounding like she's on the verge of coming undone right now. I reach around her, running my fingertip around where we're joined to gather her wetness before rubbing tight circles on her clit. The poor thing is probably aching so bad. I just want to give her another release.

I continue working her over, feeling her muscles as they clench around me again. "Give it to me, Mayhem," I grit out. "I want that cum. It belongs to me." With that, her orgasm hits, making her scream my name so loudly, that anyone on that beach down there knows exactly who's making her feel so good.

I slow again, giving her another minute to come back to earth before I pull out and lie on my back beside her. She melts into the mattress, but she's crazy if she thinks we're done yet.

"Nope," I say, reaching over and pulling her on top of me, her limbs flopping around like a rag doll. "You're giving me one more."

"Riggs, I can't," she whines, making a valiant attempt to snuggle into my chest. It's adorable, but I'm still not letting her off that easy.

"It's cute that you think you have a choice," I say with a devious grin. Lifting under her ass with one hand and holding the base of my cock with the other, I slowly lower her onto it. She gasps as I bottom out again, and even though I know she's completely overstimulated, I feel her get even more turned on as I wrap my hands around her hips and begin sliding her up and down.

"Look at you," I coo. "Not broken at all. This wet little pussy is doing everything it's supposed to. Give me another one, then I'll let you rest."

I see the determination as it passes over her face, and she sits up, bracing herself on my chest. I loosen my grip, resting my hands on her thighs as she slowly begins riding me. "There you go, sweet thing. You're doing such a good job," I praise, and I feel her clench in response.

"Riggs. You feel so fucking good," she breathes, throwing her head back in pleasure. "I love your cock."

Well, shit. Listen to the mouth on this one.

"Use it, baby. Use it to make yourself come," I reply, watching her in awe as she takes what she needs. She's breathtaking, and I'm so goddamn proud of her for doing this.

She returns to bouncing, and it doesn't take long before her moans crescendo, echoing off the windows in the room. Her inner walls clamp down and she comes on a loud scream, continuing to ride me through the entire thing.

When she's spent, she leans down, placing open-mouthed kisses along my neck. I still haven't come yet, and the sensation of her wet lips on my skin is pushing me dangerously close to the summit.

"Monroe, baby," I grit out. "If you don't stop, I'm going to come inside you. You have to get off me." As much as I'd love to fill her up, I know I can't. She told me to pull out the last time, and I won't cross her boundaries.

She resumes moving her hips, and I do everything I can not to blow, but I'm hanging by a fucking thread at this point. Holy fuck, she feels good like this. Her pussy is all used and swollen, practically begging to take my load.

"Monroe," I say firmly. "I can't hold back much longer."

She sits up, placing her hand around my throat and squeezing. I'm caught off guard by the exchange of power, but I feel my balls draw tight as she bounces up and down, using me like a goddamn fucktoy. Black clouds the edges of my vision and electricity snakes its way up my spine, letting me know I'm almost past the point of no return.

"Monroe," I choke out in a final attempt to make her stop. But she just tightens her grip, smirking down at me before uttering the single hottest thing I've ever heard.

"Shut the fuck up and take this cunt like a good boy."

Gone. Dead. Good-fucking-bye.

Every muscle in my body contracts as I come, filling her up so much that it gets pushed back out, making the most beautiful mess between us. It shoots out of me so hard and fast, that it triggers *another* orgasm for her, which I barely even register until I feel her thighs shaking against mine. She works herself through it, falling forward onto my chest when she's physically unable to stay upright any longer.

We're both completely exhausted, breathing heavily as we try to recover. My heart is pounding in my chest, and I can't tell if it's from the overexertion or the fact that I'm falling so hard for this girl that it forgot how to work properly. Could be either one, to be honest.

When I have the strength to move, I gently ghost my hands along her sides, earning a contented sigh as she snuggles into me. "You are everything, baby," I whisper into her hair. "I'm so proud of you."

"Mmmm," is all she can manage as I wrap my arms around her tightly, listening as her breathing eventually evens out and I know she's fallen back asleep.

We lie there, just existing, until my alarm goes off, forcing me to leave her. I carefully roll her onto her pillow, slide out of the bed, and cover her with a blanket so I can get ready to go to the stadium. I should be a gentleman and clean her up, but knowing she'll wake up with the feel of us still between her thighs does something to me, and I can't bring myself to wipe it away.

I shower and get dressed quickly, knowing I've officially made myself later than normal, praying that I don't hit traffic on my way through the city. It would be worth it if I did, though.

I head toward the bedroom door, pausing and turning to take one more look at the beautiful woman who stole my heart, and thanking my lucky stars for bringing her back to me.

TWENTY-THREE
MONROE

I RUSH THROUGH STADIUM SECURITY, the still-wet underside of my hair brushing along my back as I hurriedly run to my seat. As much as I enjoyed the luxury seating and easy access to food in the WAGs' suite, I'd rather be near the field. I did my job up there last time as Riggs' fake girlfriend, spending some quality time with Mr. Durst and showing him how serious this relationship really is. Hopefully, he bought it, and the idea of making a trade with another team is off the table.

To be honest, none of this has felt like acting for weeks. Riggs and I have long forgotten the animosity that used to hang in the air between us, and although we haven't talked about *what* we are, I can tell that we're not just doing this for show anymore. He's treating this like we're real, and I'm struggling to keep myself from doing the same.

On one hand, I know I'm about to become a business owner, and I need to focus on that until I establish a decent clientele and make a name for myself. Also, I left Rolling

Hills to live life for myself, without having to answer to anyone else. So, should I even be considering a relationship at all?

It's all so confusing, and my head and heart haven't stopped battling each other since I realized he's nothing like I thought he was. I expected to move here and dread being near him every day, needing to dig into my old bag of tricks to convince outsiders that we actually liked each other. I did it with Conrad for so long that I knew I could pull the wool over people's eyes long enough to take the heat off Riggs. But other than the first week or so when I refused to admit that he still had a little bit of a hold on me, everything I've said and done has been genuine.

There's no need to act like I'm crazy about him... because I am.

And it scares the shit out of me.

I know there's no easy answer here. If I stay, I'll feel like I left home for nothing, even though Riggs hasn't given me a single reason to believe he'd ever try to control me. Is he the most possessive man I've ever met? Yes. But do I really think he'd keep me from doing whatever the fuck I wanted? No. Not really. He's been completely supportive of the things I've been doing since I got here, but in the back of my mind, I'll always wonder if that'll change.

On the other hand, I already know it wouldn't be easy to leave. As much as I've spent the last couple of years convincing myself that Riggs Valentine is nothing but a selfish manwhore who never takes anyone else's feelings and desires into consideration, I can't hide behind that anymore. I'm forced to face the way my heart and body gravitate to him. How he's shown me that he knows exactly what I need, and that he'll do whatever it takes to give it to me.

What a nice little mess you've created for yourself, Monroe.

Well. Fucking. Done.

Thankfully, I don't have much time for self-loathing today, making my way down to my seat on the third baseline just as the team begins funneling out onto the field. I wait in anticipation, staring at the entrance to the dugout for number fifty-seven to make his appearance. Butterfly wings tickle the inside of my stomach, and I wring my hands together in an attempt to contain my excitement until he finally comes into view.

As if he knows I'm impatiently awaiting his attention, his gaze finds me immediately, and an ear-to-ear grin blooms across his face. Although he probably isn't really supposed to be focusing on anything happening off the field, he runs my way, and the butterflies go into fangirl mode, flapping around so hard that I almost lose my breath.

"Hey there, Mayhem," he says, looking up at me as I lean over the railing, trying to get closer to him. "I almost thought you weren't going to come. I looked out here three times, only to find an empty seat."

I laugh. "Yeah, well somebody let me sleep in. If it weren't for your sister incessantly calling me for our weekly gossip session, I'd probably still be unconscious in your bed."

"Hmmm," he says, as if he's mentally conjuring up the visual. "That might be fun to play around with." My eyes go wide, and I look around to make sure nobody is within earshot, but I have to admit that the thought of giving him permission to fuck me while I sleep wakes up a dull throb between my thighs.

"Stop looking at me like that, sweet thing," he says, snapping me out of my fantasy. "These pants are way too tight to be thinking about what I could get away with in that situation."

Jesus Tapdancing Christ, this man's mouth is lethal.

"Valentine!" Ace yells from where he's waiting behind home plate. "Let's go!"

Riggs looks back at him, giving a tight nod before taking a few steps back and climbing the wall just like he did the first time I sat here. He holds the railing with one hand, using the other to cup my cheek. I can feel several sets of eyes on us as he slowly leans in, gently pressing his lips to mine in a sweet kiss. I know he wants to deepen it —because so do I—but I'm sure there are a bunch of cameras pointed our way. We have to keep things PG in front of everyone.

He pulls away, a small grin tugging at the corner of his mouth. "I'll see you in a bit, baby," he says quietly before dropping back down to the grass and running toward the mound. My pulse is racing, and a silly smile is plastered across my face as I turn to my seat, stopping when I hear a small giggle come from beside me.

"Your boyfriend is really cute," a little girl, no more than eight years old, says shyly. "You're so lucky."

I turn, looking back to where Riggs is warming up, firing pitches into Ace's waiting mitt. As if he feels my stare, he glances over his shoulder, shooting me a sexy wink.

"Yeah, I am," I reply, and even with all the uncertainty I'm feeling, that's the one thing I'm completely sure of.

RIGGS

"That's how we do it, boys!" I yell as we make our way into the locker room. I pitched seven innings and although my shoulder is screaming, I feel amazing after beating the New York Imperials by five runs. My guys' bats were on fire, and we all played the field like the well-oiled machine I know we are.

"We going out to celebrate tonight?" Ace says, sitting down next to me on the padded bench as the rest of the team yells and laughs around us. We have a night game tomorrow, which means we could hit the clubs tonight and sleep it off before we have to be back here in the afternoon. We do it all the time, but I'm done with that shit. I have better things to do.

"Nah," I reply, rotating my shoulder slowly to combat the cramp I feel coming on. "Gotta spend some quality time with my girl. I feel like I've barely seen her." Even though we were together all of last night, it just wasn't enough. It never is.

He whistles quietly. "I never thought I'd see the day where Riggs Valentine actually settled down. I'm a little disappointed that I won't get to be your wingman anymore, but I have to say…being in love looks good on you, my guy."

I snap my head up, eyes wide as I look at him like he's speaking a different language. At first, I want to deny it. Tell him that's not what this is. But I can't bring myself to actually spit out the words.

Normally the thought of committing myself to the same girl for longer than one night would scare the shit out of me. I've enjoyed living the single life. It was easy to move from woman to woman, never worrying about anyone's feelings getting involved because they all knew the score. I never allowed myself to think about a future with any of them because I was never willing to put my heart on the line. But with Monroe?

She can fucking have it. It's all hers if she wants it.

As much time as we lost being mad at each other, I can't even pretend like we haven't fallen into something since she moved to Daytona. I was stupid to think I'd get through this without my feelings getting involved, blurring the lines of our arrangement. I was lying to myself every time I said I hated her. I was masking the hurt from her rejection with animosity, and even though deep down I knew it never really felt right, I thought I could keep that going while she was here. If anything, I figured I could continue matching her energy until this thing was over and we could go our separate ways.

But now…there's no fucking way I ever could. I want her. *For real.*

I'm falling in love with Monroe Decker.

I shake my head at the revelation, huffing a laugh—because *holy shit*—before standing to quickly pull my uniform off. I just want to hit the showers, see the trainer, and get the fuck out of here so I can finally talk to my girl. As risky as it is to bring this up when we agreed to keep this thing professional, I feel like I might explode if we don't sort it all out.

I just hope it doesn't blow up in my face when I lay it all on the table for her.

TWENTY-FOUR
MONROE

"MMMM," Riggs hums, coasting his lips across the heated skin of my neck as we ride the elevator to our floor. Sometimes there's an attendant on duty, but because it's a Sunday, we're all alone. Thank God for that. I'm not sure an extra body in here would've stopped him from pushing me up against the wall as soon as the doors closed, anyway. "Fuck, you taste good."

I moan quietly, feeling the warm moisture between my legs as it begins to slowly soak my panties. I'll never get over how quickly and easily he can turn me on. He barely even has to try and I'm a puddle at his feet. Now that I've come to grips with the fact that I don't hate him and love the way he makes me feel, it's been so much easier to enjoy all of this. I still have the same stupid hang-ups about getting into a relationship in the back of my mind, but I'd be lying if I said I hadn't thought about what it would be like.

The elevator dings and the doors slide open, but Riggs apparently isn't paying attention because he doubles his efforts, biting down on my neck while reaching both hands around to palm my ass. I'm about to just let them close and take us to the next floor, when a throat clears from the hallway. My eyes snap open and I'm mortified to see a young porter staring back at me. I gasp, attempting to shove Riggs away, but of course, the horny mother-fucker isn't deterred.

"You know it makes me hard when you fight back, Mayhem," he growls, gripping even harder with his hands as I maintain eye contact with the poor soul who's literally just trying to do his job. I internally beg the floor to open up and swallow me whole, but obviously, it doesn't.

"Riggs!" I whisper-yell, slapping at his shoulder.

"Love it when you say my name," he replies into the skin of my neck, still attempting to devour me. "But why don't you shut the fuck up so I can make you come before the elevator stops?" He reaches his hand between my legs from behind, making my face flame with embarrassment as I finally rip my eyes away from our one-man audience and focus on getting this asshole back on the same planet as us.

"We *are stopped*," I say loudly, finally making him unlatch from me as he turns to see the guy, who now has his hand in the door to prevent it from closing.

"Oh, shit," Riggs says, clearing his throat and not-so-subtly adjusting his massive erection before turning around. "Sorry, Tim. Got a little carried away there."

"Not a problem, Val," he replies, pretending like he didn't just witness amateur porn in the middle of this very classy building. "I actually just delivered some boxes outside your door. They're large and fairly heavy, so feel free to leave the cart in the hallway when you're finished, and I'll swing back by to pick it up."

I hide behind Riggs as he steps forward, fishing his wallet from his pocket before plucking out a hundred-dollar bill—*hush money, probably*—and handing it to the porter. We exit quickly, waiting for the doors of the elevator to close, signaling to us that we're alone before he turns to me like *I* did something wrong.

"Why didn't you tell me he was there?" he says in an accusing tone.

My eyes go wide, and my jaw drops in surprise. "I did!" I yell. "Several times! Maybe if you weren't such a feral beast, you'd have heard me!"

He smirks. "I've got your feral beast right here, baby," he says, palming his dick and squeezing. I want to scoff and tell him how disgusting he is, but as I watch the veins in his hand when he flexes it, my throat goes dry. I imagine those same salient ridges running along my center, eliciting the kind of teasing pleasure that only he can give.

I shake my head rapidly, attempting to eradicate the dirty thought before he notices, but I'm already busted. I meet his eyes to see a cocky expression, his tongue pushed into his cheek as though he's stifling an arrogant response.

"My dirty little slut," he mumbles, making me roll my eyes sarcastically as we approach the door. Sure enough, there are several large shipping boxes stacked onto a rolling cart, all labeled with Riggs' name and address. He opens the door, ushering me in before reaching back out to wheel it inside.

"What is all this?" I ask, even though it isn't really my business. He gets deliveries all the time, but I'm intrigued by the size of these.

He pulls the cart into the living room, unloading the boxes one by one onto the sofa. "It's your new recording equipment," he replies.

I tilt my head, brows pulling tightly in confusion. "My *what?*"

He disappears into the hallway with the empty luggage rack before coming back inside and closing the door behind him. Returning to the room, he begins unpacking everything like I'm not standing there completely perplexed and awaiting an explanation.

"Riggs," I repeat, attempting to recapture his attention. "What do you mean it's my new recording equipment?"

He pulls a large tripod out of the first box, reaching back in to grab a massive softbox. I've seen these on commercial sets when I worked at the marketing firm in California, but I've certainly never considered using one. "You said you wanted to film how-to videos for your website. I did some research and found out what kind of setup you'd need to make them look professional, and I ordered it on my way home from Philly."

I stand there, dumbfounded as he opens another, smaller box and pulls out a top-of-the-line DSLR camera kit. I go to speak but stop because I honestly don't know what to say. My heart squeezes in my chest as he sets up the tripod and screws the heavy device onto the plate, making sure it's secure enough before letting go.

"I was just planning on using my phone to record them," I say quietly. "We don't even know if this thing is going to take off, and you're out here blowing all kinds of money." I plop down onto the couch, anxiety creeping up and tightening my throat. He must've spent ten thousand dollars on this stuff alone. What if I end up failing him the same way I failed Claire and the boutique?

My eyes fill with tears as I stare blankly at the wall of windows that overlooks the beach. Riggs notices the change in my demeanor, abandoning his task and rushing over to kneel in front of me.

"Hey," he says softly, turning my chin with his finger so I'm looking at him. The sincerity in his eyes opens the floodgates, and tears begin streaming down my cheeks. Using his thumbs, he wipes them away. "You are the smartest, most determined woman I've ever met. You love what you do, and that shows in the way that you care for your clients. I have absolutely no doubt that you're going to crush the shit out of whatever you end up creating. Even if we didn't have this arrangement going on, I'd still be the first in line to invest in your business. I believe in you, Monroe. Anyone who doesn't is out of their mind."

I look into his eyes, and I can feel the wall around my heart shudder as it crumbles into a heap of rubble, leaving me completely open and vulnerable to him. When I got here, I wasn't even expecting us to be able to form a friendship. At the time, that was the furthest thing from what I wanted. I was just praying that I'd be able to tolerate him long enough to fulfill my duties as his fake girlfriend and move on with my life as quickly as possible. But all of that has changed.

I'm falling for him. I've known it for a while. I've tried my hardest to ignore the feelings, but they refuse to go away. The effects of the life I ran from still plague me when it comes to relationships, and although it'll take time for me to work on those, he makes me want to try.

"You're so much different than I thought you were," I whisper, giving him a grateful smile.

"So are you," he replies, leaning in and pressing his forehead against mine. Memories from that day at the boutique after our night together flood my mind, and suddenly, I feel awful about the way I treated him.

"Riggs," I choke out, more tears escaping my eyes and falling down my face. "I'm so sorry for all the time we lost."

He wipes them away again, shaking his head rapidly. "No," he says firmly. "I had just as much of a part in that as you did. I knew I wanted more with you before I even got you back to my room. So when you left, then acted like it was nothing more than a night of fun, I lashed out at you. You were completely honest with me. You told me that was all you wanted, and I agreed. I had no right to degrade you the next morning. I don't blame you for hating me for that."

"I never hated you," I reply. "I hated that I still wanted you after I promised myself I wouldn't."

He closes his eyes and his shoulders sag in relief. "You have no idea how good it feels to hear you say that. I told myself I could move on from what we shared, but as soon as I got you here, I knew that I'd never be able to. Can we stop fighting this now? *Please?*"

I nod before leaning forward and pressing my mouth to his in a gentle kiss. His hand comes up, cupping my cheek, and when his tongue slides along my lower lip, I open for him. This is unlike anything else we've ever shared. This isn't about sex or making our bodies feel good. It's about finally opening our hearts to the things we've been denying ourselves for too long.

We sit there, making out and breathing each other in for what seems like forever. But when he finally pulls back, it feels like I didn't get enough. I whine, making him chuckle before he takes my hand and pulls me up to stand.

"As much as I'd love to be inside you right now, I think we should give one of these videos a try," he says, moving back toward the boxes on the couch. He busies himself, assembling the lighting fixtures while I watch him with a silly grin on my face.

"I don't know if I'm ready," I say. I honestly don't need a script because I've gone through this with clients so many times that I could do it in my sleep. But the thought of actually creating something so important to my success has me feeling all the nerves.

"Well," he begins, turning back toward me, "let's give it a try and see how it goes. If you hate it, we'll delete it and try again. You have all the time in the world to get this right, Monroe. And I'll be here by your side until you feel good about it."

I've never experienced this type of situation before. The only reason my parents even allowed me to go to college was that they thought it would make me more agreeable when it came to their future plans for me. They could hold it over my head, reminding me of all the things they've done for me when they asked me to marry the person they chose to further our family's success. They footed the bill but never once asked how my classes were going or if I needed anything. I truly believe that they were waiting for me to fail so I'd come running back. Unfortunately for them, that was the fuel I needed to make sure I achieved every one of my goals.

As far as my relationship with Conrad, I know he

planned on making it so I wouldn't be able to work. Every generation before him, the wife stayed at home and raised the children with the help of a team of nannies while the husband controlled everything, including the finances. I wanted to have a say in my own future. I wasn't ready to be out from under one thumb, just to go right under another. That's why I had no choice but to leave when I did.

It's also why having so much support from Riggs feels foreign to me. I was programmed at an early age to depend on others to get by. My parents provided every material possession, getting me used to living that lifestyle so they could pass me off to someone who was able to maintain it when I was old enough. Now that I'm working to take care of myself, it's hard to think about letting that go. I know he isn't like them, though. He truly wants to see me do well on my own, and the fact that he's here right now assembling this camera setup tells me everything I need to know about what a future with him could look like.

It isn't going to be easy to just forget everything I've known my whole life, but I really do want to try. I've felt more love and support from this man—who up until recently, barely even knew me—than I have from my own flesh and blood since the day I was born. None of it will happen overnight, but I know I don't want the alternative. I want to be here with him. I want to see where this thing could go.

I walk over, wrapping my arms around his waist from behind as he flips the switch to turn on the studio lighting. He turns, pressing a kiss to the top of my head before giving me a light smack on the ass. "Have a seat,

Mayhem," he says, motioning toward the armchair near the window. "Tell me how to fuck shit up on Instagram."

I roll my eyes, barking a laugh at his words. "Well, we can start by not using phrases like *fuck shit up*," I reply sarcastically. I'm feeling more confident already, now that he's lightened the mood. I swear he knows just how to calm me.

We spend the rest of the evening recording, deleting, and re-recording until I feel like everything is exactly right. My website isn't live yet, but uploading the first video feels better than anything I've ever experienced in my career. Without Riggs, I'm not sure I ever would've had the courage to do this. Now all I want to do is make him proud.

TWENTY-FIVE

RIGGS

"HURRY UP, SLOWPOKE!" Monroe says, practically vibrating as she runs ahead of me, making her way up the stone walkway. We're playing against Boston tomorrow, and we decided to fly in a day early so we could visit Tanner and Grace. I had to clear it with the team, but since I'm not pitching and have been keeping my nose clean, they didn't see an issue with it.

"Jesus, Mayhem," I groan. "It's my day off. If I wanted to be bossed around, I'd have flown in with Clyde."

"Whatever, Grandpa," she sasses as I *slowly* make it up the steps, just to piss her off. Even though we've had a major breakthrough in our relationship, I still enjoy pushing her buttons. I don't think I'll ever get sick of that.

She goes to press the doorbell but hesitates, turning back to me with wide eyes.

"What?" I ask. She's frozen, looking like she's seen a ghost— a total one-eighty from the giddy excitement she was exuding just seconds ago.

"What if they ask if there's something going on

between us?" she whispers. "I can't lie to Grace. I've already omitted so much by keeping the fact that we slept together before I met her. That's bad enough, and it eats me alive as it is."

My expression softens. I understand her apprehensions. My sister is her best friend, and she's held onto this secret for two years. I know it hasn't been easy for her, and I just want that weight to be lifted from her shoulders.

"We're not going to keep it from them," I say softly. "That shit snowballs. One omission turns to two, then that turns into a lie. Before you know it, five years have gone by that you've been kept in the dark. And that's a lot harder to forgive." She knows I'm speaking from experience. My best friend fell in love with my sister, broke her heart, and left us all—then I found out years later from my mother what had gone down. That hurt more than I've ever admitted out loud. I don't want to put Grace in that position with Monroe. "We don't have to offer up any information that you aren't comfortable giving. But if they ask, it's better to just rip off the Band-Aid." I cup her cheek with my hand, and she leans into me. "We're in this together, baby. Everything is going to be okay."

She closes her eyes, then nods her head before she stands up straight and smiles. She's so goddamn pretty, I'm almost knocked off my ass as she turns around and pushes the doorbell. I want to kiss her. Touch her. Tell her every single emotion that flows through me when she allows me to calm her raging nerves. But I don't get a chance before the door opens and my sister lets out a high-pitched squeal. She reaches out, pulling Monroe into a tight embrace, both of them swaying from side to side as they hug like they haven't seen each other in years.

"You're here!" Grace says, pulling back and grabbing her best friend by the cheeks, inspecting her face as if she's looking for something new. Her eyes slide to mine. "Are you taking good care of her?" she asks. "Because if not, I'll fuck you up like I did that one summer when Mom and Dad were in Cabo."

I roll my eyes. "First of all, I had the flu. I could barely stand up straight. And you didn't *'fuck me up'*," I say, using air quotes on the last part. "You sucker punched me while I was chasing your stupid little boyfriend off the porch."

She scoffs. "Whatever you have to tell yourself, dipshit. Just another first kiss ruined by you and Tanner. No wonder I was a virgin until I was eighteen," she mumbles.

"No regrets here," Tanner says, coming into view behind her. "That shit always belonged to me anyway." He wraps his arms around her from behind, dropping a firm kiss to her cheek.

Goddamn it.

"Okay, bye," I say, turning toward the steps. But I'm stopped when Monroe darts her hand out, fisting the sleeve of my t-shirt and yanking me back toward her. I throw my head back, annoyed, before facing them again.

"Stop being a baby," she says with a smirk. "They're in love."

I scoff. "They do this on purpose, you know. I told them I didn't want to know about their sexual"—I pause, searching for a word that doesn't make me want to heave myself off a cliff—"*experiences.* They just want to see how far they can push me before I freak the fuck out."

She rolls her eyes. "Riggs, relax. They're newlyweds. They fuck. It's not a big deal." She takes my hand and squeezes, and I breathe a sigh of relief, feeling all the tension as it leaves my body.

"Fine," I say quietly, only to her, and she rewards me with a smile. I look over to see Grace's mouth hanging open slightly, her eyebrows furrowing in disappointment.

"We almost had him that time," she whines, making her husband chuckle.

These fucking shitheads. I knew they were just trying to get a rise out of me. I fall for it every damn time.

"Come on in, guys," Tanner says, opening the door wider for us to enter their massive house. It's everything you'd expect from a well-paid professional football player who likes to keep his life private. He had this place built, hoping that one day Grace would forgive him and they'd get a second chance, so it's every bit the cozy family home they've made it into. Large windows illuminate every room, with views of the hundred-acre lot we're nestled away in. Soaring ceilings with rich mahogany beams and bright modern light fixtures hang overhead, embodying parts of each of their personalities.

Grace has always been the sunshine to my best friend's intense demeanor, and although I may not love the thought of what they do behind closed doors, I'll be the first to admit that they belong together. Since we were kids, he's put her comfort and happiness above his own, even when it nearly killed him to do so. I'm truly glad they found their way back to one another.

I just wish they wouldn't have sex. Or kiss. Or touch each other at all.

"Oh my God!" my sister says, grabbing Monroe by the hand as Tanner closes the door behind us. "I have to show you the dress I made for Bella to wear to the home opener. You're going to *die*!"

"I'll never get over the fact that you make clothes for the world's biggest pop star. It's fucking insane," Monroe replies with a smile as Grace pulls her toward her sewing room.

"Go do guy things," she says, waving a dismissive hand in our direction. "We'll be back."

We watch them go up the stairs like two lovesick puppy dogs until they disappear down the hallway. I only realize I'm still staring when Tanner blows out a quiet whistle and sucks his teeth.

"So, you're gone then, huh?" he asks, a cocky smirk tipping up the corner of his mouth.

"Deader than a fucking doornail, bro," I reply, not even trying to deny it. I'm crazy about the girl, and I'm exhausted from holding it in. I need to talk about it. I can't tell my teammates the truth since they all think my relationship with Monroe was real from the start. I was honest with my family about why we were doing this, including my best friend, but I can tell he knows that everything has changed. And I'm glad because I think I need his advice.

"Let's go downstairs," he says, leading me to the basement, where he has a fully stocked bar. I go willingly, because I'm about to lay it all out for him and say some things I've never uttered out loud, so a little lubrication is definitely necessary.

I pull out one of the lush high-back stools, sidling up to the bar as he reaches for the top shelf, pulling down a bottle of Macallan Single Malt Scotch and pouring two fingers into each of our glasses. He turns, setting one down in front of me. I tip it back slowly, allowing the dark liquid to burn my throat as I swallow.

"Alright," he says, leaning forward with his elbows on the shiny wooden surface. "Talk."

I slump in my chair, dragging both hands down my face. "I don't know what's happening," I groan. "One minute, we're at each other's throats. Next thing I know, she's in my bed and I feel like I can't breathe when we're apart." It feels good to let the words out. I told Monroe that I was tired of fighting the way I feel about her, but I'm afraid that if I let her know how deep it all runs, it'll scare her away. Plus, it terrifies me that she won't feel the same. She's still holding back parts of herself. That fact is painfully clear.

"Let's rewind," he says, raising a brow. "How about you stop leaving out the beginning of this story? The *real* beginning." This motherfucker is the most observant human being on the planet, so I'm not surprised that he noticed there's more to Monroe and me than we've let on.

I start from the beginning, telling him all about our mind-blowing night in Boston. I don't leave out a single thing, including the way I felt that she was different from the very first sentence that came out of her mouth. He listens intently, taking in every detail. If he's surprised by any of it, he doesn't let on. He just absorbs all the information, letting me purge the emotions I've been holding inside like the good friend he's always been. When I'm done, I look at him with pleading eyes, desperate for him to tell me what to do.

He throws back what's left of his whiskey, setting the glass down onto the bar before looking at me. "I don't know what I was expecting out of this conversation, but it wasn't *that*." I roll my eyes, but he continues. "Have you told her you love her?"

"I don't—"

"Oh, shut the fuck up," he says, cutting me off. "I've known you since you were shitting your Pampers. I've seen you with plenty of girls, but you've *never* been this bent out of shape. You can lie to yourself if it helps you sleep at night, bro. But I know the truth. You love that girl. So, when are you going to tell her?"

I sigh in defeat. "Maybe never," I reply. "I know she has a past, but she hasn't opened up to me about it. The first night we were together, she refused to give me any personal details, and I know I hit a nerve in Hope Harbor when I told her she needed me as much as I needed her. At first, she acted like every kind thing I did was going to be used against her at some point, and I still think a part of her feels that now. Somebody fucking hurt her, but she obviously doesn't trust me enough to tell me who."

"I know you don't like hearing about my past with Grace, but I'll tell you that the worst fucking thing I ever did was leave words unsaid with her," he says. "I thought I'd be able to keep shit between us strictly physical, so when I realized I was in love with her, I panicked. I should've laid all my cards on the table, and we could've worked through it together. But I didn't."

He hangs his head, looking into his empty glass. I can tell he still struggles with the regret of leaving my sister behind all those years ago.

"Eighteen hundred and ninety-six days went by that I didn't get a chance to tell her I loved her. Don't make the same fucking mistake I did, man. You'll never get that time back."

I squeeze my eyes shut, trying to rein in all the emotions that are running rampant inside me. I may be new at all of this, but I know he's right. I'm not doing either of us any favors by not telling her exactly how deep this shit is for me. If she feels it too, we're wasting precious minutes not saying it. If she doesn't, I'm only giving myself false hope and she's going to feel worse for leaving me when she decides it's time to go.

As scary as it is, I know I'm going to have to say the words soon.

TWENTY-SIX

MONROE

"SO THAT WAS A LITTLE WEIRD," Grace says, plopping down onto the couch in her sewing room. She showed me all the game day outfits she's started for the Blizzard wives and girlfriends, and now I'm feeling a little inquisition coming on—one I'd literally give my left boob to get out of. And the left one is *my favorite*. "In all the years I've been his sister, I've never known Riggs to be calmed so easily. Telling him to relax generally has a much different effect." She lowers her head, eyeing me suspiciously. I sit down, leaving space between us and averting my gaze, feeling beads of sweat as they erupt across the back of my neck. "Anything you want to tell me?"

"Not really," I mumble, hoping she lets it go. But of course, I could never be that lucky.

"Okayyyyyy," she says, drawing out the word. "Maybe I didn't phrase that correctly. Let me try again. When did your relationship with my brother go from fake to real?"

I snap my head up, eyes widening at the sheer audacity

of this woman. If she wasn't my best friend I'd throat punch her ass right here. But she is…and I won't lie to her.

"I'm not really sure," I reply quietly. "It didn't happen all at once. It was a bunch of little things he's done to show me support. You know that's not something I've experienced much in my life, and it made me see him—and myself—in a completely different light. It made me hopeful for the future."

She tilts her head, giving me a sympathetic look. "I've told you so many times that you had him all wrong. I said the same to him about you. I just wish you wouldn't have judged each other so harshly when I introduced you."

This is it. I need to tell her the truth. I've been hiding the details about the way Riggs and I met for too long, and now that I've admitted that I have feelings for him, I need to lay it all out for her. Maybe she'll hate me, maybe she won't. But either way, I can't do this anymore.

"Grace," I say, swallowing thickly. "There's more."

"More *what*?" she asks.

My knee bounces nervously and I wring my hands in my lap. I need to get this over with before I have a fucking heart attack. I gnaw on my lip, considering my words before finally beginning my confession.

"That day at Praya, where you thought you were introducing us?" I say, pausing to look at her.

"Yeah?" she replies.

"We sort of…already knew each other."

"I—" she sputters. "I thought you arrived in Hope Harbor that morning."

"I did," I rush out. "But the night before, I decided to stop in Boston for a drink. My nerves were shot, and I was second guessing leaving Rolling Hills. I thought that if I could remind myself of the life waiting for me now that I wasn't under anyone's control, it would give me the courage I needed not to turn back around. I had every intention of finding a hot guy, spending the night with him, and moving forward as a new woman. I found the nicest bar in the area, ordered a drink, and waited for someone to approach me. That someone was Riggs. I'll spare you the details, but I ran out the next morning without saying goodbye, and the next thing I knew, you were introducing me to your brother."

She blinks rapidly, as if she's trying to process everything before her brows pull tight. "Why didn't you just tell me? Why go all this time lying to me about why you hated him?"

My shoulders sag and I try to swallow, but the lump in my throat feels like a golf ball as I attempt to find the words to express my remorse. "I was scared. At first, seeing him was a shock. I didn't think I'd ever cross paths with him again, and we both said some things we didn't mean. After that, there never seemed to be a good time to tell you. I had never had a genuine friend before I met you. Someone who wasn't just there because they thought they could get ahead by being around me. You were so kind to me for no reason at all, and I selfishly didn't want to give that up if you hated me for being awful to him. Which, I was. I was so mean, and he didn't deserve that. Neither did you. I'm so sorry I lied."

The tears I was trying to hold back finally spill over, and I bring my hands over my face to hide my sobs. I have no right to be crying here when I was the one who betrayed her by not being truthful. But the thought of losing my best friend now that she knows everything is almost too much to bear.

Warm arms slide around me as my body trembles. She presses her cheek to the top of my head, and the comfort of her closeness is like a balm to my undeserving heart.

"Please don't hate me," I whisper.

"I could never hate you," she replies softly. "Believe it or not, I understand why you didn't tell me."

I look up at her, my eyes widening in surprise. "You do?"

"Yeah," she says, popping a shoulder. "Tanner and I hid what happened between us for five years. And even after we reconnected, we still didn't tell Riggs right away because we were afraid of his reaction. It wasn't because we didn't love him. It was quite the opposite, actually."

Relief washes over me, and I turn so I can return her hug. "I really am sorry, Grace. I'll never lie to you again."

She laughs, squeezing me tightly. "This is karma, isn't it?"

I pull back, raising an eyebrow in question. "What is?"

"Being forced to think about my brother banging my best friend, like he has to think about me banging his."

I bark out a laugh, batting at the last of the tears still staining my cheeks with my fingers. "Yeah, you're probably going to regret putting so much effort into winding him up with all your dirty innuendos."

"It's fine," she replies, slapping my thigh before standing up. "I had it coming. Let's go find our guys before they drink all the good whiskey."

Our guys.

I don't hate the sound of that.

TWENTY-SEVEN
MONROE

"YOU DON'T HAVE to worry if you don't have tons of followers right off the bat," I say into the camera. "TikTok is just like the platforms we've discussed in the previous videos. It takes time to build a presence, but as long as you're using trending sounds and not overdoing it on the hashtags, you'll slowly see your views rise. Don't get discouraged, and make sure to download the free social media content creation kit on my website for ideas on how to get started. Thanks for watching and I'll see you in the next one!"

"Aaaaand cut!" Riggs yells through his cupped hands as if we're on a full recording set, instead of in our living room with a crew of zero, other than us. He stops the camera and runs over to where I'm sitting by the window, scooping me up into his arms and pressing his lips to mine. I squeal in response, throwing my head back with laughter as I wrap my legs around his waist. "You're a fucking natural at this, baby. I'm so proud of you."

I'll never get sick of hearing him say that.

I got word last week that my LLC was approved, and immediately went live with my website. I opted to do a rapid release of my instructional video series so potential clients can see examples of my work before deciding whether or not I'd be a good fit for them. Today, I'm recording the third video, which I plan to edit and upload in the next few days. Web traffic has been better than I expected, and I even have a few consultations set up for next week. The encouragement I've gotten from Riggs has lit a fire inside me to make this business succeed, and I'm beyond grateful to have him in my corner.

"I was hard through that whole thing," he says, burying his face in my neck. I sigh, tightening my legs around him and feeling for myself that he's not lying. He walks us over to the couch, gently laying my head onto the soft cushions before lowering his body between my parted legs. Sparks go off behind my eyes as he grinds his erection against my throbbing clit, and suddenly, I'm *famished*.

I reach down, yanking at the waistband of his sweats, attempting to push them past his ass. "I need to suck your cock," I say on a breath, feeling like I might die if I'm not gagging on him within the next ten seconds. I'm frantic, bringing my feet into the mix and using them to assist in removing his pants. But much to my dismay, he stands, putting me face-to-face with the tented material. I go to reach for it, but he backs up, making me whine in frustration.

"Bring him back here!" I yell, kicking my heel into the couch like a child having a temper tantrum.

"Calm down, killer," he says with a snicker. "I wanted to get home to help you with this, so I skipped my post-practice shower. I can assure you that you don't want any part of me in your mouth until I'm clean."

I sit up, pushing my bottom lip out in a pout. He leans down, nipping at it before hurrying toward the stairs. "Give me fifteen minutes. If Tim stops by, hand him the tickets in the envelope on the entry table. I'm still secretly trying to buy his silence from when he found us almost fucking in the elevator." I cringe, anxious about the thought of looking the poor kid in the eye again after what he saw.

"Fine, hurry up," I say loudly, crossing my arms over my chest and throwing myself back into the cushions as I hear the door to his ensuite bathroom close. Unlocking my phone, I commit to doom scrolling until he returns, but not even five minutes later, there's a knock on the door. I stand, walking over to the table and picking up the envelope so I can get this over with. Damn Riggs for making me interact with this kid.

I'll be demanding extra orgasms for the inconvenience.

I don't bother looking through the peephole, swinging the door open and stopping in my tracks when I see who's standing in front of me. I flinch, fighting my instinct to slam it in his face while I try to figure out how he even found me.

"Dad?" I choke out. "What are you doing here?"

I haven't heard from this man in *years*. He cut off all contact the day I left, froze my bank account, and I'm pretty sure the only reason he allows my mom to talk to me is because she tries to get me to come home every time she calls. She's his way of keeping tabs on me now that he can't control my every move.

"I'm here to bring you home," he replies. "You've had

your fun, but these games are over. I've just put in my bid to run for governor. It's time to come back to California and fulfill your duties to the Decker family."

I huff a laugh, because he's out of his mind if he thinks I'd ever return to that hell hole. "And what are those? Go back to Rolling Hills, marry some douchebag that isn't capable of love, and hate my life until I die? That might be good enough for Mom, but I deserve more."

Holy fuck, I can't believe I just said that.

"You ungrateful brat," he seethes. "After everything we've done for you. We set you up for a successful future, and you took off to blow it all on some shitty career that'll never get you anywhere. You think you're going to live a different life here? You think this guy gives a shit about you? He doesn't. He's probably fucking someone thinner, prettier and classier as we speak."

A devious grin pulls at his mouth as he steps forward, making me cower slightly. "Face it, Monroe. You're not enough on your own. At least we were raising you to be a woman who knew her place. Now look at you." He looks me up and down, his top lip curling in disgust. "He might be happy to have you as his whore, but it'll take more than a set of fake tits and a bad attitude to make a man like that love you."

"What the *fuck* did you just say?" Riggs booms, running down the stairs at full speed wearing only a pair of sweatpants. He puts his large body between me and my dad, and I can hear the bones in his hands crack as he clenches them tightly at his sides. I peek out, wrapping my fingers around the rock-hard muscles of his bicep, practically able to feel the blood flowing through his protruding veins.

My dad lifts his chin, but I can tell he's terrified as he attempts to look unaffected. "I'm here to speak with my daughter. She doesn't belong here. I'm taking her back home."

"Like hell you are," Riggs replies, his entire body vibrating with rage. "This *is* her home. She belongs with *me*."

My dad scoffs, rolling his eyes. "You'll get bored with her. You'll cheat, break her heart, and I'll be back to get her. So, why don't we just make the exchange now before you realize she's nothing more than a warm hole to stick your dick i—"

He's cut off when Riggs grips him by the collar of his shirt before shoving him to the ground. I stand there, unable to move or see through the unshed tears in my eyes as I watch it all happen like a horror movie on a screen. My dad scoots backward across the hallway, stopping when his back is against the opposite wall as Riggs prowls toward him, crouching down and speaking quietly.

"You're lucky I have neighbors, otherwise I'd beat your ass right here," he grits out. "If you ever try contacting Monroe again, I'll fucking kill you. I promise that nobody would miss your sorry ass—least of all, this angel of a woman you don't fucking deserve," he says, pointing a finger back in my direction but never taking his eyes off my father. "Now, get the fuck out of here before I call the cops, you piece of shit."

He stands to his full height, and my dad hurries to his feet before taking off toward the stairwell. It isn't until I hear the quiet *snick* of the door that I break from my stupor, choking out a loud sob. Riggs turns and rushes my way, catching me just as my knees wobble and give out. I claw at his bare chest, desperately trying to grab hold of something to ground myself. Swollen tears flow down my face as I attempt to catch my breath, but I feel like my whole world is caving in.

I knew deep down that my dad felt that way, but part of me hoped I was wrong. Now that I've heard the words, there's no denying that my own flesh and blood never saw me as anything more than a bargaining chip to become richer and more powerful.

Riggs carefully lowers us to the floor, pulling my trembling body into his lap and holding me tightly as I dig my nails into his skin. I let out heaving sobs, releasing every ounce of pain that's flowing like hot lava through my veins.

"Shhh, baby," he whispers softly, rocking back and forth in an attempt to soothe me. "I'm right here. I've got you." He kisses my hair as I continue to break in his arms, whispering gentle words that I can't make out over the sound of my own cries.

It seems like hours have passed before the tears begin to slow and I'm able to catch my breath, finally settling into his lap and praying that he never lets me go. If we never make it off this floor, I'd be perfectly fine with that, as long as it means I never have to know the feel of my skin not pressed against his in such a cruel fucking world.

"Monroe," he says quietly. "I'm so sorry I wasn't down here. I don't even know how he got onto our floor. I swear I'll make sure he never comes near you again."

"Don't be s-sorry," I stutter, still trying to calm down completely. "You h-had no idea that he even existed. I should've t-told you why I moved to Hope Harbor, but I didn't want to relive any of it." I drop my head back down, attempting to fight more tears as they threaten to erupt again.

"Look at me," he commands, lifting my chin. "You don't have to tell me anything you don't want to. It doesn't matter."

I nod before nuzzling back into his warm chest. I want to tell him everything, but I'm too shaken up from hearing my father's hateful words to even know where to start. I can't force the conversation, but it needs to happen sooner or later. Riggs deserves to know the whole story—the reasons why I am the way I am.

"What if he's right about us?" I whisper, letting another tear fall down my cheek.

"Baby, no," he says, nudging me so I'm sitting up straight, facing him. "None of what he said was true. He was just trying to tear you down so you'd second guess everything you've done. We're solid. I'm all in with you."

I sniffle. "Yeah, you are *now*. But what happens in five years when you're ready to move on to someone younger? Or someone who doesn't push back every time she gets upset?" I pause, swallowing. "I know I'm a lot sometimes. What if the newness wears off and you decide I'm not what you want? What if *I am* only good enough to be your whore?" I whisper, shame washing over me at the thought.

"This is fucking crazy," he says, standing abruptly and taking me with him as he stomps toward the stairs. I try to pull away, but he only tightens his grip, not letting go as we make our way down the hall

"Riggs, no! Put me down!" I cry, kicking my feet in an attempt to make him release me. But he just keeps walking, not stopping until we're standing in front of the full-length mirror in his bedroom. He sets me down, holding me still so I'm face-to-face with my reflection. I'm shocked at my appearance. My eyes are swollen and red from crying. The skin between them is scrunched together from stress. My shoulders slump forward, and I look every bit as defeated as I feel. I turn my head, ashamed of how I allowed myself to be broken so quickly, but Riggs grabs my chin roughly, forcing me to focus on my own face in the mirror.

"Look at her," he demands roughly. "Tell me what you see."

"Please don't make me do this," I beg. "I can't." I don't want to tell him that after a few hurtful words from my father, I've lost sight of the girl I fought so hard to be.

"You can," he replies. "I'm not letting you leave this room until you do."

I stare, taking in my reflection before I speak, almost so quietly, that I'm surprised he can even hear me. "She's weak."

Without a word, he yanks the straps of my sundress down my shoulders, making me gasp in surprise. Pulling it below my waist, he releases the garment, letting it fall in a heap at my feet. He disappears for a moment, plucking something from the dresser before returning to his place behind me. It's not until I feel it gliding along my bare skin that I realize it's the permanent marker from the day I had him sign things for my charity basket. He takes his time writing something before looking up at me in the mirror.

"What else?"

I swallow, tears stinging the backs of my eyes. "She's not pretty enough."

He unfastens my bra, letting it drop alongside my dress before working my panties down my legs. I stare at my naked body, numb and hardly blinking as he returns the marker to my flesh and resumes writing.

"Again," he demands.

"She's a whore," I whisper, choking on the word as it comes out. Tears slide down my cheeks, and he growls in response, putting the marker to my skin again and writing out the word.

"Again."

"She's unlovable," I sob, dropping my face into my hands. My body shakes as I cry, but he doesn't allow me to hide it, spinning me to face him. He gathers my wrists in one large hand, pulling them down until they drop at my sides.

"Listen to me," he says firmly, cupping my face with the hand not holding the marker and smoothing my tears away with his thumb. "While you're looking at yourself and seeing all those things they've made you think you are, I'm behind you with the truth. I know the real you, Monroe." He grips my chin, turning my head so I can see the reflection of my back in the mirror. My sobs come harder when I see the words written in permanent ink across my body.

"They told you that you were weak, baby. But you aren't." He angles me so that the word *STRONG* is in clear view. My heart speeds up and I turn to look at him, watching his eyes as they fill with moisture.

"They told you that you weren't pretty enough, but you're the most breathtaking creature I've ever seen." He angles me the other way, and I turn to see the word *BEAU-TIFUL* written below my shoulder blade. I stare at it for a few more seconds before he speaks again.

"They told you that you were a whore for wanting to

feel pleasure, but you're a fucking goddess, Monroe. And I'll drop to my knees every day to give you what you deserve," he says, and I turn once again to see the word *SEXY* across my hip.

I've never felt more adored in my entire life as I stare back at myself, letting his words erase every negative thought that's ever been put into my head. I was conditioned from as young as I can remember to beg for crumbs of affirmation, always getting just enough to keep me desperate for more. My parents used that as ammunition to get me to do what they wanted, showering me with praise when I did what I was told. I caught on as I got older, but no matter how hard I tried to remind myself of my worth, I guess I didn't realize until just now that the damage they had done was far deeper than I ever knew.

He leans down, ghosting a gentle kiss over my lips, and I feel a tear fall from his cheek to mine. He pulls back, lifting my chin as he returns the marker to my chest and writes again. "Fuck anyone who's ever made you feel unlovable, baby. You aren't," he whispers, turning me to face the mirror. The word *LOVED* is in big, bold letters directly over my heart. I suck in a breath, meeting his eyes in the reflection.

"I love you, Monroe Decker," he says quietly. "And I'll spend the rest of my life reminding you how fucking special you are."

I spin toward him, barely able to hold the words inside for another second. "I love you too," I breathe, crashing my lips to his. I hear the marker hit the floor before his hands come up to my face, holding me tightly as his tongue slides against mine. I pour every piece of myself into the kiss, hoping he can feel even an ounce of the gratitude I have for him in this moment. He was right. This is my home. I belong with him.

When I got here, I pretended to hate this man. I made up a completely inaccurate persona of who I wanted him to be, so it would be easier not to fall for him when I had convinced myself he wasn't part of my plan. But I fell anyway, and now I realize that I'm stronger with Riggs by my side. He doesn't hold me back. He holds me *up*. I know I can achieve my biggest dreams with him cheering me on, believing with all my heart that he'll never let me down.

The kiss becomes frantic, and a dull throb blooms to life between my thighs as I become so needy for him that I can barely think. I reach for his sweats, pulling them down and dropping to my knees as his hard cock bobs between us. He steps out of his pants and boxers, and I dive forward, desperate to get him to the back of my throat as fast as I can. I open as wide as my jaw will allow, wiggling my head from side to side in an attempt to take his full length and fighting my gag reflex as his head pushes roughly against it.

"That's it, sweet thing," he grits out. "Take my fucking cock." He sounds like he's on the verge of coming already, and it makes me feel exactly like the goddess he sees when he looks at me. He pushes in deeper, reaching down to wrap his hand around my throat as he fucks it.

"There's that throat bulge," he says. "I fucking love feeling you swallow me from the outside. You're my sexy little cock slut, aren't you?"

I try to nod, but the way he's holding me prevents it.

"Be my polite girl and answer the question, Monroe. Are you my sexy little cock slut?"

"Mmhmm," I mumble as best as I can, involuntarily constricting against him as I do.

"Fuck!" he yells, pulling himself from between my lips. I stare up from the floor, breathless as I wait for him to tell me what to do next. "As much as I want to obliterate that tiny little throat, I need to fill you. Stand up."

TWENTY-EIGHT

RIGGS

HOLY FUCKING SHIT. I've never wanted anything more than I want Monroe's pussy wrapped around me right now. I'm doing everything I can to avoid going to that place where I can't control myself, but I feel like I'm walking on a tightrope, ready to fall at any second. I need to be present for this. *For her.*

She stands, and I spin her so she's facing the mirror before taking her hair in one hand and sliding the other down her back until I can feel her dripping center. She's hot and ready as I spear two fingers inside her, curling and thrusting them until she moans for me.

"What a dirty girl you are," I coo. "Does the thought of choking on my cum really make you this wet? You're a mess."

"Yes," she replies, raising to her tippy toes as I fuck her hard. Her inner muscles begin to close around me quickly, but I'm not ready to make her melt yet. Just as she's about to come, I yank my fingers from her body and stuff them into my mouth hungrily, making sure I'm close enough to her ear for her to hear me suck her arousal onto my tongue. She whines in frustration, no doubt because I denied her the release she so desperately needed.

"You don't come unless it's on this cock," I say, stepping up behind her and sinking myself into her wet cunt. I see stars as she tightens around me, almost like her body is forming to the way I fit inside it. We're perfect for each other. I've known it since the second I laid eyes on her. I'm just glad she's finally catching up.

I thrust in and out, listening to the sounds of her heavy breathing and quiet moans as I fuck her from behind. Her head begins to hang forward, but I tighten my grip on her hair, pulling it up so she's looking straight at the mirror.

"Look at her again, Monroe," I demand. "Tell me what you see."

She watches as I fuck her, a lazy smile tipping up the corners of her lips. It's like she's seeing herself for the first time. In a way, she is.

"She's beautiful," she says, letting her eyes roam over her body as it bounces against me. Her pierced nipples glint in the light and I'd give anything to sink my teeth into them right now.

"Good fucking girl," I praise. "Rub your clit for me and tell me what else."

She obeys, diving a hand between her legs and rubbing wildly at her swollen bundle of nerves. "She's strong," she says on a moan.

"Fuck yeah, she is. What else?"

"She's sexy." Her eyes meet mine in the reflection and I wink back at her.

"Sexiest girl I've ever seen," I reply, leaning over her shoulder so my lips are at her ear. "What else?"

She exhales, her hooded eyes connecting with mine again. "She's your whore."

Fuck yes.

I let go of her hair, digging my fingers into her hips for leverage as I pick up my pace, pounding into her. My grunts and her moans mix with the sound of our wet skin slapping together, and I've never felt more complete than I do in this moment.

"That's right, baby," I reply. "You *are* my whore. In here, I'll defile every one of your holes whenever I want." I spit on her back entrance before abandoning where I'm holding her side, pushing the tip of my thumb into the tight bud and earning a gorgeous gasp from her plump lips. She clenches at first, but releases quickly so I'm able to slide in even further. Every part of her is made for this. *For me.* "You'll submit to me and let me take what I need in this room. But out there, in the world? You're my fucking queen. I'll fall at your feet and give you everything. You'll never have to question how loved you are, because I'll remind you every day that you own me."

"Oh my God, I love you," she whimpers as her inner walls begin to tighten around me. I reach between her legs, batting her hand away and taking over, rubbing tight circles on her clit while she arches her back in pleasure. Her legs become more and more unsteady with every one of my thrusts, so I wrap my free hand around her waist, supporting her weight.

"I love you, sweet thing. Let go and come for me so I can fill you up," I say, just as her pussy grips me tightly. She cries out and her legs buckle, but I keep going, refusing to let her fall as she climaxes so hard that the pressure almost forces my cock right out. I fight against it, waiting until her muscles have stopped contracting before I finally let myself come, shooting my load inside her with a loud growl. It goes on forever, and I revel in the feeling of filling the woman I love with this part of me, that'll one day hopefully create another life. The thought triggers an aftershock so intense that I come again, almost dropping us both to the floor where we stand.

Fuck.

I pull out, watching as a mixture of our pleasure falls between our feet before lifting Monroe into my arms and carrying her to the bathroom. As dead as I feel, and as much as I'd love to slide right into bed with her, we made a mess and I can't let her go to sleep without cleaning her first.

I walk into the shower, carefully sitting her on the bench and turning on the water, allowing it to warm completely. When it's at a comfortable temperature, I pull down the detachable head, using it to wash her body and hair as she leans back against the wall with a sleepy smile on her face. The permanent marker stays put, but it'll be a good reminder of who she is when she gets dressed tomorrow. When the words eventually fade, I'll continue to repeat them to her every day until she's sees what I see when she looks in the mirror.

When I'm done with her, I quickly wash myself before drying us both and carrying her to the bed. She's combative the entire way, complaining about how extra I'm being, but I don't give a fuck. I'm prepared to take care of her until my last breath—and that begins right here, right now.

"YOU FEELING OKAY, BABY?" I ask, drawing gentle circles with my fingertips along the soft skin of Monroe's back. We've been awake for almost an hour this morning, but neither of us has even made any attempt to move. Last night was intense in so many ways, and I want to make sure she isn't feeling any leftover emotions from everything she went through. I'm sure it isn't easy for her to relive all the vile things her father said to her, but my instinct to mend her heart when she's hurting won't allow me to let them plague her mind.

She breathes a heavy sigh. "Yeah. I think I need to completely cut ties with my parents. Even my mom. I know she's the one who told him where I was. She does anything he tells her to, and I can't trust that my secrets are safe with her anymore."

"If I had known about them, I would've never asked you to do all of this for me. It was only a matter of time before photos of us were taken and plastered all over the internet. I wish I could've protected you from that," I say, tightening my arm around her body.

"I should've told you about my life in California a long time ago, but I hate going back to that place, even if it's only in my mind." She pauses, thinking before she speaks again.

"Growing up, I wasn't shown a lot of genuine love. My parents provided the best of everything for me, and made sure I never wanted for anything, but when it came to being nurtured? I'm not sure they were ever really taught how.

"As a kid, it wasn't so bad because I had nannies that raised me to know how unique and special I was. But as I got older, and didn't need them any longer, it was up to my parents to give me the emotional support every teenager needs while they're trying to figure out who they are. They didn't even give me a chance to do that. They just told me what was expected of me, and I wasn't allowed to ask questions."

I remain quiet, allowing her to continue her story. I'm thankful she's sharing all of this, and I want her to know that I'll always be here to listen when she needs me.

"When I was seventeen, they told me I would be marrying a classmate named Conrad Astor. I was to date him throughout college, then we'd have a big, extravagant wedding after graduation. They never asked me if it was something I wanted, or if I even liked him, but I certainly wasn't given a choice. It was a business move that would make both of our families richer and more powerful in their circle, so we were expected to go along with the plan. They treated me like a little doll, creating the perfect future wife for him. On my eighteenth birthday, they paid for me to have a breast augmentation because they thought it would make me more attractive to him. I didn't complain because I was young and just wanted to have what society called a *perfect body*, but looking back, how fucked up is it that they encouraged me to alter myself for a man? Every time I'd try to change my appearance, whether it was a new haircut or a new style of clothing, they'd tell me to ask Conrad first. We weren't even living together yet, and it was like they were already passing ownership of me over to him.

"I tried to do what they wanted. I dated him, but I knew pretty early on that if I ended up marrying him, my life would be miserable. I wanted to do my part for my family, so I did everything I was told for years, even though I felt in my heart that I was meant for more. Some nights I would stay awake, staring at the ceiling while thinking of ways to make myself disappear. Some of those thoughts were pretty dark, but in the end, I just decided to pack up everything I could…and I left. I was thankful that my parents had allowed me to go to college, even though my father insisted I wouldn't need a degree, because it gave me the qualifications to get the job at Praya. I waited until everyone was asleep one night, got in my car, and drove across the country with about five thousand dollars to my name. I didn't know if any of it would work out, but the alternative was something I wasn't willing to accept for myself. I deserved better."

I lean down, pressing my lips into her hair, doing my best to hold back the tears that are gathering in my eyes for this poor girl. She was so brave, leaving everything that she had ever known because she knew she was worth more. I'll never be able to tell her how grateful I am that she found her strength, because without it, I never would've met her.

She goes on. "As soon as I was out of the state of California, I felt like I could breathe again. Even though the future was uncertain, I knew I had done the right thing. I was so excited to erase every memory of the girl I never wanted to be, that I found a salon along the way and dyed my blonde hair brown. The week after our night in Boston, I was feeling so empowered, that I googled the nearest tattoo shop and had my nipples pierced." She chuckles under her breath. "It was like a giant *fuck you* to my parents for expecting me to conform to what they said I should be. It felt so good, that I decided to get my first tattoo immediately after."

I reach under her knee, dragging her thigh across my lap and ghosting my fingers over the art that covers her smooth skin. I've had time to study it, and I wondered what the meaning behind the piece was, but now that she's telling me her story, it all makes sense. The face of the woman is hers, and the puppet strings attached to her head and arms represent the hold her parents had on her. There's a blindfold over her eyes as well, no doubt a symbol of her upbringing, being shielded from the great big world that awaited her if she could just find the strength to cut herself free.

Monroe Decker is the most awe-inspiring woman I've ever met in my entire life. From the outside, it probably looked like she had it all, but she knew better. She knew that she was too special to be caged up, so she left it all behind to give herself what she deserved.

I use my fingers to tip her chin, dipping down to take her lips in a soft kiss. I breathe in her scent, making a promise to myself that I'll never let her down. I'll love her and support her in anything she wants to do, just like her parents should've done from the start. Someday, we'll build a family of our own, and I vow to make sure our children know that whatever choices they make for themselves, their parents will always be there to catch them if they fall.

I was crazy for ever thinking that this wasn't exactly what life is all about. I spent so many weekends having meaningless sex with women I never intended to be with, but I know now that I was just buying time while I waited for Monroe to walk into that bar and change me forever. I'm not that guy anymore, and I couldn't be more thankful that my eyes are finally open wide. This woman has become the most important piece of me, and I'll never be able to thank her enough for allowing me to care for her the way I do. She's it for me.

"I love you, Riggs," she says quietly, nuzzling back into my chest as I hold her tightly. "I know with everything that went down last night, I should probably feel immense loss, but because of you, I don't. If anything, I feel like I finally have a family that loves me unconditionally."

"You do, Mayhem," I reply. "You do."

THIRTY
MONROE

"OH, FUCK OFF!" I yell at the television, clutching the remote tightly in an effort to channel my anger. The Fury are playing tonight in Atlanta, and Riggs is pitching. The umpire has been calling balls all night, even though he's hitting the strike zone almost every time. They're losing by six runs late in the fifth inning, so unless some kind of miracle happens, it's looking pretty bleak.

"Come on, Val," I say under my breath, sitting back down on the sofa as I shove my thumbnail between my teeth. It's practically down to the cuticle at this point, but it's been a rough game. I either bite my nails, or I heave this remote through the screen. This is a financial decision.

Ace gives the signal and Riggs shakes his head, clearly not liking the call. His catcher tries again, earning a nod right before he stands and winds up to fire the pitch. It's low and inside, but still a strike according to the white square I'm staring at, yet the umpire calls another ball, and the player walks. I can tell by the look on his face that Riggs is getting pissed. Apparently, so can Clyde, because before the next batter makes his way to the box, he's on his way to the mound. Ace hops up from behind home plate, joining the men as they speak quietly. Riggs shakes his head, his brows pulling inward as if he's about to argue before he rolls his eyes and heads to the dugout. The camera follows him as he flings his glove into the brick wall before throwing himself down onto the bench. The crowd above him cheers at his misfortune, and I wish I was there so I could nut punch every single one of them.

I knew I should've flown there when he offered for me to come along. I had a video call with a potential client earlier today, and I thought I'd feel more confident if I were in my own space rather than in a strange hotel room. Looking back, I wish I were there, because I'm sure he's not going to take it easy on himself after this one. It's not his fault, but I know he'll take the loss as his own, and it'll eat away at him.

I turn off the TV and make my way upstairs to take a shower. It doesn't take long, so I go through a full skin care routine before falling into bed and waiting what feels like hours for my phone to ring. I'm in the middle of editing my last how-to video when it vibrates next to me, a photo of Riggs planting a messy kiss on my cheek while I scrunch my face in fake disgust filling the screen. I slam my laptop shut, tossing it onto the mattress and answering the FaceTime call.

"Hey," I say, giving him my best sympathetic smile because I'm sure he's not in the best mood.

"Hey, baby," he replies solemnly. "How's my sweet girl?"

I get comfortable, settling myself back onto the pillow as I pull the comforter up over my chest. We've made it our post-away game ritual to talk until we fall asleep. I miss him so much, but this is his job for a lot of the year, so I'm getting used to not feeling the heat of his body beside me at night.

"I'm good," I say, a small smile tipping up the corner of my mouth. I feel like an asshole for wanting to celebrate, but I know he'd be pissed if I didn't tell him about my day. "I got the account."

"I knew it!" He says triumphantly, an ear-to-ear grin blooming across his face. "Congratulations, Mayhem!"

I laugh, not knowing why I expected anything less than this reaction out of him. Even though they just lost and he didn't pitch his best, he's setting that aside to experience this big moment in my life.

"Thank you," I reply. "The instructional videos were a huge hit, and the shop owner said she's already seeing an improvement in her online sales now that she's getting social media engagement. I convinced her to sign up for three months of consulting, and hopefully, we can make an even bigger impact on her business in that time." I pause, tears of joy filling my eyes. "*I fucking did it.*"

"I never doubted you for a second, my little badass." The look on his face is full of pride, and it makes me feel so good knowing that I'm not letting him down. I know that his investment in me was a part of the hook to get me down here, but that doesn't change the fact that I want to succeed for both of us. I'm just grateful that things are moving in such a positive direction.

I yawn, giving him a tired smile as I pull the pillow from his side of the bed toward me, propping the phone against it. It smells like him, and if I close my eyes and listen to his breathing, it almost feels like he's here.

"You tired, sweet thing?" he asks, and I nod my head in response. He mirrors me, lying on the opposite side and propping his phone up on what would be my pillow if I were there, taking a deep inhale and letting his eyes fall closed.

"Good night, baby," he whispers. "I love you."

"I love you too." The words are barely out of my mouth before I'm drifting off, almost able to feel his protective arms wrapped around me as I fall asleep alone in our bed.

I wake abruptly, the alarm on my phone blaring in my ear. Normally, when Riggs and I fall asleep together, neither of us hangs up until our batteries die in the middle of the night. His must have gone first this time, because mine is still above twenty-five percent.

I sit up, trying to get my wits about me as I reach over and kill the loud noise. It takes me a minute to remember that Taylor asked me to meet with her this morning before she has to be at work. Apparently, she's butting heads with some people on their marketing team about something, and she wants to pick my brain since Riggs told her all about my new business. I agreed because she's been so kind to me since I moved to Daytona, and I truly want to help if I can.

Deciding to do the bare minimum today, I throw on a pair of cotton shorts and a baby tee, with all my tattoos on full display, and finish the outfit with my brand-new white sneakers. I pile my hair up on top of my head in a messy bun and brush some tinted moisturizer over my face to cover the subtle dark circles I always get when Riggs is out of town. I can't even deny the fact that I sleep a million times better when he's home. It's quite the change from living by myself and doing everything I could to keep my distance from him.

I chuckle at the sentiment, heading down the stairs and toward the kitchen to grab my wallet and keys. We're meeting at a café, so I skip breakfast in lieu of the large macchiato I plan on having when I get there.

I make my way down to the lobby with every intention of having the valet pull my car around, but when I see what a gorgeous day it is already, I decide to walk the four blocks. Pushing through the door, I'm thankful that the humidity is low and there's a slight breeze.

I turn toward the café, taking in the sights around me. I haven't really spent much time getting to know the city, but now that I am, it really is a beautiful place.

Riggs and I haven't discussed what the future looks like, but I'm starting to think that maybe it wouldn't be so bad to stay here. I love Hope Harbor, yet the thought of leaving him to go back there twists my stomach into knots.

Maybe I should call a realtor to see if it would be worth selling my house. It's bittersweet because I worked so hard to buy it on my own, but I really want to put in the effort for this relationship. Riggs shows me every day that he's all in, and making a commitment to move down here would show him that I am too.

I wait for the feelings of unease to settle in as I consider packing my entire life and starting over yet again, but this time, they never come. I don't even have to wonder why that is. Last time, I was running from something. This time, I'm running *to* it.

I smile at the thought, putting a little extra pep in my step as I approach the café entrance and go inside. I spot Taylor immediately, raising a finger in the air as if to say *I'll be right there*, before heading to the counter to order my macchiato along with a glazed doughnut, because I walked all this way and now I deserve some extra carbs. Waiting at the counter, I stuff a twenty-dollar bill into the tip jar before taking my breakfast and joining Taylor at her table.

"Thanks for coming," she says cheerfully. "I know it's early."

I shrug. "I had to be up anyway. It's nice to get a jump on the day."

She takes a sip of her coffee as I get settled, waiting until I've taken the first bite of my doughnut before she breaks the silence. "Okay, so here's the deal. The fans seem to have forgiven Riggs for the most part, but his jersey sales are still at an all-time low. He's usually one of our best-sellers, but right now, we can't seem to move them at all. The marketing department is claiming that it's not a PR issue, but I feel like it is. That's why I asked you to meet me. I was hoping that you might be able to come up with some ideas on how we can get him back into the fans' good graces, because apparently, pitching well and winning games isn't enough. Short of letting Friggle beat the shit out of him on the field, I feel like there's not much that'll make them happy, you know?"

I make sure she's finished, pursing my lips in thought while I go over everything she said. I've been to several home games, and I've noticed that people don't cheer for Riggs until he starts striking batters out. There's little excitement when he's warming up, unlike there is for every other pitcher in the rotation.

The solution hits me like a freight train, and I try to work out the details before I say it all out loud. "We need to convince the fans that the two of them have buried the hatchet. Riggs made a public apology for his outburst, but he never went out of his way to say he was sorry to Friggle. That's setting a bad example for the younger kids, and their parents aren't going to support him by buying his jersey."

She tilts her head, and by the look on her face, she agrees with what I'm saying. "Alright, so what do you suggest?"

"Well," I begin, "I think the best thing would be to choose an upcoming home game and make a whole event out of it. You could brand it as Friendship Day and offer a two-for-the-price-of-one deal on tickets for kids, encouraging them to bring a friend. I'm sure there are sponsors who would gladly pay to have their logo put on friendship bracelets that you could hand out at the gates. Friggle could throw the first pitch to Riggs, and they could exchange bracelets in front of the whole stadium."

Her jaw is slack as she stares at me, blinking rapidly for several seconds. "Holy shit, he was right," she whispers. "You *are* a genius."

Warmth washes over me at her words, and a wide grin blooms across my face. Knowing that Riggs is out there telling everyone who will listen how amazing he thinks I am still gives me butterflies, even though he's told me himself a hundred times.

"Sometimes you just have to think outside the box," I reply.

Her shoulders slump slightly as she lets out a forced exhale. "But how am I going to convince the marketing department that this'll work? They're all old and set in their ways. They've been using the same strategies for the last thirty years, and they aren't always open to new ideas."

I smirk, lifting a brow. "I have a motto, Taylor. *Sin now, ask for forgiveness later.* How can they say no if you've already gone out and secured a massive sponsorship for the event?"

She barks a laugh, shaking her head at me in disbelief. "If they fire me for this, I'm telling them it was all your idea."

"Well," I say, popping a shoulder. "If it works like I think it will, the last thing they'll want to do is fire you. They might even put up a statue in your honor in front of the stadium."

"Let's not go off the rails here, Monroe," she replies with a sincere smile. "Thank you. Riggs is lucky to have you. We all are."

I sip my drink, thankful that I've been accepted into the Fury family—first by Mr. Durst, and now by Taylor. I feel welcome in a way I've never experienced before, and the thought of her coming to me for help with something so important just solidifies the fact that I made the right choice by coming to Daytona.

All my life, all I've ever wanted was to make my own path. Leaving California was just the first step in creating the future I had always dreamed of. If I decide to leave Hope Harbor, a piece of me will always be there. That little beach town was the beginning of my rebirth, and I'm thankful for the safe place it provided while I figured out who I really was.

If you would've told me three months ago that Riggs Valentine would be a puzzle piece in my story, I'd have never believed you. But here I am, actually considering putting down roots in this city because I've never felt more empowered than I do with him by my side.

We finish our breakfast, and Taylor heads off toward the stadium for what I assume will be a long day of pitching the idea of Friendship Day to all the major Fury sponsors. I'm excited to see what they come up with, and I'm ready for the fans to finally see what a kind, funny and talented player they've been blessed with in Riggs.

Now, I just have to find a way to convince him to go along with my crazy plan.

RIGGS

"Listen to me carefully, Mayhem," I grit out. "There's *no fucking way* I'm doing anything with that long-armed dildo. I'd rather take a cleat to the nuts than trade friendship bracelets with him. As a matter of fact, *he* should be apologizing to *me*. I only reacted to him booing me in front of everyone."

She sticks her bottom lip out, pouting. "Are you sure?" she coos, sliding her center over my hardening erection. Just minutes ago, I was lying on the couch, minding my business while watching game highlights. Next thing I knew, she was straddling me and asking me to make a fool out of myself in front of tens of thousands of fans. "There isn't *anything* I could do to convince you?" She reaches up and palms her braless tits through her tight white tank top, pinching her nipples as she moans. I close my eyes, losing myself in the hot friction that's being created between us, almost forgetting what she asked as I grip her hips and help her grind against me.

"You're a fucking she-devil, you know that? You're preying on a weak, innocent man here. How do you even sleep at night?"

"Usually full of your cum," she replies, winking down at me.

She's gonna pay for that one.

"Fine," I growl, thrusting my hips upward. "I'll do it. But if he tries to hug me, he's getting knocked the fuck out again."

She stills her movements, leaning down and pressing a chaste kiss to my mouth before hopping off of me. "Thank you!" she sing-songs as she walks away, leaving me gaping like a fish with my rock-hard cock staring up at me.

"What the fuck just happened?" I mumble to myself, throwing an arm over my eyes in frustration.

She really is a she-devil. But she's *mine*.

Minutes later, she comes back into the room, flopping down onto the sofa next to where I'm still attempting to make my dick deflate. "I texted Taylor and told her you were happy to participate in the event. The Children's Hospital has agreed to sponsor it, so they'll be donating the bracelets and picking up the tab for all the free tickets the Fury will be giving away. The marketing department wasn't happy with her for going above their heads, but

Mr. Durst loved the idea, so they had no choice but to go along with it."

As much as I don't want to do this, the girls are right. My fans have not been nearly as enthusiastic as usual, and although I haven't allowed it to affect my pitching, it still doesn't feel good knowing they have negative feelings toward me. Even though I'm known as the Bad Boy of Baseball, I've always made sure to connect with the people who fill our stands at every game. I think that persona mainly came from my wild dating life and hot temper.

But all of that has changed now that Monroe is here. The things I used to think were important no longer matter, and I'm happy to trade my old life for this new one with her. My days of partying and acting like a fuck-up are over. I just want to be the man that my girl and my team deserve. If that means playing nice with the team mascot —even though he's the creepiest thing I've ever seen—so be it.

I'd do anything for her.

THIRTY-ONE

RIGGS

"ARE you absolutely sure there's no other way?" I say, pouting as Monroe runs her fingers through my hair. We're standing in the hall just outside the locker room, getting ready to walk to the field for the Friendship Day first pitch. Taylor came in about fifteen minutes ago, telling us that there isn't an empty seat in the entire stadium.

"I *did* suggest a Celebrity Death Match between you and Friggle, but for some reason, the idea was shut down. So unfortunately, no, there's no other way," she says, doing a terrible job of hiding her sarcasm.

I reach up, grabbing her face between my fingers and thumb, squeezing her cheeks. "That smart mouth is going to get you in trouble, Mayhem," I reply through clenched teeth before leaning in to kiss her.

"That's fair," she giggles, and the sound makes me less irritated. "I'll tell you what. If you're a good boy and do as you're told, I'll let you do whatever you want to me later. How does that sound?"

I reach out, sliding my hands along her waist before

reaching around to palm her ass. "Why didn't you lead with that, baby? I've been dying to use your body for all kinds of depraved things," I say so only she can hear. She swallows thickly, and I watch as a pink blush spreads across her face and chest, making me smirk. "Ooh, I think you like the idea of being my free-use little whore. I bet your panties are already wet."

Her eyes flutter closed, and I back her against the wall, diving a hand down her shorts and checking for myself. Sure enough, she's soaked, and I have to fight the animal inside me as he bares his teeth, knowing we can't have her the way we want to right now. As much as it pains me to do, I pull my hand out, sucking her arousal off my fingers before pressing one last kiss to her lips.

"You're *mine*. I hope you're ready to get torn apart," I growl, knowing we're playing with fire right before I need to be on the field. Hopefully, being this worked up doesn't fuck with my game, but if it does, it would be worth it.

"Okay, it's time!" Taylor's voice bounces off the brick walls, and I look to see her standing there covering her eyes. I'm guessing she did it as a precaution, but had she been here a minute ago, she'd have had an eyeful of my semi as I rubbed Monroe's pussy when I definitely shouldn't have been.

Small miracles.

I say my goodbyes, making sure Monroe is escorted to her seat by security before I walk through the dugout and onto the field. I sidle up next to where Ace is crouched behind home plate, tapping his shoulder to let him know he can move aside for this shit show. He stands, a silly grin stretched across his face as he sweeps his arms out as if to say *it's all yours*. I nod back at him, trying my hardest not to let my grumpy expression break through as I get down on one knee and put my glove out in front of me.

Friggle stands on the mound, oversized glove on one hand and a baseball in the other. He's wearing what looks to be my jersey, and his googly eyes wiggle back and forth as he pretends to stretch.

"Hurry the fuck up," I mutter under my breath, wanting to get this thing over with. But of course, he can't just make it easy. His arm stretches turn into full-on lunges before he finally decides we've had enough. He places the hand that's holding the ball into his glove, looking at me as if he's waiting for a signal. Since I refused to rehearse any of this, I have no idea what I'm supposed to do here. I doubt he knows what each hand gesture means anyway, so I rest my hand between my legs and point down to the ground, telling him to give me a fastball. He makes a giant show of winding up, abandoning any kind of form and opting for a windmill, circling his arm around several times before he finally lets go of the ball. It flies straight up in the air, and I throw my head back, waiting what feels like decades for it to finally drop into my glove. I breathe a sigh of relief, glad he didn't actually know the signal and end up hitting me in the nuts in front of all these people.

I stand, walking toward the mound with my hand in my back pocket. Pulling out the oversized friendship bracelet, I step up next to him and hold it out. Any semblance of hope I had that he would just be cool and take it goes down the drain when he holds his furry wrist out between us, waiting for me to attach the braided band.

Mustering up the realest-looking fake smile I can produce, I wrap the bracelet around his arm and tie it in a knot. He brings it over his heart in an exaggerated movement, swaying back and forth with happiness before opening his hairy purple hand to reveal a smaller version of what I just gave him.

I grunt in annoyance before thrusting my arm between us, allowing him to attach the Velcro ends of the bracelet. Since he doesn't have fingers, they had to make it special so we could do this. It's itchy against my skin, and all I want to do is shake it to the ground, but I refrain. Monroe said I had to be a good boy to get what I want, so that's what I'm going to be.

I smile at the mascot, giving him a tight nod and turning to walk back toward the dugout. I don't get far before I feel a fuzzy hand around my wrist, tugging me back.

"Don't you fucking dare," I growl quietly, but he just looks at me with his stupid, creepy face before he lunges forward and wraps me in a hug. I stand there frozen as the crowd cheers, obviously a lot happier about the embrace than I am. I try to remember that I need to stay cool, because I know if I lay him out again, it'll probably cost me my career.

Thankfully, he releases me, throwing his arms up in triumph as the fans go wild. My eyes lock on Monroe, where she sits in the front row with tears of laughter streaming down her face. As mad as I should be, the sight of her enjoying herself at my expense calms me down, and I roll my eyes before leaving my new best friend to continue his antics alone.

"Not gonna lie," Ace drawls as I make my way into the dugout. "I'm a little jealous. I thought we had something special, Val. But you never look at me the way you just looked at Friggle."

"Sit and spin, Mathers," I grump, flipping him off. He barks a laugh before standing and patting my shoulder, then walks away.

I sit back a little longer, watching as my teammates start funneling onto the field. Standing, I smooth my pants and fit my glove over my hand before walking up the steps and heading to the mound. Immediately, I notice louder than usual cheers coming from the stands. I look up, watching kids jump on their chairs as their parents laugh beside them.

Holy fuck. She did it.

I'll be the first to admit that I thought Monroe's idea wasn't the best when she first pitched it to me, but in true form, she knew exactly what she was doing. I don't know if this'll translate into jersey sales, but it's amazing to walk onto the field and feel the love. My hot temper has gotten me into some trouble over the years, but up until now, I never realized how quickly that could be detrimental to my career. Having her here to keep me in check has certainly opened my eyes to what my life could look like if I don't stop reacting before thinking.

I'll never be able to thank Monroe for being exactly what I need, but I have no problem spending the rest of my life trying.

THIRTY-TWO
RIGGS

RIGGS:

Remember last week when you told me if
I was a good boy, I could do whatever I
wanted to you?

MONROE:

Yes.

RIGGS:

Well, I'm ready to collect my prize.

MONROE:

Oh, God. What'll it be, Val? Blowing you
while you watch ESPN? Fucking me on
the beach where everyone can see?
Making me call you Daddy?

RIGGS:

All wonderful ideas, but no. I just want to
take you on a date.

MONROE:

That's all you want? A date?

RIGGS:

Yep. My flight gets in at 8 o'clock. I'll text
you the address for where to meet me.
Wear running shoes.

MONROE:

If this date includes cardio, I already
hate it.

RIGGS:

Well, I hated getting dry humped by the
team mascot, but here we are. No
arguing. Be a good girl and follow
directions.

MONROE:

Ugh, fine. See you tonight.

RIGGS:

Love you, sweet thing.

MONROE:

Love you.

I POCKET MY PHONE, leaning my head back and closing my eyes. After our home game last week, I spent a couple of hours interacting with fans, so we were both exhausted by the time we got home. The next morning, I had to leave for some road games, so this'll be my first night home. I've set up a night that, if all goes according to plan, neither of us will ever forget.

I try my hardest to rest for the remainder of the flight, but I'm way too excited to get any sleep. By the time we touch down and I tell Monroe where to meet me, I'm vibrating with anticipation. The drive from the airport to the stadium is short, so I swing by the groundskeeper's office with about fifteen minutes to spare before my girl arrives.

"Hey, Albie," I say, rapping a knuckle on the thick wooden door before stepping inside. He's an older man, probably in his late sixties, and I became fast friends with him when I was first brought up to the majors. I wanted to show my dedication to the team, so I arrived on game days before everyone else and always left last. I took the time to get to know a lot of the staff members, and that's something that's about to pay off for me in spades.

"Hey there, Riggs," he says with a smile. "Welcome home." He stands before rounding his desk and extending his hand between us. I shake it and give him a tight nod.

"Thanks, man. Good to be back. Everything all set for tonight?" I ask.

"Sure is," he replies cheerfully. "The man door next to the main cargo bay is propped open with a brick. All the other entrances are locked, so make sure that one is closed tightly before you leave. I gave my overnight security guards the evening off. It's all yours." He raises a suspicious brow, eyeing me. "I don't know what you're up to tonight, but if you get caught, I had nothing to do with it."

I chuckle quietly. "Of course. Thanks for your help. I owe you one."

He gives me a thumbs up, shuffling out of the room and leaving me by myself. When I'm sure he's gone, I make my way to where the main breakers for the entire building are. I stand, shifting my weight from foot to foot, nervous that Monroe won't be down for the things I've planned for us. I'd be perfectly okay if she wasn't, but this is all I've thought about for the last week, and I'm practically salivating at the thought of what could possibly happen here.

Before I met her, the beast inside me was destined to live his life in a cage. I restrained myself so much that I wondered if I'd ever feel true fulfillment during sex. I think that's part of the reason why I never had an issue moving from woman to woman. They were using me in the same way that I was using them, and we were all in agreement that it would never be more. They'd never see the real me and I didn't have to worry about getting my feelings involved, because I was convinced that I'd never find someone who matched me so perfectly in every sense of the word.

That's exactly what Monroe is to me. Not once have I ever wondered whether she liked me because of my job, since I never told her who I was that first night. By the time she found out, she had already made up her mind about me, and we wasted two whole years convincing ourselves that we hated each other. I know I was wrong for being dishonest back then, but I can't say it didn't help me get past the fear of her ending up just like the rest when I had already begun to feel things for her that I had never experienced before.

Hearing her backstory and fully understanding the kind of upbringing she had brought everything full circle for me. In Boston, she just wanted to have an evening of fun and freedom for herself. Not giving personal details was her way of taking control of the situation. While it threw me off back then, now I get it.

Her first night in Daytona, I was taken aback by how unimpressed she was with my condo. I chalked it up to just being her bitchy persona, but that wasn't it at all. She grew up with the best of everything, so when she saw my lifestyle, it was nothing she hadn't already been around since the day she was born.

Finding out about her past also explained her behavior on the night of our first charity function. I played it over and over in my head, trying to understand why she was able to change her demeanor as if a switch had been flipped, even though I had upset her on the way over. My sweet girl spent her life acting in front of people who were nothing like her, putting on a show because she wanted to make her parents happy. Looking back, I feel like an asshole for asking her to do the same, but from here on out, I vow to make sure she never feels like she needs to be anyone but herself ever again. I love her exactly as she is, and so does everyone who's crossed her path since the day she left California.

"The stadium? Really? *This* is how you're wasting your reward?" she says, making me spin around to where she's standing thirty yards away. She looks absolutely gorgeous in a tight black cotton dress, complete with a pair of white Air Force Ones. Her long, dark hair is hanging over her shoulders in waves, and although she's wearing very little makeup, I've never seen her more beautiful than she is right now.

"Oh, Mayhem," I drawl as a smirk pulls at the corner of my mouth. I want to walk over and touch her, but I need to keep some distance between us. If she consents to this, I need to give her a little room to run. "I can't think of anywhere I'd rather do this than right here in the dirt that makes me feel the most powerful."

She quirks a brow. "Oh yeah? You want to let me in on why we're here?"

"I'm glad you asked," I reply, walking toward the wall that houses the main breaker. "I thought we could play a little bit."

"Play?" She exhales harshly, letting me know she's aware of *exactly* what I'm thinking. I'd be crazy to assume she couldn't feel the energy as it leaves my body.

"Mhmm," I hum. "For tonight, I want you to be completely mine. To let me do whatever my instincts tell me to do. As always, if either of us says stop, we stop. Otherwise, anything goes."

I watch as her breath hitches, her chest moving up and down rapidly as she becomes more aroused. As nervous as I was that she wouldn't want to go along with my plan, I should've known this would be her reaction. But I need the words from her.

"Yes," she says quietly.

A devious grin spreads across my face. "Any limits you have before we start?"

She swallows thickly, shaking her head. "No." She knows she just has to say the word and it'll all end, so I'm okay with her response.

"Good," I reply, flipping the door to the breaker box open and pulling down on the lever, shrouding the entire stadium in complete darkness. "You better run, sweet thing. Because if I catch you, I fuck you."

She freezes for a second, then I hear her back up a couple of steps before she turns and takes off. The light of the moon illuminates her silhouette just enough for me to see the direction she turns in, but once she's out of sight, I'm relying on all my other senses to find her. I give her a little while to get away, but when I hear nothing but the blood pumping between my ears, I begin my hunt.

She's spent enough time on the lower levels of the stadium that she knows her way around this particular area, but not as well as I do. I could navigate this place in my sleep. All I need to do is find her, and then she's mine to do whatever I please.

I start walking the way she ran, trying as hard as I can to stay light on my feet in case she makes any noise. The smell of her perfume still lingers in the air, but it's weak. I turn in the opposite direction of the door she entered, taking my chances that she's headed toward the field.

"Mayhem," I sing darkly. "Why don't you come out? I promise to take it easy on you if you give yourself to me." She knows that's a lie just as much as I know she'd never reveal herself that easily, and the thought of what I'll do once I find her makes my heart race in my chest. I can feel my blood hammering against every pulse point in my body as I continue searching, trying to focus on what little of my surroundings I can see for clues. I put my nose in the air, inhaling to see if I'm even moving in the right direction, but it's not her signature perfume that permeates around me.

It's her cunt.

"Baby," I say in a taunting voice. "I know you're here somewhere. I can smell how wet you are. That poor, aching pussy of yours is begging you to stop hiding and let me rip her apart."

I continue in the direction I was going, stopping dead in my tracks when I see a small movement out of the corner of my eye. A smirk pulls at the corner of my mouth, and I watch her stand from the shadows, looking like a deer in headlights.

"Gotcha," I say, but before I can get to her, she takes off

running. I follow as she shuffles down the steps, making her way toward the railing that separates the first level of seating from the field. My heart rate picks up as she hits the landing, a whoosh of air leaving her body as her ribs press against the hard metal pipes. "Looks like you're trapped, Monroe. Game over. You're mine." I slowly descend, watching as she looks in every direction, attempting to find an escape. Right as I hit the third step from the bottom, she turns and swings a leg over the bar, immediately following with the other so she's standing on the ledge of the wall.

My little badass.

I reach my arm out, attempting to grab her wrist, but she lets go, making the ten-foot drop down onto the dirt that surrounds the field. She takes off running while I follow, knowing she's truly fucked herself now. No matter where she goes, every exit to the place is locked. I slow my pursuit, attempting to save some energy while she gasses herself out. By the time I get to her, she won't have anything left to fight me with.

She passes both dugouts since she knows the layout from when she was down here with me last week. There's a short hallway that leads to the locker rooms, but she's smart enough to assume that they'd be locked. They are. I can get in with my fingerprint on the keypad, but that won't do her any good. Stalking across the field, I watch as she yanks on the door to the bullpen. In a surprise to us both, it opens, and she closes it behind her. I'm sure she thinks she's home free, but she couldn't be more wrong.

"Aww, baby," I say sweetly, turning the knob to find that it's been locked. I expected that, so I walk further, reaching the end of the padded wall where it meets the chain-link fence. Scaling it with ease, I fling myself over and drop to the other side, landing on the floor next to the metal staircase that leads directly to where she's caged herself in. If I were anyone else, she'd have gotten away. But she's in my house.

As quietly as I can, I make my way down the steps and into the bullpen. My gaze lands on her immediately, and she knows she's fucked. Her eyes go wide as she turns toward the door, but I'm done with the chase. Now, I want my reward. I dart my arm out, snaking it around her waist and lifting her from the ground. She kicks against me, attempting to fight, but my grip is like iron around her. There's no fucking way I'd ever let her go.

"Tell me to stop if you don't want it," I say quietly against her ear. She doesn't respond, giving her consent. I turn us, dropping her on her hands and knees straight into the dirt and laying my body on top of hers until she flattens out under me. She attempts to thrash around, fighting to bring air into her lungs, but I'm pressing down on her so forcefully that she can barely move. My cock is so hard, I'm surprised it hasn't torn through my pants already. I've never experienced this kind of euphoria in my life, and I'm not even inside her yet.

"Uh-uh, sweet thing," I tut. "Little holes like you don't need to breathe. You can stay there and struggle under my body weight, or you can willingly give me what I want. Either way, I'm taking it." Her thigh muscles twitch at my words, and I can't stop myself from reaching down to see if she's as turned on as I am. Thankful for her choice of attire, I slide my hand up her dress and yank her thin lace panties to the side. As soon as my fingertips touch her flesh, the beast inside me roars with need. The outside of her pussy is completely soaked, and when I press against her swollen clit, she moans loudly.

"My dirty little whore," I say, rubbing in tight circles over her pulsing bundle of nerves. "Being hunted really turns you on, doesn't it?" Her only answer is another moan before she gives one last, half-hearted effort to break free from under me. I grab a fistful of her hair with my free hand, and tear her underwear into pieces with the hand between her legs before spearing two fingers inside her tight heat. I give her no time to adjust as I begin fucking her, but she's so aroused that it wouldn't be necessary if I did. I keep a steady tempo, changing angles often to make sure I'm hitting every part of her. It isn't long before her inner muscles contract around me, so I pick up my pace, tapping against her g-spot as she explodes around me in the quickest orgasm I've ever seen.

"Fuck. That's it, baby. Come hard," I growl as I work her through it, feeling her body shake under me as pleasure consumes it from head to toe.

After what feels like minutes have gone by, she begins to slowly go limp, exhaustion already trying to pull her under from all the fighting. Normally, this would be my cue to slow down, but the vulnerability I feel coming from her in this position has me finally unleashing the animal inside me, giving him free rein to do whatever he pleases. Other than listening for the sound of the word *stop* leaving her lips, he's in complete control.

THIRTY-THREE
MONROE

I'M BARELY conscious as Riggs lifts his body from where he was pinning me down. Even if I didn't want this so badly, I'm not sure I'd be able to muster up the energy to get away. The pleasure from my orgasm is still somehow ebbing as I hear the sound of him tearing at his clothing behind me. My dress is bunched up around my stomach, along with the waistband of what's left of my underwear. He ripped them down the middle, leaving my used, dripping pussy on full display for him. My knees, elbows, hips, and cheek burn from where they were rubbing in the dirt, but the pain only makes me wetter as I anxiously await his next move.

When he told me to run, the adrenaline that coursed through my body sent every nerve ending into high alert. I had barely taken two steps before I felt my clit begin to throb with need. Half of me wanted to let him catch me easily, but the other half knew that we'd both come even harder if I forced him to hunt me like a true predator.

This is us. Perfect for each other in every way.

Strong hands grip my hips, pulling me to my knees and spreading my legs apart. I don't even have the energy to lift my head, so I focus on the cool dirt against my cheek, feeling its abrasive texture as it scratches my skin. My pulse races and my back heaves with my harsh inhales, but I feel safe and secure, fully aware that Riggs knows exactly what I need.

"Mine," he growls, right before I feel the flat of his tongue slide from my clit all the way back to my ass, gathering the wetness that soaks my skin before pushing inside the tight hole. I can't hold back the moan that tumbles out as he eats me like he's starving, stopping every now and then to spit everything that I'm giving him right back onto me. The sounds are obscene, and my toes curl at the thought of what we must look like from the outside. I'd give anything to be watching him from the shadows as he loses himself in this moment. I imagine every vein in his body bulging under his skin as his muscles flex. I can tell he's breathing just as hard as I am, each exhale coming out with a forced rumble that vibrates along my core as he licks and sucks.

I hear more rustling, and all my senses tune in to figure out what he's doing. When I hear the quiet *click* of what sounds to be a plastic cap, followed by something cold running down the crack of my ass, I clench my fingers into the dirt.

Oh, fuck.

"Your holes are my property, Monroe," he grits out. "It's time for me to finally feel this one."

I moan loudly. The thought of him pushing his huge cock into my ass is both terrifying and exciting. I've done anal before, and it's one of my favorite things, but I'll admit that his size has made me hesitant to ask for it up until now. I know I could tell him to stop and he would, but I want him to take it from me.

"Say you want it, whore," he whispers darkly into my ear as I feel one slick finger slip inside, slowly pumping in and out. I focus on the pleasure, attempting to regulate my breathing so I can answer him, but I'm at a loss for words when I feel more lube followed by a second finger. My eyes roll back and I feel my inner muscles accept him as he coaxes me open. The way he's twisting his hand around, pushing on every part of me, has me ready to explode right here.

"Don't go brainless on me yet," he says. "Answer the question. Do you want me to fuck your ass right here in this dirt like the filthy animal I know you are?" He slides his fingers all the way in, stilling when I'm completely stuffed, waiting for my reply.

"Y-yes," is all I can muster. I want him so badly I feel like I might cry.

"That's my perfect girl," he says quietly. "I'm not going to take it easy on you. You know how to make it stop." I nod, listening as he squeezes more lube onto himself and works it over his cock. Just the sound has me dripping with anticipation, panting like a dog in heat as I wait for him to finally take me. I feel his tip press against my hole, and I do everything I can to relax. We're both so slick, that when he does begin to push forward, his head slips in easily. He stills, heavy breaths leaving his body as if he's still restraining himself. But I don't want him to. I want everything. I want him fully unleashed for this.

Knowing that there's only one way to get him to move things to the next level, I push back as hard as I can, taking his entire length inside as I do. Pain radiates up my spine, but as I bear down on him, it turns to complete ecstasy for us both.

"Goddamn it. I can't wait to blow my load in your ass," he growls through clenched teeth, finally giving into his instincts and taking me the way I know he's wanted to all night. He wraps a hand around the back of my neck, holding my body in place as he pulls out and brutally thrusts into me. The stretch is a sweet relief as I finally allow myself to let go of every thought in my head and just exist. The sounds our bodies make as they come together are utterly pornographic, making my clit throb with the need to release.

As if he knows exactly what I'm feeling, Riggs grabs a chunk of my hair, lifting the upper part of my body from the ground and immediately sinking his teeth into my neck. His free hand wraps around my front, roughly massaging my swollen bundle of nerves as he continues fucking into me. I'm weightless, electricity flowing through every one of my limbs and gathering deep within me as I near a climax unlike any other. I push back into him, somehow needing to be filled even more as I finally tumble over the edge of my orgasm. My body tightens to the point of pain before it all releases, launching me into a freefall. I cry out, allowing myself to be consumed by the feeling until Riggs tightens his grip in my hair and stills behind me. He comes with a loud roar, only removing his teeth from my flesh to turn my head and plunge his tongue into my mouth. I allow him to control the kiss, my limp body hanging in his arms as he takes the last of what he needs from me.

Taking a few more slow and languid thrusts, he loosens

his arm around my waist but doesn't let go as he runs his tongue along the bite marks he left behind. There's a slight sting, but it's quickly soothed away as he cares for me. I love the way he fucks me, but this is my favorite part. The part where I allow him to thank me in his own way for being exactly what he needs.

He carefully pulls out of my body, never letting me fall back into the dirt as he lifts me from the ground and pushes through a door I didn't see in the midst of my panic. It's camouflaged by the padding that covers the entire wall, so unless you know it's there, it doesn't stand out. I rest my head on his shoulder, fighting the urge to fall asleep as we make our way—both almost completely naked—down a quiet corridor. He leaves warm kisses along my forehead and hair the entire way, and I sigh contentedly at the feeling of his lips on my skin. We reach the end of the hallway, and he presses his finger to a pad that's installed next to a metal door, waiting for it to beep before he pushes through. When it closes, he sets me on my feet, and just by the sterile smell alone, I know we're in the empty showers of the locker room.

I open my eyes, looking around to find that the stall we're in is set up with our soaps and shampoos from home. He really went out of his way to plan this entire night, and my heart tightens in my chest because even though it's unconventional, this whole thing has been pretty romantic. That sounds ridiculous to say, but I wouldn't change it for the world.

We shower together, and as usual, Riggs refuses to let me wash myself. This is just one of the many ways that he shows his love for me. I allow him to do it because I know it means just as much to him as it does to me when he provides aftercare. It's an intense bonding experience for us both, and I love the way he places just as much importance on our interactions after sex as he does during.

Once I'm clean, he washes himself quickly before drying us both and helping me over to a padded bench. I sit down, still fighting my exhaustion as he pulls a leather duffel bag from his locker and takes out clean clothes before dressing me. I roll my eyes, attempting to do it myself, but he swats at my hand when I reach for my shirt, giving me a look that lets me know there's no way in hell that's happening.

When he's satisfied, he stands and dresses himself before reaching down and pulling me up into a hug. "Thank you," he says quietly, cupping my cheeks in his hands and lowering his mouth to mine.

"Thank *you*," I reply against his lips, truly meaning it. This man is exceptional in so many ways, and I'm forever grateful that he refused to give up on us, even when I made it almost impossible for him to want to try.

THIRTY-FOUR

MONROE

"I MISS YOU ALREADY," I say into the phone as I pour myself a cup of coffee. I'm exhausted, and my body is still sore from our date at the stadium a couple of nights ago, but I'd be lying if I said that every little mark that decorates my skin isn't a welcome reminder of the best sex I've ever had in my life—hands down. Adding that kind of adrenaline and anticipation just heightened my arousal, making me come so hard that I barely remember anything other than the way I ascended into pure bliss as Riggs gave me everything I never knew I needed.

"Mayhem, I've been gone for," he pauses, no doubt to check his watch, "eight minutes. You better be careful, or I might start to think you actually like me."

I playfully scoff. "In your dreams. This is all a ploy so I can get closer to Friggle. Now that you two are besties, how about putting in a good word for me?"

"Don't even joke about shit like that," he deadpans, making me giggle. Although it seems like the two of them have buried the hatchet, I'm still pretty sure Riggs won't really be letting up on his grudge anytime soon. They don't have a game today, but he's on his way to the stadium to meet with the trainer and get in a workout before they play at home tomorrow. The Fury are leading their division right now, and early predictions have them bulldozing their way through the playoffs, straight to the World Series. Between that, business starting to pick up for me, and all the progress we've made in our own relationship, it finally feels like I can truly enjoy my life.

"Okay, okay," I relent. "I'm going to jump in the shower and get myself together for the day. There are a few updates I want to make to my website, so I'll see you when you get back. I was thinking I would try that new lemon chicken recipe for dinner, so we'll have that while we watch our movie tonight. It's your turn to choose, but I'm warning you right now, if you pick another cartoon, I'm leaving forever."

He gasps in mock outrage. "Who hurt you so badly, that you continue to talk shit about the most innocent type of entertainment we have in this world? Cartoons are for *everybody*, Monroe. Even awful shrews like yourself."

I roll my eyes, not that he can see it. Which is good because that means I don't have to hide the silly grin that blooms across my face. "Whatever, manchild. Have a good workout. I'll see you in a bit."

"Love you, sweet thing," he replies softly, and my heart beats faster in my chest. I'll never get sick of hearing those words.

"Love you too. Hurry home."

I hang up the phone and set it on the counter next to me before picking up my mug and taking a sip of my coffee. I smile to myself, thinking back to my very first day here. All I wanted was to help Riggs fix his image so I could cash in on his end of the bargain and move forward with my life. Little did I know, I'd end up falling for him and deciding to put down roots right here in Daytona.

I spoke with a realtor in Hope Harbor, and she told me that renting my place out may be a more lucrative option right now. I definitely don't want to lose money if I decide to sell, so I'll hang onto the house for now and maybe start interviewing tenants soon. I've dropped a few hints here and there, so I'm sure Riggs knows that I'm considering moving down here for good, but I wanted to have all the puzzle pieces in place before I told him it was happening for sure.

I know how crazy this all sounds, but it just feels right. The more time I spend in this city, the more I love it. Grace has her hands full with Tanner and her new business, and it's time that I do something for my own future. I thought that was my job at the boutique in Massachusetts, but now that I'm on the path to truly having my own independence, I realize it can look however I want it to. If I decide six months down the road that Florida isn't where I'm supposed to be, I can go somewhere else. This business gives me the freedom to travel wherever life takes me. But to be honest, I can't imagine being anywhere that Riggs isn't. I love him, and I want to savor the newness of our relationship.

I finish my coffee, getting up to place the mug into the sink before grabbing my phone and heading upstairs to shower. Just as I turn on the water to warm it, my phone rings on the counter. It's definitely a Rolling Hills area code, but I don't recognize the number flashing across the screen. I'm sure it's one of my parents, and as much as I don't want to talk to either of them, I need a clean break. I need to let them know that as long as they're unwilling to respect my decisions about how I live my life, there's no need for them to contact me at all.

After the night my dad showed up at our door and spewed the most vile, hateful words at me, there's no way Riggs would let him anywhere near me. But I was too stunned to say my piece then, and I deserve that.

I turn off the water and take a deep breath before answering the call. "Hello."

"Monroe, how are you, sweetheart?" my mom says, and her cheerful tone immediately pisses me off. Either she knows what went down and she's okay with her husband speaking to her daughter that way, or he's keeping her in the dark about it. No matter which one of those options is true, it's equally fucked up.

"Spare me the fake concern, Mom. Unless you're calling to tell me that you finally grew a backbone and decided to think for yourself, I'm not telling you shit," I reply. She gasps in surprise, but I don't let her tell me how unladylike my language is before I continue. "Did you know Dad was going to come here?"

She stays quiet for a moment, no doubt attempting to come up with a story that doesn't make her look just as bad as he does. I spent way too much time thinking she was remaining neutral in our situation, but I should've opened my eyes long ago to the fact that he's got her completely brainwashed into thinking he's a good man.

"Yes," she says, solidifying what I already knew. "He's running for office now, and we need you to come back so we can show that we're a strong family unit."

I choke on a laugh. "You're kidding, right? We've *never*

been anything close to that. I was a little doll that you dressed up and paraded around, making me think I had no other choice but to go along with the life you forced on me. I almost did it too. I guess I can thank you for giving me the strength to run away, because after looking at your miserable existence for so long, I knew I deserved better than that."

I wait for her to say something, but as usual, her silence doesn't surprise me. The woman doesn't have an independent thought in her head as long as my dad continues to provide the lifestyle she's used to.

"You know what?" I say. "Fuck this. I'm living my best life right now, absolutely no thanks to the two of you. I have a man who loves and supports me, and I don't need to beg him for affirmations because he gives them freely. Shame on you for wanting me to settle for less in this world. I don't want to hear from you ag—"

"Goddamn it, Monroe!" my dad booms, the phone rustling as I hear him take it from my mother. "I was trying to play nice with you, but since you're deciding to be a spoiled fucking brat, you leave me no choice. Either come home, or I release the video of your boyfriend attacking me."

"What?" I ask, immediately feeling my stomach drop. "What video?" He was alone that night. When Riggs went down to the property manager's office the following morning, they checked the lobby cameras and saw my dad come in by himself. They still have no idea how he got past security, but they were able to see him slip through the door to the stairwell that leads to our floor. They apologized profusely and vowed that it wouldn't happen again. I begged Riggs to let it go because I was afraid that if we dug deeper, the whole debacle would somehow make it to the media, and I just wanted to move on.

"You didn't really think I'd let him get away with that and not cover all of my bases, did you?" he says, and the darkness in his voice sends a chill right up my spine. "From what I understand, that guy can't keep himself out of trouble. It would be his word against mine. Do you really want to be the reason he loses everything? Come home, and I'll delete the video. Nobody else will ever see it. Or don't, and it'll be all over social media. It's your choice, Monroe."

"You're bluffing," I whisper, unsure of whether I should believe him or not. I know the kind of lying, cheating, and stealing he's capable of. I've watched him do it all my life.

"I wouldn't be so sure about that," he replies. "This surveillance video has no audio, so my story about how I showed up to tell you how much I missed you, only to be met with your angry boyfriend shoving me down and threatening to kill me will be quite believable." Just then, my phone vibrates with a notification and a grainy black-and-white video pops up on the screen. Just as he said, there's no audio, and I watch as Riggs grabs him by the collar and pushes him down, towering over him. Even though the details of their faces are hard to make out, you can tell that my father is terrified. The beginning of the video, where I answered the door to his disgusting words, is cut off. But it wouldn't matter anyway since we wouldn't be able to hear them.

This is bad.

I stay silent, trying to fight back the tears that are gathering in my eyes. He has no idea how close to the real truth he is. That Riggs was already on his last strike with the team even before my dad showed up. If this video sees the light of day, the work that we've done to clean up his image won't matter. Assaulting what appears to be an innocent man isn't something we can talk our way out of, especially when we can't prove that Riggs didn't fly off the handle for no reason again. He was defending me, but with his track record, I don't think anyone would give him the benefit of the doubt.

It's way too risky to leave it up to chance.

"Give me two days."

THIRTY-FIVE
RIGGS

"EVERYTHING OKAY?" I ask as I bring my glass of water to my mouth. Monroe has been acting weird ever since I got home. She's much quieter than usual, and all she's done since we sat at the table is push her chicken around on her plate. I know something is up.

"Mhmm," she replies quietly, keeping her eyes glued to her food. Her lip quivers and she quickly pulls it between her teeth to mask the movement, but it's too late. I already saw it, and now I'm freaking out a little. She was fine when I left for the stadium. She told me she loved me when we said goodbye on the phone, so why can't she even look me in the eye all of a sudden?

I set my fork down and push my chair back to stand. After rounding the table, I crouch down beside her and turn her chair toward me. Her head doesn't move with her body, so I gently place my fingers under her chin, attempting to pull her gaze to mine. But she's still avoiding eye contact, and her expression looks unsettled.

"What's going on?" I try again. I'm doing my best not

to lose my temper because something is obviously bothering her, but if I don't find out what it is, I can't fix it. And I *need to fix it.* I can't stomach seeing her this way, or knowing that whatever it is, she doesn't feel comfortable telling me.

She looks up, and I don't think I've ever felt further away from her than I do right now. Her expression is nearly blank, her posture caved in as she holds her forearms tightly over her midsection. This is not the girl I left earlier today.

"I—I," she stutters right before her eyes go wide. She throws an open hand over her mouth, stands abruptly, and knocks me on my ass as she takes off toward the stairs, hurrying up them and disappearing into the hallway. I stand and rush after her, making it through the door to the bathroom just as she heaves into the toilet. Kneeling behind her, I gather her hair into my hands and hold it while she vomits violently.

"Riggs, go," she says weakly, batting a hand back in my direction to shoo me away. She's fucking crazy if she thinks I'm leaving her here alone, but I don't even get a chance to tell her that as she turns away again and continues throwing up.

"It's okay, baby," I say softly. "Get it out." She finally gives up and drops her head forward, taking slow, steady breaths to quell the nausea. We sit there, her sniffling softly while I rub her back, until she finally stands. I follow, leaning against the wall while she brushes her teeth, hoping she'll tell me what's making her feeling unwell. She turns to face me, still completely avoiding eye contact.

"I'm going to sleep in my bed tonight. I don't want to get you sick," she whispers. "Goodnight."

"Wait," I rush out, grabbing her by the arm. "Let me take care of you." I'm desperate to close the distance between us—both physically and emotionally—but I can tell she's checked out. I just wish I knew why.

She shakes her head. "Riggs, you're getting ready to pitch in a couple of days. Whatever this is," she pauses, resting a hand over her stomach, "could take you out if it's contagious. I shouldn't be breathing on you all night. I'll sleep in my bed, and we'll talk tomorrow."

I let her go because if she really is sick, she has a good point. But the way she's acting still feels very alarming. I don't like the thought of being apart tonight if something is on her mind.

"Okay," I relent. "But at least let me tuck you in." She nods weakly, turning down the hall and walking into her old room with me only a few steps behind. Instead of undressing and putting on one of my t-shirts like she usually does, she pulls back the covers and gets into bed, still wearing her cropped crewneck and leggings. All of this is so unlike her, but maybe she just doesn't have the energy to change. I think better of offering to help her, instead opting to pull the covers up over her before pressing a lingering kiss to her forehead.

"I love you, sweet thing," I say softly. "I'm just down the hall if you need anything."

"Night," she whispers, rolling away from me and pulling the blanket over her head. Reluctantly, I stand and slowly walk toward the door. Looking back one last time, I wonder what happened in the past six hours that has put so many miles between us.

I kick the blankets off my legs, tossing from one side to the other. I've barely gotten a wink of sleep all night. I don't know if it's because I'm thinking about my exchange with Monroe earlier, or simply the fact that she's down the hall instead of in bed with me where she belongs. Either way, I've given up on getting any rest. Every possible scenario has played in my head, but I can't figure out what she isn't telling me. At first, I considered that she really does have a stomach bug, and she just wanted to keep me from getting sick. Then my mind went in another direction, wondering if she could possibly be pregnant and doesn't want to say it out loud for fear of my reaction. I know she's on birth control, but we haven't used a single condom since we started having sex again, so it isn't out of the realm of possibility. Whatever it is, I'm not going to leave this house until we talk about it.

Turning to my phone that's propped up on the charging stand, I see that it's four o'clock. I don't have to be at the stadium until this afternoon since we have a home game later today, so I should be enjoying a very rare morning off. Maybe I just need to go check on her, and I'll be able to salvage the last couple hours of darkness that I have left.

I stand and pad quietly out of the room and toward hers. I expect to be met with silence, but I'm caught off guard when I hear small sobs coming from the other side of her door. I immediately twist the knob and push my way in, panic taking over at the sight in front of me.

Monroe is on her knees in front of the dresser, frantically stuffing articles of clothing into her suitcase. Even though she's been sleeping in my bed for weeks, all of her belongings stayed in here because it was easier. Now I'm regretting not moving her into my room fully. Another suitcase stands in front of the closet door, and two duffel bags are stacked next to it. This is pretty much everything she brought to Daytona.

"What the fuck is going on?" I ask, startling her. She turns abruptly, tears running from her red-rimmed eyes. She was so entranced in what she was doing, that she didn't even hear me come into the room.

"Nothing," she says, swiping at her cheeks as if she can erase the evidence. Like I wouldn't question why in the fuck she's awake in the middle of the night, sobbing as she packs her luggage.

"No," I say, moving toward her and kneeling on the floor. "You're not fucking leaving me again, Monroe. Tell me what's wrong. Whatever it is, we'll get through it."

Her eyes finally connect with mine, making my heart shatter in my chest. She looks utterly defeated. Her shoulders hunch forward, and she releases a long, slow sigh. "We can't get through it, Riggs. I *have* to go. Please trust me when I say I'm doing this for you." Her chin quivers as her eyes fill with more tears. I reach for her, attempting to provide comfort—anything to ease her pain—but she pulls away, shaking her head as she puts out a cautious hand between us. "Don't," she says. "You're making it harder."

"Baby," I plead, "please just tell me. There's nothing more important to me than us. If you're trying to save me from something and you think the only option is leaving, you're wrong. If you're—" I pause, unable to bear the thought of losing something so precious. "If you're pregnant, I promise I'll be the best dad ever to our baby. I can't think of anything I'd want more than to have a family with you. Just don't leave me. *Please*," I choke out, letting my own tears of desperation fall. I drop my head forward, my shoulders shaking as I break down, hoping she understands that nothing in this world could ever mean more to me than she does.

I press my palms to my eyes, trying to breathe deeply before her warm arms wrap around me. She squeezes tightly, and we cry together for several minutes before she pulls away.

"I'm not pregnant," she whispers, and I have to admit that the words aren't a relief in any way. From the moment the thought popped into my head, a sense of calm washed over me, despite the lingering unease from not knowing what was going on with her. I'm completely positive that a future with Monroe and whatever kind of family we're blessed with is exactly what I want out of life. I just have to make her stay.

"Then what's wrong?" I ask. "Why are you trying to sneak out in the middle of the night?"

She loosens her hold on me, backing up slightly but staying angled toward my body. I miss the warmth of her touch immediately, so I reach out and rub my thumb along her thigh. I just need some type of connection right now, and I'm grateful she's allowing it.

"My dad called," she says, making my eyes go wide as I whip my head up to look at her. I told that piece of shit not to contact her again, and now I'm finding out that, not only did he not listen, but he said something to upset her. My nostrils flare and my fingers flex, but I try to repress my anger long enough for her to tell me everything.

"He has a copy of the surveillance video from the night he was here. I don't know how he got it, but it's from the camera above the archway. There's no audio, and the beginning is cut off, but it looks really bad. He told me that if I come home and show that we're a strong family unit while he runs for governor, he'll delete it. I need to go back to California so he doesn't drag your name through the mud."

"No," I say, my whole body tingling with the rage I'm holding in. I won't let him take her from me, just so he can treat her like garbage and make her life miserable. She deserves better. "We'll just be honest. We'll tell the truth. People will have to believe us."

She huffs an incredulous laugh. "Why would they? You've been in trouble twice for attacking what appeared to be innocent people. You already had one foot out the door with the team prior to me coming here. My dad has somehow managed to create a fake persona that people associate with integrity and honesty, even though he's anything but. You're the Bad Boy of Baseball, and I'm just his rebellious runaway daughter. It'll be our word against his, and I promise you, he'll win. He *always* does. I have to do this, Riggs. You'll lose *everything*."

Fuck that. She *is* everything. I don't give a single shit about playing baseball if it means losing her in the process. I'll hang up my cleats right now.

"I'll ask the security manager for the video. We'll watch the uncut version and see if there's anything we can do," I say in an attempt to grasp at straws.

"No," she replies quickly. "My dad obviously knows somebody here, otherwise he wouldn't have been able to get it in the first place. We can't trust anybody. Plus, what good would it do to have the rest? The camera didn't pick up the audio, so it'll still look like you were in the wrong. You'll get kicked off the team. I wouldn't put it past him to press charges and sue you for millions, either. I was stupid to think I'd ever be out from under his control," she whispers, her face twisting in pain. "I finally find real happiness and he comes to swipe it away like it's nothing. I'm a pawn in his game. That's all he'll ever see me as."

"Hey. No," I say softly, pulling her trembling body into my arms. "I'm not letting him do this to us. Give me one day. Just let me fight for us, Monroe. You took that choice from me after our first night together when you left without saying goodbye. Please let me show you how much I need you." I'm desperate for her to say yes, but I can't force her to stay if she doesn't want to. I just have to hope that she trusts me enough to figure something out.

She looks up at me, swallowing thickly. "One day. That's all we have."

I shake my head, smiling softly down at her. "We have the rest of our lives, sweet girl. I promise."

"I love you, Riggs," she whispers, pressing her lips to mine. I pour everything I have into the kiss, hoping she understands the lengths I'll go to keep her here with me. I'll burn this whole fucking world to the ground if I have to.

Without breaking our connection, I stand, pulling her with me and walking us back to the bed. I carefully lower her to the mattress, dropping down between her parted legs. Cupping her jaw with my hand, I trail wet kisses down her face, stopping to suck on the sensitive skin below her ear. I feel her hips rotate slightly, creating the sweetest friction between us as needy whines fill the air around us. I help by grinding down, kissing her neck as the head of my erection rubs her clit through our clothes. Even with the barrier separating us, stars explode behind my eyes at the feeling of her warmth seeping through the fabric. This woman owns me in every way. There isn't a chance in hell I'd ever let her go.

I bring my lips back to hers, claiming them in another kiss that's filled with all the love I have. I know she feels it. She *has to*. Her body trembles under me, and I'd give anything to ease her mind about the future. I know I need to let my actions speak in this situation with her dad, but for now, I'll do whatever I can to help her escape.

I reluctantly pull away, sitting back on my feet while I peel her shirt over her head. My mouth waters as her tits peek out from the top of her bra, and I go lightheaded with the need to feel her piercings against my tongue.

"Arch your back," I command, waiting for her to obey before I reach behind her, unfastening the clasp that separates me from what I want. Pulling the lace material away from her body, I lean down and suck one rose-colored bud into my mouth, using my teeth to graze the metal barbell that decorates it.

"Riggs," she gasps, and I swear I feel like I could come right here as she sings my name. I know I'd never let anyone take her from me, but in the back of my mind, I can't help but hope this isn't the last time I make love to her. I need it to be perfect, so that if we end up apart, even for a little while, she's unable to forget the way I'll worship her until my last breath.

"I'm here, baby," I whisper, fusing my lips back to hers as I peel her leggings down past her knees, yanking them off and throwing them to the floor. Her panties meet the same fate, and by the time I ghost my fingertip along her sensitive clit, we're both ready to lose ourselves in one another. I rub gentle circles around it, savoring every one of the sweet little cries that escapes her swollen lips.

I shuck my thin sleep pants and boxers, working them down my legs and kicking them onto the heap of her clothing that lies at the foot of the bed. Bringing my focus back to my girl, I leave room between us so I can continue moving my hand along her flesh.

Monroe clings to me as I coax her orgasm to the surface, sliding down and just barely entering her with one finger as she clenches her inner walls in search of more. I want to make her forget everything that isn't the feeling of being mine. Even if it takes hours, there's nowhere else I'd rather be than right here, showing her that I'll always be here to fight the monsters that come for us. I'll never let her down.

I finally take mercy on her, sinking two thick fingers into her impossibly wet cunt. I slowly work them inside until my palm is cupping her hot skin, curling them forward as her hips lift off the mattress.

"There she is," I say softly, knowing I'm grazing the part of her that makes her insides turn to mush. My heart rate speeds at the thought of making her come undone, over and over, until she feels nothing but pleasure. As much as this is for her, I need to lose myself just as badly.

I continue massaging her g-spot until she's gripping me so tightly, that I'm not sure I could pull out even if I wanted to. "Good girl," I praise. "Come for me." Keeping my fingers bent as I thrust in and out, I do my best to make sure she has everything she needs to explode. She moans loudly and her legs begin to shake as a small gush of wetness runs out of her and into my hand. I can't tear my eyes away from her face as the orgasm washes over her. Her mouth is parted and her eyes are squeezed shut, yet she looks as though she doesn't have a single worry in the world. My beautiful girl deserves this every hour of every day, and all I want is to be the lucky man who gets to give it to her.

The pleasure begins to ebb, and her muscles relax as she returns to earth, sinking back down into the mattress. I press gentle kisses along her shoulder and neck, listening to the soft, rapid breaths that come from her sated body. I continue coasting my mouth over her skin, and it doesn't take long for her arousal to build again. She wraps her small hands around my biceps and pulls me between her open, trembling legs.

"You're my fucking world, baby," I whisper, capturing her lips with mine while I line up at her entrance and slide home. She's so warm and tight, there isn't a question in my mind that she was made just for me. We're two halves of the same whole, and no matter what goes down after this, we'll always be connected. We're incomplete when we're apart, and we're unstoppable when we're together.

I push all the way inside, gritting my teeth as we both get used to the stretch. My heart pounds in my ears as I move slowly, making sure that I'm not going to blow before I can get her over the edge again. Pulling back so I'm using my hands on either side of her head for support, I focus on her face as I begin thrusting harder. A beautiful flush covers her damp skin, and her mouth hangs open as she pants and moans my name. She grinds down, meeting my hips with hers, urging me to give her even more.

"There you go, sweet thing," I coax. "Make that beautiful pussy feel good on my cock. You're doing such a good job." The praise hits its mark, making her shatter under me for a second time. Her body convulses and her cunt contracts so tightly, I don't even get a chance to let her finish before I'm pulled under right alongside her. My release hits me like an explosion, launching me into pure ecstasy as I empty everything I have inside her. It feels like it goes on forever, wave after wave of electricity shooting through us both until we have nothing left to give.

I collapse, doing my best to support my weight with my shaking forearms so I don't crush her. We're covered in sweat, gasping for breath, trying to grasp onto the final moments of bliss before reality settles back in.

"You're mine," I whisper against her cheek, feeling a lone tear slide across her skin and onto mine. "Nobody's going to take you from me. I promise."

She sighs, snuggling into me as I lie there inside her, praying that she trusts me to fix everything.

I don't care what it takes to make it right. The only thing I'm unwilling to give up is Monroe.

THIRTY-SIX
RIGGS

"HAVE A SEAT. We'll call you in a few minutes," Mr. Durst's assistant says, gesturing toward the waiting area outside his office. I spent the entire morning racking my brain, trying to figure out a way to fix this shitstorm without having to get anybody else involved. I even went as far as dropping down to the security manager's office in my building to ask a few questions. Monroe's worst fears were confirmed when he told me that none of the cameras lining the hallways capture audio. I didn't dig any further because if the video surfaces before I get a chance to at least try to control the situation, I can kiss my career goodbye.

Which is exactly why I'm here.

Knowing I was out of options, I decided to throw up one last Hail Mary before pulling the pin and tossing a grenade that's sure to blow up my entire life. If it doesn't work, my endgame really doesn't change since the most important thing here is that she doesn't go back to California. But I have to try to save my job.

Minutes go by as my anxiety builds, wondering if I made a mistake by even coming today. Although I've been trying to do better, my track record with this team isn't great, and I have no idea if being here will make the situation better or worse.

"C'mon in, Riggs," Mr. Durst's voice rings through the room, startling me. I stand, shaking out my arms in an attempt to rid my body of the jitters, but it's a lost cause. I feel like every one of my bones is vibrating as nervousness passes through me, terrified of what this meeting will bring. I love baseball and I don't want to give it up, but if I have to choose between the game and Monroe, I'll pick her every time. It's not even close.

"What brings you in today?" he asks as I round the chair opposite his, sitting down and wiping my sweaty palms along my pant legs. I know I need to be honest here, but the whole situation isn't pretty. I'm not innocent. The parts of the video that are going to matter show exactly what happened. I shoved her dad. I towered over him, barely restraining myself as I threatened him. Even though the words I said will never be heard, it doesn't take a genius to figure it out.

"Sir, I want to say thank you for continuously giving me chances with this team, even when I didn't deserve them. I appreciate that more than you'll ever know." I swallow the lump in my throat as he leans back, the leather of his chair groaning as he relaxes against it. He purses his lips and raises a questioning brow, urging me to go on.

"There's a video of me that's about to be released, and it looks really bad." I pause, shaking my head. "It *is* really bad. But I wanted to tell you about it myself before it makes its way around the internet. I've given you no reason to believe anything I say, but you deserve to know that the guy you've continued to support isn't the one you're about to see."

"I'm afraid I don't understand," he says, prompting me to pull my phone out of my pocket. I cue up the video I had Monroe send me, pressing play before reaching across his desk and handing it to him. He watches, and I can tell the moment it happens because he shakes his head in disappointment.

Fuck.

"Who is he?" he asks, looking up at me. I'm surprised he's giving me a chance to explain, and I'm going to make sure he has the whole story before he decides what to do with me. He may toss my ass out of here either way, but I'll go down fighting.

"Monroe's dad," I reply. "He slipped past security and said some repulsive things to her. I overheard it and reacted on instinct. I shoved him and told him I'd kill him if he ever tried to contact her again, and now he's threatening to release this video and drag me through the mud unless she moves back to California. I know I was wrong, sir. But I can't apologize. He deserved all of that and more," I say, gesturing to the phone he still has clutched in his hand. "If it costs me my career, so be it. I love her and I'll protect her until the day I die. Absolutely nothing is more important to me than she is."

He reaches forward, returning the device to me before sitting back and crossing his arms over his chest. Sweat beads at the back of my neck, and my mouth feels like it's full of cotton balls as he stares at me in silence. It seems like hours have gone by before an ear-to-ear grin erupts across his face. I look around the empty room, attempting to figure out why he isn't ripping me a new asshole, but I find nothing. At least, not until he speaks.

"It's about time," he laughs, clapping his hands slowly. I scratch at my cheek, unsure of what to say because I have no idea what he means. Shutting the fuck up has worked for me so far, so that's what I do while he continues.

"Since the day we drafted you, I've been waiting for you to show me the kind of man you are. You hit speed bump after speed bump along the way, but deep down, I knew that the Riggs Valentine I saw through the media's lens wasn't the whole story. You may not think anyone noticed the way you got to know each and every employee at this stadium your rookie year. Or how you sincerely enjoy connecting with the fans, even when there aren't any cameras around to capture it. You remind me so much of myself when I was your age, so I knew we'd get another side of you eventually. When I first met Monroe, I felt it in my soul that she would be the one to bring it out of you. I'm so glad she finally did."

My brows pull in tightly. "Wait," I choke out. "You're not going to fire me?"

"Do you want me to?" he asks.

I bark a laugh. "Respectfully, sir. Fuck no. I love this team, and I want to continue being a part of it."

He gives me a tight nod. "Alright, then. I'll do what I can to control the narrative of this situation. Hopefully, we can keep the fans on our side. But either way, this organization has your back. As long as you promise to take care of your family, we're proud to have you."

"Absolutely, sir. I won't let you down," I say, relief washing over me. I was hoping this meeting would end on a positive note, but I definitely didn't expect it to go this well. Any other team in the league would have told me to pack my shit, but Mr. Durst values things in this life that are more important than money and winning. For that, I'll always be grateful.

I extend a hand between us, and he shakes it before I turn and walk out of the room with a renewed sense of belonging as a member of the Daytona Fury family. None of my past fuck-ups matter to me anymore. The only thing I want to focus on moving forward is being the best player, teammate, and partner I can be. The people who have stood by and supported me deserve that. Nobody more so than the woman I love.

THIRTY-SEVEN
MONROE

I NERVOUSLY PICK at my nails as I pace the floor, practically wearing a hole in the marble as I move across it. Riggs said he needed to go to a meeting two hours ago, and I've been a ball of anxiety ever since. I have no idea what it was about, or where he had to be, but I've played every terrible scenario over in my head since he walked out the door. I know he was being vague so I wouldn't worry, but it's having the opposite effect.

He asked me to trust him, and I do. But if he can't find a way to prove that he didn't attack my dad for no reason, I'll have no choice but to get on a plane to California. I refuse to let this be the end of Riggs' career, so I'm fully willing to do what I have to do for now, but I'm running out of time. If I take too long, that video will be uploaded to social media, and it'll solidify the public's wrong opinion of him.

Riggs Valentine is the best man I know. He may have made some poor, reckless decisions in the past, but he's not that guy anymore. He's fierce, protective and loving.

He doesn't deserve to have his dream ripped away from him over some bullshit lie.

Just as I'm about to crawl out of my own skin, I hear the door open and close. I whip around to see Riggs standing there with a cocky smirk. He takes his time, dropping his keys into the dish on the entry table like I'm not over here dying with worry.

I stand there frozen, waiting for him to say something. *Anything.* I just want to know that he's okay.

He looks up at me, his smirk morphing into a wide smile. "It's over, baby," he says, and that's all I need to take off across the room and launch myself into his waiting arms. He laughs as I squeeze him tightly, lifting me off the floor and spinning me around.

"Wait!" I shout, kicking my feet in an attempt to get him to put me down. "What exactly does that mean? *What's* over?" He keeps me in his arms, walking us over to the sofa and setting me on the plush cushions before plopping down beside me.

"I decided that honesty was the best policy here. I tried to work out ways to prove that the video isn't what it looks like, but I knew without the audio, it wouldn't matter. So I went straight to Mr. Durst and I told him the truth." I wince, making him chuckle, and he continues. "I told him what happened that night, including the way your father spoke to you. I told him I had to protect you, and that's why I did what I did."

"He wasn't mad? You've been such a problem child over the years, and we knew he was ready to send you packing. What changed?" That video showed him doing exactly what he had done to Tanner when he found out about him and Grace. He was protecting his sister, but because the videos didn't pick up the conversation between them, it just looked like an unprovoked attack. Even after they spoke about it to the media, the public had already made up their minds. That was one of the reasons Riggs was in hot water when I got here, so I'm curious to know what's different between now and then.

"You did," he says softly, leaning forward and pressing his forehead against mine. "You make me a better man, Monroe. The whole world can see it."

Tears prick at the backs of my eyes and I press my lips to his, inhaling the scent of his woodsy cologne as it wraps around me. He can say it was me who made the difference in his life, but the truth is, we did it together. I may have been a catalyst in him wanting to show people who he really is, but that guy was always in there. He just needed someone to pull him to the surface.

"So, we're staying in Daytona?" I ask, swinging a leg over his lap so I'm straddling him. It's not sexual; I just feel like I can't get close enough. I'd crawl into his skin right now if I could, and I don't even care how creepy that sounds.

"*We*, huh? Is that your way of saying you want to move in with me, Mayhem?" he chides, grabbing my ass and squeezing.

"Ew, no," I say with a scoff. "I could never live with a guy who clips his toenails at the dinner table."

He rolls his eyes. "I still can't believe you called my mom about that. You really are a she-devil," he replies, a small smile lifting the corner of his mouth. "Move in with me. I know it's a lot, and if you want to keep your house, you can. But let's give this thing a real shot. We can stay in Hope Harbor during the offseason, and—"

"I'm interviewing new tenants next week," I say, cutting him off. "I hired a moving company to pack everything up and ship it here. Your mom is supposed to be meeting them tomorrow to get started."

His eyebrows shoot up, nearly disappearing into his hairline. "You're fucking with me. Right?"

I giggle. "Nope. I decided weeks ago that I didn't want to leave. I just needed to work everything out before I let you in on my plan. Are you happy?"

"Baby, I'm the happiest guy in the world."

Two hours later, we're snuggled up on the couch, a chick flick queued up on the TV and a plethora of snacks in front of us. We decided to celebrate by ordering all the McDonald's fries we could handle and calling it a balanced dinner, then spending the evening with a movie of my choice. If I wasn't already feeling worshiped, I definitely am now.

I'm doing my best to push all the heavy stuff with my dad out of my mind, but I have to admit that I still have a few worries. We may have the support of the Fury organization, but if he decides to press charges, I'm not sure that'll be much help. That's a bridge we'll have to cross when we get there, but I hope it doesn't come to that. With any luck, my dad will back off and let us live our lives. He doesn't need me appearing as his doting daughter to run for governor when he already has the entire state of California fooled into thinking he's a good person. I'm sure my mom will portray the picture-perfect wife, making all sorts of excuses for why I'm not around. He'll win the election on a foundation of lies and get everything he wants, just like he always has.

"You good?" Riggs asks, pulling me into his warm body. "Something on your mind, sweet thing?"

I snuggle into him, letting all the stress melt away as he holds me tightly. "No," I sigh. "I just wish there was a way to take my father down a peg."

He kisses the top of my head, grabbing the remote and pressing play. "Karma has a way of coming back around. It'll catch up with him eventually, and I'll make sure you have a front row seat to his downfall."

THIRTY-EIGHT
RIGGS

"I FUCKING LOVE BASEBALL," Monroe says quietly as I bend down to pull a pan out of the cupboard.

I freeze with my hand in mid-air, turning my head to see her taking a very generous eyeful of my ass. "Really?" I ask, raising a brow in question.

She pops a shoulder. "I mean, I love baseball *butts*. That's basically the same thing."

I stand and turn abruptly so my back is against the counter, away from her prying gaze. "First of all, stop objectifying me, you pervert. Secondly, the only baseball butt you better be looking at is mine."

She pushes her lip out in a patronizing pout. "Aww, does it bother you that I look at the entire buffet of cake at every Fury game?" I growl in response, spurring her on. "I have a question. Will yours get as round as Ace's, or is that"—she waves her hand in a circle, gesturing at my midsection—"your final form? I just need to know if I picked the wron—"

I drop the pan and dart around the island as she

screams and runs the other way. She's laughing hysterically as I chase her into the living room, reaching out when I'm close enough and throwing her over my shoulder like she weighs nothing. She beats her small fists against my back trying to get me to release her, but I tighten my hold until I reach the sofa. I toss her down, and her laughs get louder as I dig my fingers into her sides.

"Riggs! No!" she screams as I tickle her, thrashing around to avoid my attack.

"You little brat," I say, finally relenting before leaning down and dropping a firm kiss to her lips. "You're lucky I'm hungry or I'd turn that ass red."

"Oooh," she replies. "We'll circle back to that later."

I chuckle, standing and turning away from her with my arms stretched out at my sides. She takes the invitation, jumping onto my back and wrapping her legs around me as I bring us to the kitchen.

I haven't been able to wipe the smile off my face since Monroe told me she was staying in Daytona. It was a subject I had planned on bringing up eventually, but the fact that she made the decision on her own makes it that much better. It may seem like we're moving fast, but with her new business taking off, she's able to work from anywhere. My job already has me away for several days at a time throughout the season, so putting over a thousand miles between us during such an important stage of our new relationship sounds terrible. I want to have her here when I'm home, then I'll follow her wherever she wants to go during the offseason. It'll take some sacrificing from us both, but it'll be worth it.

I drop her onto the counter and return to the cupboard to retrieve the frying pan. Opening the refrigerator, I take out a dozen eggs, bringing them to the stove and cracking them one by one. We talk and laugh as I cook, and I can't help but be grateful for the growth we've experienced, both separately and as a couple in the months that she's been here. Although it started as a fake relationship, I knew deep down that I'd fall for her. If I'm honest, it started for me the night we met. Monroe is the exception to every rule I ever made for myself, and I'll never take her love for granted.

"I was thinking," I say, pushing four pieces of bread down into the toaster. "We have a five-day break coming up in a few weeks. How would you feel about going to Hope Harbor for a visit? I want my parents to meet my new girlfriend."

She raises a brow, tucking a piece of chocolate-brown hair behind her ear. "I've met your parents a million times, Riggs. No introduction necessary."

I scoff playfully. "Yeah, as my sister's best friend. I want to re-introduce you as the woman I love, their soon-to-be daughter-in-law, and the mother of their future grandchildren."

Her eyes go wide, but a smile pulls at her lips. "Who are you? Certainly not the same Riggs Valentine that had a different girl on his arm every weekend because he was allergic to feelings."

The toast pops up, but I ignore it, walking over and pushing her knees apart with the backs of my hands so I can step between them. "Uh-uh," I say, shaking my head. "Fuck that guy. He didn't know what he was missing." I cup her cheeks and press my mouth to hers in a gentle kiss, inhaling her scent as I do. "I meant it when I said I wanted a future with you, Mayhem. We may not be able to get the time back that we missed out on with each other, but from here on out, I'm all in. We can go at whatever pace you want to, but just know that my endgame will always be the same."

"I want that too," she says quietly, leaning her head into my chest as I wrap my arms around her. The feeling of holding her will never get old, and I'm a lucky mother-fucker to be able to do it whenever I want.

Kissing the top of her head, I return to the stove, turning it off and preparing our plates. "Here you go, baby," I say, setting her breakfast next to her before taking my own and leaning against the counter as we start to eat.

"What's your plan for the day?" she asks. "I know you have to be at the stadium later, so I was thinking I'd work on the marketing plan for that new salon chain while you're gone. Unless you need me for something."

I wiggle my brows. "Oh, I need you for all kinds of things."

"That's not what I meant," she deadpans. "Why are you so horny all the time?"

I shrug, shoving a fork full of eggs into my mouth and chewing. "It's just who I am, Mayhem. Don't act like you don't love it."

She smirks. "Maybe a tiny bit."

I chuckle as I finish my food and place the empty plate into the dishwasher. Just as I go to head toward the stairs, the sound of the doorbell fills the air.

"I'll get it," Monroe says, hopping off the counter. "You take longer to get ready than any girl I've ever met. Go shower or you'll be late."

I roll my eyes, but don't say anything because she's kind of right. I really do need to get going, but the last time I let her open the door when we weren't expecting company, it turned out to be a disaster. So instead, I follow as she walks into the entryway and pulls it open, a loud gasp escaping her as she does. I'm immediately on high alert, closing the distance between us so I can protect her from whoever has her reacting this way. Part of me is expecting to see her dad. Instead, a thin woman who looks just like Monroe, only older and with blonde hair, stares back at us. It's very clear that she's her mother, but this is anything but a happy reunion. I swear I'm going to rip the entire security team in this building to shreds after this. This is the second time someone has gotten past them and ended up on our doorstep uninvited. I've never considered buying a house of my own that's far away from other humans the way Tanner's is—more than I am right now.

"Did he send you?" she spits. I step behind her so my front is pressed against her back in a silent show of protection and support. I want her to know that I'm here to take over if she needs me to, but I have a feeling there are a lot of unsaid words that she'd like to get off her chest.

"No, sweetheart," her mother pleads, putting her hands up as if she's surrendering. "I promise he didn't send me. I left."

Monroe stiffens in front of me. "What do you mean, *you left*?"

"Can I come in?" she asks, glancing down the hallway to make sure we're alone. I don't like this one bit, but it's completely up to Monroe. I'll let them talk, though I definitely won't be leaving them alone while they do it. I'm not about to let this woman hurt her any more than she already has.

She turns her head, looking over her shoulder at me. I

swallow the lump in my throat, nodding my head and backing away just enough to make room for her mother to pass by.

"Riggs, this is my mother, Jenna Decker. Mom, this is my boyfriend, Riggs Valentine," she says, introducing us.

"Hello," I say, extending my hand between us. I don't say it's nice to meet her, because I don't know if it is yet. I need to hear what she has to say before I decide whether I'll give her a chance or not. She wraps her fingers around mine, and we shake hands before she enters the apartment. I make sure the door is closed and locked, because who knows if she's really here alone? Maybe I'm an asshole, but I definitely don't trust either of Monroe's parents. At least not yet.

We make our way into the kitchen, and I gesture for the two women to sit down at the island. Jenna does, but Monroe continues standing as though she may need to make a quick escape. But she's crazy if she thinks she's going anywhere. If anything, I have no problem showing her mother the door at the first sign of my girl's discomfort.

"Talk," she says, shifting nervously from one foot to the other. My instinct is to go over and wrap my arms around her, but I want her to do this by herself. She deserves to have complete control of the situation, and to take it wherever she wants it to go.

Her mother lets out a deflated sigh, and I watch as her eyes fill with tears. "I let him treat you poorly for so long," she whispers. "I've been a horrible mother, and I don't blame you for running away from everything we put you through. I stood by and watched as he planned the same exact life for you that my father planned for me, and I did nothing to stop him. I'm so sorry." She drops her head into her hands as sobs rack her body. I can tell that Monroe is restraining herself. She wants to comfort her mother, but there are too many details that she isn't clear on to feel like she can. Instead, she moves in closer, taking the barstool next to Jenna and sitting down. I feel like this is a conversation that isn't meant for me, but I can't bring myself to leave her here. I'll never forgive myself if she needs me and my hand isn't available for her to hold. So I stay quiet, allowing them to interact without me interjecting.

"Mom, what happened?" Monroe asks. "Tell me why you're here."

THIRTY-NINE
MONROE

TO SAY that I'm shocked to see my mother would be a massive understatement. The trip from Rolling Hills to Daytona isn't a leisurely drive. It's something that requires planning and plane tickets—and in Jenna Decker's case, an entire arsenal of wardrobe changes. But here she is, sitting in my kitchen wearing jeans and a hoodie with only a Dior tote in tow. Unless she stopped at a hotel before she came here, she's looking a lot like a runaway herself.

"Well?" I implore. I'm so confused and need to know what the hell is going on.

She blows out a shaky breath, thinking carefully about what she's going to say. I hope she doesn't lie to me. If she does, I'm ready to cut her from my life completely. Now that I have real love and support, I'm not accepting anything else. I deserve more, and now I know that.

"I'm sure you already know that your father has made me keep tabs on you since you left home. Every time I called, he was right there next to me, listening as we talked. Every conversation you and I have had in the last two years was planned ahead of time. He wanted to make sure there was always doubt in your mind about whether you made the right choice. He said it was only a matter of time before we broke you down enough to get you back home."

I drop my head to hide the tears that are stinging the backs of my eyes. I refuse to shed any more over my father, when all he's ever wanted was to use me to get ahead in life. I thought the way he spoke to me the day he came here was the final nail in the coffin, but hearing that he pulled my mother into his plan just makes it worse. I was a pawn to him. And so was she.

She continues. "I knew what I was doing was wrong. Let me just make that clear. I don't want you to think I'm placing all the blame on him. I'm a grown woman, and I chose to let him control my actions instead of being the mother you deserved. I think part of me was a little jealous and bitter that you got out and I was left there, pretending to live a perfect life when we both know just how awful it really was. I believed the only way to stop it from getting worse was to do what he said, so that's what I did.

"I knew he was planning to come and bring you home, and I prayed that you'd find the strength to see through his manipulation. It may not seem like it, but the last thing I wanted was for you to ever return to Rolling Hills. Just from the way you sounded so happy the last time we spoke on the phone, I could tell that you had found the life you always dreamed of."

I look up at Riggs, giving him a soft smile and letting a single tear fall down my cheek. She's right. I did find that. I may have left California on my own and started creating something special, but it wasn't until I admitted my feelings for him that I finally felt like I really had it all. He winks at me in a silent show of understanding before my mother continues her story.

"When your father came home from that trip, his efforts to regain control over you went into high gear. I knew when Conrad started coming back around, that something was up. So I did my best to snoop around to figure out what they were planning. At first, they were very careful about what they said when they knew I was there, but eventually, they slipped up.

"Last week, a man I had never seen before showed up to the house. He was young, wearing all black with a hood and sunglasses, which made me curious about what he was hiding. I pretended like I was meeting my friends for dinner, but instead of leaving, I snuck back in. That's when I found the three of them hacking into the security footage from your building here in Daytona. Apparently, Conrad met the guy through a mutual friend and told your father that there would be a way to get security camera recordings if he could provoke Riggs into assaulting him. They already knew about his shaky situation with the team, and thought threatening to release the video would be enough to get you to come home. They knew you'd want to protect him. I listened carefully from the hallway as they retold the entire situation to the man in black while he pulled footage from his computer."

I scrunch my brows in confusion. "But you called me after that. You tried again to get me to come home, knowing that he had the video. Why would you do that?" I'm trying my best to put myself in her shoes, but I can't imagine choosing my shitbag husband over my own child.

No matter how many times I've played this out from a different perspective, I just can't understand it.

"I decided that I was going to leave as soon as I heard their plan. But you have to remember, he controls everything in our household. Other than the allowance he gives me every week, I didn't have access to any money. So, I was stuck. As soon as we got off the phone, I told him I was going shopping, threw as much jewelry as I could fit into my bag, and went to a pawn shop in LA. I took the cash they gave me, drove to the airport, and here I am. I'm never going back there, Monroe. I shouldn't have stayed as long as I did. Please forgive me for not being a better mother. I'll do anything to gain your trust back."

She hangs her head, soft cries shaking her body as the consequences of her complacency finally hit her. I place my hand over hers on the counter, squeezing and hoping the little bit of comfort is enough. Right now, I can't give her anything more. I don't know if I'll ever be ready to, but it breaks my heart to see her like this. This could have been me. If I hadn't found the strength to leave home when I did, the woman I'm looking at is living the life that was destined to be passed on to me. For the first time in two years, I can truly look back and say how proud I am of myself for not accepting anything less than what I deserve.

"What happens when he realizes where you are? You know he's going to come looking for you. He would've been able to run for governor without his adult daughter, but it'll raise a lot of red flags if the voters find out that his wife ran away too."

She looks up at me, blotting the tears from her cheeks with her fingertips. "I hadn't really thought that far ahead," she replies. "My main priority was coming here to apologize in person. I know I don't want to go back there, and I was able to get enough money from my jewelry to last a few months if I'm careful. Other than that, I don't really know what I'm going to do to keep him from coming here and dragging me home. But I promise I'll do everything in my power to make sure he never comes near you again."

I shake my head, blowing out a forced breath. "There has to be a way to take him down. We both know he's done so many immoral and illegal things. Somebody out there has to have something we could use to stop him. At the very least, show the voters of California that he's not the man they think he is."

"Oh my God," she whispers, her eyes going wide. "I do."

FORTY
MONROE

"MILLIONAIRE AND GOVERNOR CANDIDATE, Edmund Decker the third has been released from Los Angeles County jail this morning after being arrested at his Rolling Hills home two nights ago. He's been charged with fourteen counts of solicitation after anonymous videos catching him in the act were sent to police," the reporter says as I keep my eyes glued to the TV, where the news covers the story of my dad's arrest. "Additionally, the FBI has discovered several offshore bank accounts where it's been speculated that Decker was funneling money in order to commit tax fraud. Sources close to the family say that other parties were involved, but no further charges have been filed. The investigation is ongoing, and we'll keep you updated on any new developments as they come in. Back to you in the studio, Barbara."

I take the remote, turning the television off before throwing myself back into the couch cushions. "Holy shit," I say on a relieved exhale, a slight smile breaking through my shocked expression as I look at my mother.

As soon as I mentioned taking my father down, she pulled out her phone and showed me more than I needed to see of him engaging in questionable acts with women that weren't her. Thankfully, I was spared from the nauseating details, but there was plenty of evidence that he solicited and paid for sex multiple times over the years.

When we decided to send the videos to the police as an anonymous tip, we were hoping that it would at least change the public's opinion on him, forcing him to drop out of the election. It didn't seem right that a man like him would be in control of an entire state, so we crossed our fingers and hoped for the best. We certainly weren't expecting them to dig any further into his dealings, resulting in the uncovering of so many other potential crimes that we had no idea he was involved in. He's out on bail now, but they've launched a full investigation, which means he's unable to leave the state of California. My mom and I are safe from any retaliation he may have been planning, and his indiscretion with the escorts voids their prenuptial agreement. Not only is it very likely that my mom will be able to get a restraining order if my father doesn't get put away for several years, but she's also going to walk away with enough money to take care of herself for the rest of her life.

When I asked her what made her hire a private detective to follow my father, she matter-of-factly said that all the women at the country club have videos like that of their husbands. They keep quiet, acting like model wives, knowing that they always have some extra ammunition in their back pockets. None of it makes any sense to me, but the lifestyle out there never has. My happiness and independence have always been worth way more to me than all the money in the world.

"That escalated quickly," my mom says quietly. "Am I a terrible person for not feeling bad? He wasn't always like this, you know? Although our relationship started the same way that yours and Conrad's did, there was a little while where he tried to be a good husband. I don't know exactly when it changed, but over the years, I became okay with sacrificing my own happiness for his. That was my fault. The thing that tears me up the most is that I had no problem allowing him to do it to you. I really am sorry, Monroe. I don't expect you to sweep this under the rug or forgive me anytime soon, but please know that I love you and I own every mistake I've made. I want to be better for you. And someday, if you have children of your own, I promise to always put them above everyone else."

My eyes fill with tears and I lean forward, finally wrapping her in a tight hug. When she showed up here a couple of nights ago, I was honestly too disgusted and hurt to even touch her. I wasn't sure of her intentions until we sent the videos. Now, I see that she wants to repair the things that have been broken between us. I'm not there yet, but I'm going to try. Even if it takes years for me to fully trust her, I know I don't want to cut her out of my life.

"I love you too, Mom," I whisper as we hold one another. "We'll get through this. Everything is going to be okay now."

"Hey, ladies," Riggs says, startling us both. "How's it going?"

I stand, walking over and throwing my arms around him. He presses a quick kiss to my cheek, which is so different from the way he normally greets me. I know he's behaving himself for my mom's sake, but I can't say I don't miss the horny comments and advances that I pretend to hate. She's been staying at a hotel downtown at night, but she's come here both days while he's been at the stadium. It's nice being able to talk to her without my dad around. She seems like an entirely different person from the woman I've known all my life. She's funny and sarcastic, always ready with a witty comment when it's needed to lighten the mood.

Now I know where I get it from.

"Good," I say, squeezing him tightly. He's been so attentive for the last couple of days, making sure I'm okay after my dad's arrest. I probably shouldn't be, but I think my heart and head disconnected from him after the night he came here and degraded me to the point where I almost fell back into the dark hole he kept me in as a kid. If it weren't for Riggs reminding me who I am that night, who knows where I'd be right now?

"Atta girl," he replies, making the butterflies in my stomach flutter around wildly. I'll never get over the way he can make me feel so adored with barely any words. Just as I press onto my toes to kiss him again, the doorbell rings. I throw my head back in exasperation as Riggs chuckles quietly. "You want to grab that for me, sweet thing?"

"No, thank you," I reply. "I don't have the best track record when it comes to opening the door."

He barks a laugh. "Trust me. After I threatened to move out, taking every other Fury player in the building with me, they hired several new security guards. No more unexpected guests will be knocking without checking in first. Now, go," he says, patting my ass as I walk toward the entryway.

I grip the knob, taking a deep breath before swinging the door open. Without so much as a greeting, my best friend barges in, steam practically coming from her ears as she makes a beeline for the living room.

"Douchebag!" she screeches, pointing an accusatory finger at Riggs. I can tell the look of bewilderment painted across his face is fake, even from where I'm standing. Whatever he did to piss her off is something he's well aware of, and likely planned on purpose to get this very reaction.

"Wow. Nice to see you too, sis," he says. "How was your flight?"

She grits her teeth. "My *flight* was great. The full-body cavity search at the security desk downstairs, though? Not so much!"

He tries to hide his laughter by tucking his lips tightly between his teeth, but fails miserably as he bursts into hysterics, bending down with his hands on his knees as he loses it.

"Really, Riggs?" she yells. "You told them I carry weapons from time to time, *just in case I need them*? You made me sound unhinged! I had to take off my shoes and socks while they wanded me *three times* before patting me down!"

"Seriously? They did?" he says as he continues laughing. "Oh my God, that's gold!"

She straightens, tossing her long blonde hair over her shoulder. "Yep. Last time I was that up-close and personal with a wand, your best friend's dick was in my mouth."

His face goes completely pale as horror clouds his

expression. "Jesus fucking Christ, Grace! I told you to stop fucking him!" He stomps his foot like a petulant child, and I stifle a laugh of my own.

"We're married, asshole!" she shouts. "I didn't want to say that, but you left me no choice! Maybe next time you'll think twice before you fuck with me!" I swear, these two need their own reality show. I'd totally pay for a subscription to the Valentine siblings' clusterfuck of a relationship.

God, I love them.

"Mom," I say, sauntering back to the living room. "This is my best friend, Grace. She's Riggs' sister."

Grace stiffens, realizing we aren't alone. "Oh my God," she whispers. "It's nice to meet you." She walks over, taking my mother's extended hand and shaking it.

"Jenna Decker," she says, holding back her smile. "Your Thanksgiving dinners must be interesting."

"You have no idea," I reply, chuckling as I walk back over to Riggs and wrap my arms around his waist. "What are you doing here?" I ask Grace.

"I wanted to come check on you. Figured I'd spend the week out here while Tan is at training camp. You good?"

"I am," I say with a genuine smile. "I'm happy." Having the three of them here right now gives me a sense of family that I'm beyond grateful for. For the first time in my life, I feel like I'm exactly where I'm supposed to be, surrounded by all the people who love me.

FORTY-ONE
RIGGS

"WHAT'S YOUR DEAL TODAY?" I ask Ace as he moves his gaze from the stands to me. He's had a silly smile on his face for the entire game, and I swear I've had to snap him out of several daydreams so he could focus on doing his job. Last inning, he threw up two hand signals that I had never even seen before because he wasn't paying attention.

"Huh?" he asks, looking back to whatever he was distracted by moments ago. I try to follow his line of vision, but with a packed stadium, it's hard to see exactly who's caught his eye.

"I know that look," I say. "*I've had that look.* That's the *I'm getting good pussy* stare. Details, Mathers. Give me all of them." I put my hand out, wiggling my fingers as though I'm expecting him to drop something into my palm. My catcher is always down to hang out with women, but I rarely see him actually leave with any of them. He has no issue sucking face with them on the dance floor, but at the end of every night, it seems as though he goes home alone. So, if he's got a new girl in his life, I'm intrigued.

"What?" he chokes out. "No. I'm not—" His eyes are wide, and he looks like he just got caught with his hand in the cookie jar, making me laugh loudly.

"Oh, wowwwww," I say, drawing out the word. "You got a secret girlfriend? It's about time, Acey boy!"

He scoffs as if it's a crazy idea, but I don't miss the way he wrings his hands together in his lap as a silly grin breaks back through. I decide to leave it alone, because when he wants to tell me about it, I know he will. He isn't private by any means, but I suspect there are things about him that would probably surprise me. I've gotten to know the rookie pretty well throughout the season, and he's a great kid. I hope whoever this girl is doesn't break his heart.

"How about you?" he asks. "It seems like things are going well with Monroe."

Now it's my turn to smile like a fool. I turn my head, spotting her in her usual seat immediately. She's wearing a sequined jersey dress with my name and number on it, which my sister surprised her with before we left today. Her long, chocolate hair is pulled up into a bun, show-casing her beautiful neck that I can't wait to bite into later tonight. Grace sits on her left, laughing and cheering like the proud sister she's always been. Jenna is on her other side, taking in the sights and sounds around her as if she's seeing the entire world for the first time.

"She's amazing," I reply. "I've never met anyone like her before. She's been through so many things that were designed to make her jaded and closed off, but she isn't.

She's loving and strong. I know I don't deserve her, but *fuck*, I'm glad she chose me."

"Don't sell yourself short, Val. You deserve more than you think." He gives me a boyish grin before grabbing his bat and standing up. "Time to give the people what they want."

Taking off toward the dugout entrance, he goes up the stairs, stopping at the top and waiting for the intro to his walk-up song to ring throughout the stadium. The crowd goes wild as he swings his bat, doing his signature choreography while making his way to the plate. The first time I saw him do this, I rolled my eyes at the show tune he chose, but it's become quite the gimmick for the kid, and the fans love him. I'd feel differently about it if his game didn't back it up, but as long as he keeps playing the way he does, he can sing and dance all he wants.

The music stops and he readies himself for the pitch, choking up on his bat and focusing on his surroundings. As soon as the ball leaves the pitcher's hand, I hold my breath, awaiting the sweet *crack* of a connection. He lets the first one sail into the catcher's mitt, unaffected by the now o-and-one count.

He's locked in when the next one comes his way. It's a low slider, and it's exactly the kind of pitch Ace lives for. He pulls his front foot up, bringing the bat around and connecting at the perfect angle. The ball flies up in the air, shoots past the outfield, and drops down just beyond the wall. Fireworks are launched into the sky as he leisurely rounds the bases, all the while making a heart with his hands and holding it in the direction of where he was staring into the stands before. I look again, watching as a beautiful blonde, maybe in her early thirties, shakes her head in indignation. At first, she looks pissed, but a smile breaks through as she covers her red cheeks with her hands. Squinting even more, I recognize her familiar face and make a mental note to grill him like crazy for the info.

This is going to be good.

We end the game with a win and I make my way over to my girl because I can't wait another second to see her. I run toward the wall, giving no warning before I jump up, grabbing hold of the railing and waiting for Monroe to reward me for my great game. She pushes her way to the end of the row before descending the two wide steps that separate us.

"Not bad, Val," she says playfully, grabbing my face and pressing her mouth to mine. As much as I want to part her soft lips with my tongue and remind this whole place who she belongs to, I know I need to be a good boy. Just because I'm out of the woods with the team doesn't mean that can't all be flushed down the shitter if I do what I'm thinking and drag her back into the bullpen for a repeat of our date night.

"You better watch that smart mouth, Mayhem. I can think of several ways to stop it from running when I finally get you alone," I growl so only she can hear.

"Mmmm," she hums. "Well, you're in luck because my mom is going back to the hotel, and your sister is catching a red-eye back to Boston tonight because she misses Tanner."

"Thank fuck," I say on a relieved exhale, leaning in to steal one more kiss before lowering myself to the field and running toward the locker rooms. All I can think about is getting home and worshipping her body until the sun comes up.

Because as fake as we pretended this thing was when she came here, I don't think it ever really was for me. I've been blessed beyond my wildest dreams with the love of the most amazing woman I've ever met, and I can't wait to spend forever making sure she knows how grateful I am. Monroe Decker is finally free to live the life she's always imagined, and I'm the lucky motherfucker that gets to stand beside her as she makes her mark on the world.

EPILOGUE

MONROE

"OKAY, YOU REMEMBER THE PLAN, RIGHT?" I say, staring at Friggle's giant googly eyes as I wait for confirmation. He hops up and down, his long arms flapping at his sides as he does.

I sigh, rubbing my temples because I honestly don't have the patience for this. It's hot, my underboobs are sweating, and I'm literally salivating at the thought of a soft pretzel.

"For fuck's sake, Brent. We're the only two people in this hallway. You can talk." I'm questioning my decision to involve him in this little announcement more and more with every second that he stares at me wordlessly, but I thought it would be fun to rile Riggs up, so I'm trying to push through.

"Yes, I remember," he whispers, looking around like he doesn't believe me and a preschool full of children is going to jump out from behind one of the thick wooden doors at any moment. *This dude takes his job* way *too seriously. Now I understand why Riggs beat the shit out of him.* "Go out there, hand him the jersey, and turn him toward the Jumbotron."

"Exactly," I reply, patting him on the shoulder as I sneak into the dugout and hide behind Hawk, who's strategically standing near the corner. It's game one of the World Series, and Riggs is warming up at the mound with Ace before they're called to the third baseline for the National Anthem. But I have a surprise for him first.

The last year and a half since I moved to Daytona has been the most amazing time of my life. My marketing business is doing great, and I've been freelancing as a special events consultant with the Fury on the side. After the success of Friendship Day, Taylor practically begged me to help the marketing department out. At first, I tried to decline, but she brought out the big guns. I couldn't say no to Mr. Durst when he told me how much the team needed my fresh outlook, so here I am.

Riggs and I moved out of his old building six months ago, purchasing a house with our own private beach. Although it's secluded, I still go out there topless from time to time to fire him up. Let's just say the outdoor shower we built has *seen some things.*

As far as my family, so much has happened since my father's arrest. He was found guilty on all counts of solicitation and tax fraud, and just as I suspected in the back of my mind, he took Conrad down with him. Apparently, I wasn't their only mutual interest. They were working together for years, stealing from clients and hiding money in offshore accounts so nobody suspected a thing. The state of California dodged a bullet, because who knows what they would've gotten away with if my dad had become governor?

My mom and I are working to rebuild our relationship, and we've come so far since she moved to Daytona. Her divorce from my dad is almost final, and her lawyers predict that she'll end up getting every dime their broken prenup entitles her to. She's made some new friends down here, including the Fury's grumpy ass manager, Clyde. As surprising as that was to us all, it's certainly made the team's life easier now that he isn't flying off the handle every ten seconds.

"Showtime," Hawk whispers as I peek out from behind him. We watch as Friggle walks toward Riggs with the piece of white fabric clutched in his furry hand. True to form, my fiancé attempts to act like he doesn't see the mascot, but Friggle refuses to be ignored, stepping directly into Riggs' line of sight. I laugh as he throws his head back in annoyance before finally giving up and raising his hands in question.

Friggle thrusts the jersey between them, shaking it rapidly in an attempt to get Riggs to take it. He finally does, giving a thumbs up, which I can tell he's just doing so he can get back to his warm-ups. The mascot points to it, putting his hands together then pulling them apart as if to say *open it up*. Riggs does, and I watch his eyebrows pull inward as he reads the word *DADDY* that's been embroidered across the back. He looks back up at Friggle, confused before he's spun around to the Jumbotron.

Hawk moves aside and I hurry up the steps, straightening my tank top that says *Daddy's Biggest Fan* with an arrow pointing down to my still somewhat flat belly. Keeping my positive pregnancy test from Riggs has been killing me since I found out, but I wanted to make his first World Series start the most memorable night of his life.

The only person who knew prior to today was Grace, and surprisingly, she hasn't told a soul. Our stellar secret-keeping is about to pay off once he realizes what's going on here.

The crowd goes nuts as the animations begin to play across the big screen, starting with a cartoon baby in a number fifty-seven jersey toddling across, followed by text that says *Congrats, Val! You're going to be a daddy!*

He immediately whips his head to my empty seat, a look of shock painted across his expression until he catches me walking toward him out of the corner of his eye and turns my way. I point to my shirt as I close the distance between us, making his confusion turn to pure happiness as he grins from ear to ear.

"Shut the fuck up!" he says. "Seriously? You're pregnant?"

"Yep," I reply, tucking my chin as heat flashes in his eyes. It's no secret that Riggs has been trying to put a baby in me for a while, so when we decided to stop using birth control, he went into feral breeding mode. I swear the man can smell it when I'm ovulating. It's been pretty hot, to be honest.

"Come here, Mayhem," he says with a smirk, crooking his finger in invitation. A huge smile blooms across my face as I jump into his arms, immediately being lifted off the ground as the sounds of the crowd celebrating with us ring through the stadium.

"I fucking love you so much, baby," he says into my ear. "Thank you. For being everything I've ever wanted."

And whether he knows it or not, he's been the exact same thing for me...even when I pretended he wasn't.

Curious about Ace's story? Keep reading for a sneak peek of Scoring Position, book 2 of the Daytona Fury series…

SCORING POSITION PROLOGUE
ACE

"What do you mean, I don't have enough credits to graduate?" I ask, my brows pulled tightly in confusion. "My advisor told me at the beginning of the year that I'd be good with the nine credit hours I signed up for."

I hear the rapid clicking of a keyboard as my knee bounces with anxiety, because if I don't let it, I might climb right the fuck up these walls.

"Okay," the woman replies. "I see the problem." I breathe a sigh of relief, hoping she has some good news for me. "One of your courses had a mandatory lab that required you to be on campus to complete your work. Since you did your lessons remotely, your attendance in that lab was never counted, resulting in a zero for the accompanying course. So, you still need three more credit hours in order to earn your diploma."

I let my head fall back, dragging a hand down my face in exasperation. "I was approved by the dean for independent study. I was excused from all on-campus instruction."

More tapping. I clench my fist on the table in front of me, trying not to freak out on this poor woman. It's not her fault that I'm dealing with this shit.

But it isn't mine, either.

"Unfortunately, Mr. Mathers, you didn't complete the work for this course, so you'll either have to retake it and be on campus for the lab portion, or choose another elective to earn those credits. There are a few left for the summer semester if you want to graduate as soon as possible. I'm sure, given your situation, the dean will have no problem approving you for independent study again. You can register right on the app if one of the open courses strikes your fancy."

"Thank you," I say, completely defeated as I end the call. *Fuck.* I promised my grandma I would graduate from college when I was a kid. We were very close, and although we both knew I was destined for the MLB, she told me she wanted to see me walk across the stage to accept my diploma before she died. I would be the first in the family to do so, and it was important to her, so I vowed that I would earn my degree. Unfortunately, she recently passed from a blood infection, but I refuse to let her down. I have to see this through.

I slump back in my chair, huffing an annoyed breath as I pull up the university's app to search for open courses. The ones that are full are grayed out, leaving only three electives for me to choose from. I begin to look them over, not sure which one would be easiest. As a rookie in the MLB, I need to focus on our season that's already in full swing, but I also want to get this over with so I can be done with school forever.

"What's up, rook?" my teammate Jackson says, pulling out a chair and sitting down. It's a game day, and a lot of us get here early to meet with one of the trainers before we start preparing for warm-ups. As a catcher, I always make sure my legs are thoroughly stretched and massaged so I don't get any cramps while squatting and standing during play.

"Not much, man," I reply. "Just found out I need one more elective to graduate. I'm trying to choose between the three courses nobody on campus wanted to take so I can get this shit over with."

He shoots me a toothy grin. "I gotta say, I commend you for following through with this whole college thing. I did one year of that shit while I was in the minors, and it was hell trying to juggle it all. But you're almost at the finish line."

He's right. It has been hell. I was drafted right out of high school and spent just over two years in the minors before I was called up to catch for the Daytona Fury. I figured an associate's degree in business administration would be the easiest route to go, so that's what I went with. It's been far from the cake walk I expected when I promised my grandma I'd graduate. Unfortunately, with my busy schedule, it's taken a bit longer to complete everything, but I'm finally nearing the end. Now I just need to bang out one final course.

"Thanks. I'm just not sure which of these will require the least amount of brain power." I scroll through my options again, but I'm cut off when Jacks swipes the phone from my hand.

"Let's see," he says as he peruses the available options.

"Intro to Ballroom Dancing." He purses his lips as he considers it. "Sounds innocent enough, but they go kinda hard on that dancing show with the celebrities. You might get hurt."

My brows bunch together in confusion. "I'm taking it independently. How would I get hurt if I'm by myself?"

He shrugs. "You never know, dude. It's not worth the risk." Looking back down at my phone, he moves on. "Beekeeping. Is this seriously a college course? Why is everything so dangerous?"

"I'm allergic to bees, anyway," I reply, shaking my head rapidly. "That one's out. What's behind door number three?"

He scrolls to the bottom of the list, a knowing grin tugging at the corners of his lips. "Your fucking layup class, man. You could nap through every lesson and still pass, no problem. Matter of fact, you could probably teach it!"

I blow out a relieved breath, thankful that I won't have to take much time away from baseball to study. I was one of the top prospects my senior year and was drafted in the first round, but I'm young and still have to prove myself to this team. I'm not the only catcher on the Fury roster, and I can be moved back down to the minors at any time if they feel like I'm slacking. I may be a fan favorite, but as soon as my game starts to suffer, that won't mean a thing.

"Alright," I reply with a big smile. "What course?"

He winks, turning the phone toward me, and my stomach drops right into my ass as I stare at the words typed in bold across the screen. *Human Sexuality.*

Fuck.

Preorder Scoring Position on Amazon:
https://a.co/d/csUZQVj

Want to read Tanner and Grace's story?
Turn the page for the prologue of QB Keeper, book 3 of the
Boston Blizzard series…

QB KEEPER PROLOGUE
TANNER

I HOLD the thick paper in my hand, reading it for the tenth time while standing at my mailbox. I don't know what I was expecting when I took a quick run down my mile-long driveway this morning, but this definitely wasn't it.

You are cordially invited to the 40th-anniversary celebration of Bill and Libby Valentine

Saturday, April 2nd at 2 o'clock

1111 Journey Lane, Hope Harbor, Massachusetts 01125

I wish I could say I was excited to celebrate such a huge milestone for my childhood best friend's parents. Forty years of marriage is a big deal, and their love has always been an inspiration to the people who know them, but the only thing going through my mind as I think about what attending this party would mean is *her*.

Grace Valentine.

My Grace.

The girl whose anguished cries haunt my dreams every single night.

There was a short time in my life where I held her and nothing else mattered. Not football, not school, not my future. It was just us, learning, exploring…falling.

And then I fucked it all up.

I knew better than to have a secret fling with my best friend's younger sister. It started as me wanting to protect her, as I had done since the day she was born. I was only three, but our parents always joked that I was Grace's personal bodyguard. If another kid tried to play with her or touch her toys, little Tanner had no problem letting them know that wasn't an option. And as we got older, my instinct to make sure she was safe and happy only intensified. I can't tell you how many douchebags her brother Riggs and I scared off in high school so they'd stay away from her. Wrong? Maybe. But I'd have done anything to protect her heart.

Then I turned around and ripped it out with my own two hands.

What I thought was the right thing at the time ended up being my biggest regret. It's been five years, and every time I get invited to an event in Hope Harbor, I decline like a little bitch. I make some shit excuse about having practice or workouts so I can get out of them, convincing my family to come visit me in Boston instead. I even had this house built with a fully equipped guest suite so they would feel like it was a little vacation when they came here. For half a decade, everything I've done has been for Grace…or to avoid her.

Riggs and I still talk occasionally, but he's currently playing professional baseball in Florida, so our conversations rarely make it long enough for his sister to come up. Especially since, to this day, he has no idea what happened between her and me that summer.

I don't want to know what she's up to now. My guess is that she's in a relationship, if not married. Girls like Grace Valentine don't stay single for long. If her beautiful blue eyes and silky blonde hair don't reel a guy in, her kind heart and amazing sense of humor will. Some lucky son of a bitch is probably holding her right now. And I can tell you with absolute certainty that whoever he is, he doesn't deserve her.

No one does.

The day I walked away, I deleted all my social media accounts, drove myself from Hope Harbor back to Harvard, and vowed to stay away for good. I had done enough damage. The least I could do was let her have our hometown as her safe space. Let her chase her dreams in Los Angeles, being able to return whenever her heart missed home, and give her a fair chance at a happy life. Because I knew that without her, that would never be an option for me.

The thick cardstock feels like a brick in my hand as I try to tell myself to stay away. That I'm only invited because Riggs and his parents have no idea that I'm the cause of Grace's first broken heart. That for one whole summer, she gave me every single piece of herself, and I humiliated her by acting like the way she felt was just some stupid school-girl crush. Then I told her she meant nothing to me and walked away while she cried and begged me not to.

I decide right here that it's time to go back and face the consequences of my actions. I deserve to see how happy and successful she's become in spite of the way I broke her. That she's thriving while she unknowingly still carries my heart in her hands.

And she deserves to see how empty my life has been all these years, knowing that I'm the only one to blame.

Read QB Keeper now on Amazon:
https://a.co/d/aGvRHBd

ACKNOWLEDGMENTS

My husband - Riggs is the closest to you of all of my guys...which makes sense, given how much of a pain in the ass he was to write. Haha I'm just kidding. Thank you for answering all of my random, weird questions...even ones that came during the most inappropriate times. You're my favorite person in the world, and I appreciate everything you do to support me. I love you.

My kids - We're five books in now, and if you've read any of the acknowledgments I've written to you, you're grounded. I love you both.

My mom - Not gonna lie. I seriously hope you skipped this one. If not, let's never, ever talk about it. I love you and I'm so thankful that you support me in everything I do, but let's pretend you never learned to read.

Breanne - Another one in the books for the iconic duo. I'm so grateful for everything you do while I'm creating these stories. From art, to editing, to being a sounding board and voice of reason when I feel like I'm failing, you always know exactly what I need. I don't think I'll ever find the words to express how proud I am to have you on this ride with me. I love you.

Hannah Gray - We made it! We officially wrote books at the same time, and released them within a week of one another. For a minute there, I wasn't sure if we'd get through it without one of us being the sane one, but look at us. Easy peazy. I love you and I'm so grateful to have you as my mentor on this journey.

Lexi James - Even though our time zones try to keep us from loving one another, we somehow manage to find a way to be exactly what the other needs when we need it. I wouldn't be able to do any of this without you, and I'm so thankful that you get me the way you do. I love you and I'm so proud of the things you're accomplishing.

Jaime Rayyan - My baseball research queen. Thank you for all the baseball booty videos, and for continuing our Daily Dose of Bosa while I wrote this book. Also, thank you for not blocking my crazy voice messages and always having the right answers when I'm freaking out. You are such a gift to me, and I love you to the moon and back.

Maggie Marrero - I couldn't have done any of this without you. From taking some of the workload off me, to reading and loving this story the way I do, every detail you've helped me with has made such a huge impact on my career. I don't deserve you, but I'm so glad you always have my back. I can't wait to see where we go next.

Chelsey Bodkin - Bringing you into my inner circle is one of the best decisions I've made as an author. Not only have you taught me so much, but you've also been the light on some of my darker days while attempting to write this story. Thank you for all the bomb content you create, and the late-night unhinged text messages about *90 Day Fiancé*. You're stuck with me now, so get comfortable.

Amanda Mudgett - My little flower. No matter what you have going on, or how busy your life is, you continue to put our friendship on the top of your priority list. I am so grateful for everything you've done for me, and for the way that you're always there to catch me if I feel like I'm falling. ILYSM.

Ashley Boyle - You've been the best hype girl since Hot Route, and your words have given me the confidence to write on the days I've wanted to throw my manuscripts in the trash. I appreciate you more than you'll ever know, and I'm so grateful to have you in my life.

My FSBB girls - Thank you so much for always being my biggest supporters. You go out of your way to make me feel special, and I will never be able to tell you how much it means to me. I love you all, and I'm so grateful for everything you've done for me.

Autumn and the Wordsmith Publicity team - Thank you for doing all the heavy lifting for these releases. I'm so thankful to be part of such an amazing group of authors and professionals.

My beta readers - I know there are a lot of you now, but you've all become such an important part of my process. I've been told so many times to keep this group small, but I love the little family we have, and each of your input is so valuable to me. Thank you so much for the time and dedication you put into helping me create such complete stories.

My ARC team - To my OGs and my newbies, I love you all so much for taking a chance on me. I can't wait to bring you along wherever this journey takes us!

Bookstagram/BookTok girlies: Since the release of Hot Route, I've been so humbled by the support I've gotten. Your DMs, reviews, and edits are what keep me going when I'm feeling like I can't. On my harder days, all I have to do is go into my tagged posts and read about the way you love my characters. That always brightens my day and gives me the strength I need to keep on typing. I love you all!

My readers: you've given me opportunities that I never thought I'd have, just by reading my stories. I'll never be able to come up with the words to say thank you for changing my life, but please know that I'll never take it for granted. As long as you keep reading, I'll keep writing.

ABOUT THE AUTHOR

C.L. Rose is a wife and mother of two. She lives in Northeast Ohio with her husband, son, daughter, and dog, Tank. When she isn't writing, you can find her reading in front of a space heater, wrapped in a thick blanket, probably complaining that she's cold.

authorclrose.com

MORE FROM C.L. ROSE

Boston Blizzard Series

Hot Route
The Stunt: A Boston Blizzard Novella
Run Game
QB Keeper

Daytona Fury Series

Wild Pitch
Scoring Position - Coming January 2025
Double Play - Coming Spring 2025